The
Boat House
Secret

Debra Burroughs

Lake House Books
Boise, Idaho

First eBook Edition: 2015
First Paperback Edition: 2016

THE BOAT HOUSE SECRET by Debra Burroughs,
1st ed. p.cm.

Visit My Blog: www.DebraBurroughsBooks.com

Contact Me: Debra@DebraBurroughs.com

ISBN-10: 1539464172
ISBN-13: 978-1539464174

DEDICATION

This book is dedicated to my amazing husband, Tim, who loves me and encourages me every day to do what I love – writing.

TABLE OF CONTENTS

ACKNOWLEDGMENTS

*I would like to acknowledge my awesome Beta Readers,
Cathy Tomlinson, Janet Lewis, Buffy Drewett, and
Celeste Corbin, who inspire me and help me
with their words of encouragement and critique.*

*I want to also acknowledge my brilliant Editor,
Lisa Dawn Martinez.*

CHAPTER 1

"WATCH YOUR STEP," Michael Baxter warned, holding Jenessa's hand as she stepped off the dock at the lakeside marina and into the waiting motor boat. His little boy, Jake, was already perched on the edge of the padded bench that ran around the rear of the vessel, wearing an orange lifejacket and an eager smile.

The boat rocked and Jenessa felt herself begin to lose her balance, but Michael's strong arms grabbed around her waist to steady her. Jenessa blushed from the awkwardness, thanked him, and took a seat beside Jake. She snuggled an arm around him and smiled.

"I'm ready," she called to Michael, who took his place at the helm.

"Me too, Daddy. Let's go!" the six-year-old added.

It was late April and the sun hung high in the bright blue sky dotted with puffy white clouds. Winter had finally melted into spring and the temperature was hovering somewhere around seventy degrees. It was a perfect afternoon for a boat ride around Jonas Lake, not far from their town of Hidden Valley.

"Hold on," Michael called back over his shoulder as he eased the throttle forward, pulling away from the dock. Once a safe distance from the marina, he opened it up.

Jake giggled as the wind blew in his face, ruffling his dark hair. Jenessa slid on a pair of big sunglasses as she relaxed against the back of the seat, clamping her hand around her long, dark tresses to keep her hair from flopping around in the wind and becoming a tangled mess.

"Faster, Daddy, faster!" Jake hollered, his face an expression of sheer glee.

Jenessa adored that little boy.

She and Michael had been dating for about nine months and they had talked of the possibility of getting married one day. She loved Michael—his strength, his integrity, his tall and handsome good looks—but if she was truly honest with herself, the idea of mothering Jake was at the top of her list. She was approaching thirty, and, if they hoped to have a child together, she had better move things along. Her biological clock was ticking louder every day.

As she watched Jake thoroughly enjoying himself, niggling thoughts danced in her mind, visions of the baby boy she had given up when she was seventeen. She had ached for him ever since that heart-wrenching day, had never stopped wanting him, had never stopped wondering. Where was he? What was he doing today? Was he happy? Would she ever see him again?

These questions and many more were her constant companions.

As an investigative newspaper reporter, probing questions were at the heart of what Jenessa did for a living, but *these* questions were at the heart of Jenessa herself. She had relentlessly searched for answers over the years, but so far none had led her to find her son. Any time she thought she had a lead, it turned out to be nothing but hopes in the wind.

When she moved back to Hidden Valley, almost a year ago, she had reconnected with her high school friend Michael, who'd previously had no idea why she had disappeared right before her senior year. Since her return, she had shared with him the details of her unexpected pregnancy—the reason why she had left town without a word over twelve years before. She'd told him how she had given the baby up for adoption, after considerable pressure from both her parents and the father's. What Michael didn't know, at least not yet, was that she had never given up searching for her son, that she'd had periodic meetings with her attorney regarding him, or that she had suspicions that someone in Hidden Valley knew his whereabouts.

It was times like this, times when her mind was not burdened with the task of hunting down a story for the paper, that she allowed herself the luxury of feeling that missing part of herself. She didn't know how other women did it. How they managed to shut their eyes, and their hearts, and all but forget about a child that had been a part of them for nine whole months.

Still, Jenessa had to wonder…why hadn't she told

Michael about her search? Or her meetings and suspicions? Perhaps it was because of who the baby's father was…

Michael slowed the boat to an easy glide as they neared the charming lake houses and cabins that dotted the edge of Jonas Lake. He turned his head back to Jenessa. "I thought you might enjoy seeing the homes along the water."

It had been a while since she had ventured around the lake after her return to town. The place held such painful memories that she was reluctant to relive them. It was at one of these very lake houses that the trajectory of her life had veered so far off course.

Jenessa snugged her hair into a ponytail holder she had around her wrist, and then moved to Michael's side, putting one hand around his waist and the other on the dashboard to steady herself. "They are pretty, aren't they?"

"Maybe someday we'll have a cabin on the lake." He smiled down at her, then gave her a quick kiss before looking back over the shoreline. "Hey, isn't that the Alexanders' lake house?"

"I think it is," she replied, knowing full well he was right.

"Remember when we were there last summer, investigating the St. John murder? I thought Grey Alexander was going to blow a gasket when he found us searching his place."

Michael was a detective on the Hidden Valley police force, and at times Jenessa managed to weasel her way into his cases to get the scoop for her newspaper, the Hidden Valley Herald, often in spite of his protests.

"I'm sure that's the house," he declared.

Jenessa nodded. "You're right," she agreed, but that wasn't the only time she had been there.

A prickly tightness began to squeeze her chest as they motored past the beautiful lake house. Several people were sitting on white Adirondack chairs positioned in a loose semi-circle on the back deck that faced the lake. One of the men stood and waved to them. Even from a distance, she recognized him right away, the sunshine bouncing off his blond waves. A thick lump grew in her throat, her pulse quickening.

"Is that Logan?" Michael asked. Irritation sizzled through the words as he obviously also recognized her old beau.

"Yes." She swallowed hard and waved back at him, not wanting to appear rude. They had dated in high school. Logan had been her first love—and he was the father of her baby. Since her return, he had tried to rekindle their old flame, but she had chosen a relationship with Michael instead. Even so, Logan had not been shy about letting her know he was still interested in her, still in love with her, pursuing her whenever possible, which had become irksome to Michael.

She cleared her throat and struggled to keep her voice even, not wanting to let on to Michael that Logan could still make her heart skip a beat. "I wonder who that is with him," she muttered in a nonchalant tone, sneaking a quick peek over her shoulder, then immediately regretting even caring.

"No idea." Michael turned his gaze forward and sped up a little. He lifted his chin toward another dwelling farther down the shore. "There's a great little cabin."

Picking up on the clue that he didn't want to talk about Logan Alexander—which was fine by her—Jenessa played along. "Yes, it's adorable. So rustic."

Over his shoulder, he glanced at his son. "You doing okay back there, big guy?"

"Go faster, Daddy," Jake moaned, sounding impatient at the slowness of the boat's pace.

"In a minute." Michael turned his attention back to Jenessa. "See those rocks?" He pointed at an outcropping between the cabin and the next lake house. "When I was a kid, long before you moved to Hidden Valley, my dad told me about investigating a case of a body that was found there."

"Really?" *Was there an interesting story here?* "Tell me about it."

"I don't recall much. I was only about ten or eleven. Something about teenagers partying out there and something happening to one of them."

Jenessa leaned closer toward him and lowered her voice. "Was it murder?"

Michael huffed a laugh. "Possibly. Provenza thinks so anyway." Detective George Provenza was Michael's senior partner and drawing close to retiring. "As a matter of fact, the victim was Mayor Evans' oldest son."

"Really? Tell me more."

"He stopped by the station last week and asked Provenza if he would reopen the case."

"Why now?"

"He said it was coming up on the twenty-year

10

anniversary of their son's death, and he and his wife want to finally have some closure, know for certain what happened to their son."

"Parents never stop grieving for the loss of a child," Jenessa couldn't help thinking of her own loss, "no matter how old the child was or what happened to them."

"His wife has it in her head that with the advances in technology, maybe we could find out what really killed him."

"What or who?" she added.

"Yes, could be a who, I guess."

"What do you think, Michael?"

"I think she's been watching too many cop shows on TV. The medical examiner had ruled it an accidental drowning, so unless there's some new evidence, I doubt our captain would let us reopen the case."

"Daddy?" came a young voice.

"In a minute, Jake." Michael continued telling Jenessa the story. "I think that boathouse had something to do with the death."

A weathered boathouse came into view along the shoreline, not as grand as the Alexanders', which was large and pristine, holding two boats side by side. This particular boathouse, with weatherworn paint, had a sizeable deck running along one side from the land to the opening that housed a boat, and it appeared to have a room with windows closest to land, perhaps for a groundskeeper.

Sitting higher up on an incline was the large house it belonged to, which appeared to be in better condition, with a scattering of mature pine trees growing between the home and the boathouse. Who did this property belong to?

Jenessa couldn't help but be curious about the case, her sight still on the old boathouse. She imagined the partying teenagers Michael had mentioned using this boathouse, and spilling out onto the deck. What happened there that night? How did one of them end up dead?

She had to ask. "Any idea whose place it is?"

"Some relative of those Alexanders, I think," Michael muttered.

"Really," she replied, trying not to sound too interested. If Michael was right, though, maybe Logan knew the story of what had occurred at this place on that fateful night.

"Faster, Daddy!" Apparently, Jake could no longer hold his frustration at his dad's snail's pace. "It's been way more than a minute."

"Why do you care so much about what happened?" Michael asked her, seeming to ignore Jake's pleading.

Had she sounded too interested?

"You brought it up," she volleyed back.

"I was just making conversation, but you—"

"Oh, you know me," she tried to cover, "there's only so much nuptial and garden club news I can handle." Her previous job had been far more exciting, writing for a large newspaper in Sacramento. "This sounds like it might be an interesting story to write about."

"I don't see how," Michael said. "Who's going to care now?"

"Well, you did say it was the current mayor's son. I think this is something the townspeople would be very interested in."

Just then Jake squeezed in between Michael and Jenessa and tugged at his father's pant leg. "How come we're going so slow?"

"You want to go faster, big guy?" Michael asked his son while he pitched a mischievous grin at Jenessa. He looked relieved to have a reason to change the subject.

Jake nodded, his eyes wide with excitement.

Jenessa took his little hand. "Then we'd better go sit down and hang on, Jake. I think it's going to be a bumpy ride."

CHAPTER 2

IT WAS A MONDAY MORNING and Jenessa woke up thinking about what Michael had said about the mysterious death at Jonas Lake years ago. Should she leave it up to Michael to ask Detective Provenza about the incident, or should she pursue the senior detective herself to get some answers?

She slipped out of bed and headed for the shower. As the warm water cascaded over her body, visions of drunken teenagers partying at the lake swirled in her mind. One could have had too much to drink, then fell, hitting his head, tumbling into the water. Or perhaps there was something more sinister at play here.

After breakfast she called the police station and asked for George Provenza.

"Provenza here. How can I help you?"

"Hey, George, it's Jenessa."

"That's Detective Provenza," he sounded slightly irritated. After almost a year of quasi-working with him, he still insisted she give him the respect of his rank. "Michael's not in yet."

"You're the one I want to talk to."

"Oh really." He didn't sound flattered.

"Yes. Michael was telling me about a death that happened up at Jonas Lake about twenty years ago. A young man died, he said. Do you remember that?"

"Yeah, I remember, Mayor Evans' son—well, he wasn't the mayor back then. I worked on that case, but we couldn't solve it. In the end, the ME declared it an accidental drowning. Why are you asking about it? You have some new evidence to the contrary?"

"No, just curious." She decided against telling him Michael had divulged that the mayor was asking for the case to be reopened. "Do you have a few minutes to talk? I could come by your office."

"No need. I can tell you all I know right now. Let me grab the file."

"You still have it in your office?" After twenty years, and it being deemed an accidental drowning, why wouldn't it have been filed away in storage?

"Yeah, I've still got it. I was never satisfied that it was an accidental drowning, but I couldn't prove otherwise."

Maybe there was more to this story. The sound of the metal file drawer shutting popped through the phone. "What can you tell me, Detective?"

She heard papers rustling, assuming he was looking through the file.

"I worked this case with Michael's dad, you know."

"Michael mentioned that. His folks are out of town, so I thought I'd ask you about it."

"There were a number of people we interviewed at the time, but it never really went anywhere. What brought this up?"

"Michael and I were on the lake on Saturday and he pointed out a boathouse that may have been involved. Do you happen to know who it belonged to?"

"Yep. At the time, it was owned by Grey Alexander's sister and her husband. Don't know if they still own it after all this time, but as I recall, we interviewed them and their teenage daughter, but they didn't tell us much—either they didn't know anything or they were keeping tight-lipped about it."

"Anything you can tell me about the victim?" she asked.

"I guess I can share what we released to the press back then. His name was Nicholas Evans. His friends called him Nick. He was twenty years old and went to the college right here, Whitfield."

"I'm assuming, being the mayor's son, he grew up in Hidden Valley, right?" she asked, as if she didn't already know.

"That's right."

Yes, people in this town would undoubtedly be interested in a story like that. She could see the headline now: Mayor's Son Murdered.

"Anything else?" Provenza asked.

Jenessa hesitated, not sure the detective was going to like her next question. "Would you mind if I had a look at the file, *Detective Provenza*? Maybe a fresh set of eyes might see something others missed." The mayor and his wife would certainly appreciate her uncovering some new piece of evidence. Hopefully Provenza would see it that way too.

"Are you saying you think I missed something, Miss Jones?" his words rife with indignation.

"Oh no, not at all, Detective."

"You're not law enforcement, young lady, so—"

"I realize that, but what if I found something you and Michael's dad missed? Something that pointed to murder?"

"You'd like that, wouldn't you? A nice juicy murder for your newspaper."

"I won't lie, George, the thought had crossed my mind, but it couldn't hurt having another pair of eyes take a look, see the facts in a different light," she said. "You even told me yourself that the death being ruled an accidental drowning never sat right with you."

"True."

"Really, George, who's going to care about my taking a look at a twenty-year-old accidental drowning? Who knows—maybe I'll find something."

"Let me think on it. I'll let you know."

"Think quick, would you, George?"

"Don't crowd me, Miss Jones." He cleared his throat like he meant it. "Like I said, I'll think about it, then I'll let you know."

~*~

Jenessa ducked into her favorite coffee shop, The Sweet Spot, which sat at the corner of Main Street and Broadway in the quaint downtown of Hidden Valley. Stepping inside, she caught the eye of her best friend,

Ramey, who co-owned the place. She stood behind the counter waiting on a line of customers.

"Be right with you," Ramey called out with a smile, then returned her attention to a customer. Her big blue eyes sparkled and her head of red curls danced around her neck as she laughed at something the man said.

Ramey had been her best friend since she was fifteen, and now, at thirty, she was more like a sister. Several years back, before Jenessa's mother, Lydia Jones, was tragically killed in a car accident, she and Ramey had opened The Sweet Spot, a bakery and café, serving the best coffees and baked goods in town. Now, with her mother gone, Jenessa's sister, Sara, was helping Ramey run the place.

Jenessa checked her watch. If she waited through the line, she'd be late for work. Coffee would have to wait. She spun to leave, running smack into the person behind her.

"We've got to stop meeting like this," the familiar masculine voice resonated.

Heat rose in her cheeks. Surprised and a bit embarrassed, she lifted her face, locking gazes with the man. "Good morning, Logan," she offered warmly.

"Enjoy your boat ride?" His azure eyes glinted with a hint of mischief. His lips spread into a friendly smile.

"As a matter of fact, we did." She needed to rush away, but she was curious about the other people at his lake house, not to mention the mysterious death near his family's property. "You looked like you had friends up at your lake house last weekend. Anyone I know?"

"Well," his raised eyebrow appeared to take note of her curiosity, "it was my cousin Summer, and her husband, Chet. You remember her, don't you?"

"Summer?" It had been a long time, but Jenessa seemed to recall meeting Logan's cousin at a party or two he had taken her to in high school. "It's been a while."

He glanced around the café and leaned nearer to her. "Chet is going to be running the bank for us," he said in a muted tone, "so they moved back to town last week. But keep it under your hat, we haven't told the bank employees yet."

Logan's father owned one of the banks in Hidden Valley, as well as a real estate office, the newspaper, and a few other businesses. While his father was spending the next few years in prison—unless his high-priced legal team could get him out—Logan had been tasked with running the family businesses and, to Jenessa's surprise, was doing an admirable job of it. He was growing into a mature, savvy businessman right before her eyes—a long way from the entitled rich kid she had dated in high school.

As passionately as Logan continued to pursue her, there was no love lost between Jenessa and his father. Grey Alexander had always blamed her for trying to derail his son's bright future when they were teenagers, not to mention the fact that it was her dogged investigative reporting last year that had helped crack the case that landed him in jail.

"I won't say a word—promise. Perhaps I'll run into your cousin sometime." Jenessa remembered Summer was about five years older than Logan and had married her college sweetheart. Other than that, details about Summer were rather fuzzy.

"Maybe even today," Logan said. "I'm meeting her here for coffee."

"Sorry, but I can't stay. The line's too long. If I'm late again, Charles will have my head." Jenessa took a couple of steps toward the door and looked back over her shoulder. "Tell her I said hello."

She slipped out the door and found Summer walking toward the entrance.

"Jenessa?" she inquired, scanning Jenessa's face as her lips broke into a wide smile. "Those green eyes and dark hair, I would recognize you anywhere."

"Summer." Jenessa's response came across a little more surprised than she had intended, but they had only met a few times, many years ago. How could Summer have recognized her so quickly?

The same way she had realized that was Summer walking toward her, no doubt—Logan.

Jenessa politely extended her hand. "Good to see you again."

In response, Summer reached out to take it, her long shirtsleeve inching up, exposing a blue and purple bruise on her wrist.

Jenessa shook the woman's hand, pulling her gaze up to meet Summer's, and smiled. She looked good— trim and lightly tanned. Her golden hair fell in soft thick waves around her shoulders, and her azure blue eyes matched the color of Logan's.

"I'd love to stay and catch up, but I'm already late for work." Jenessa self-consciously ran a hand over her own hair, not as thick and luxurious as Summer's. "Another time?"

The woman's smile widened and appeared to be sincere. "Sure, that'd be great."

Jenessa hurried down the street to the newspaper, her curiosity piqued about Summer. She'd have to make time to find out what she had been doing the last thirteen years.

~*~

Jenessa strolled into the newspaper office and greeted the elderly receptionist.

"Good morning, Alice. You look nice today," she said as she stopped at the front desk. "Any calls for me?"

Alice feigned a blush at the compliment and waved a few yellow slips at her. "The Murphys confirming their appointment with you about their vow renewal next weekend, Mr. Goldstein, the high school principal, asking for you to interview him about the finished auditorium remodel…oh, and one from the tall, dark, and handsome Detective Baxter," she crooned, unashamedly showing her delight in the man.

Jenessa checked her cell phone, wondering why Michael hadn't called her on it. The screen was black. Apparently she had forgotten to charge her phone the night before and it was dead.

"Thank you, Alice." She plucked the message slips from the old woman's boney fingers and continued down the hall to her cubicle.

Once situated at her desk, she phoned Michael, but the call went straight to voicemail.

"Hey, Michael. I'm just returning your call. Sorry, my cell is dead. Call me at the office."

She got busy writing a few articles she had been working on for the society page and a human-interest story on the town's new humane society. These were nothing like the hard-hitting stories she was used to writing at the Sacramento newspaper, but since moving back to Hidden Valley she was beginning to appreciate the slower pace and lighter articles.

Eventually, Michael called her back. "Sorry, I was in a meeting about a potential new case and couldn't—"

"A new case?" Her interest flared. "Tell me about it."

"You know I can't do that, at least not yet anyway."

"Just a tiny clue…please."

Silence.

"A murder?"

"No."

"A jewelry heist? A kidnapping? A blackmailer?"

"Stop that."

"You didn't say no, so which one is it?"

"I can't say. But listen, I might have a question or two for you, so I was just calling to see if you wanted to get together for lunch."

"Lunch, huh?" Perhaps she could pepper him with enough questions that he would cave. "Sure. My treat."

"Antonio's?" he suggested.

"Perfect."

"And I'm paying."

She knew Michael would never let her pay, but she had to try. "See you at noon."

~*~

Sitting at a table in the middle of Antonio's Italian Ristorante, Jenessa glanced around the room. "This was where we had our first date, remember?"

"Of course I remember. That's why I suggested it." Michael smiled, but he looked a little nervous.

She considered asking why, but figured it had something to do with the new case and she'd leave the interrogating questions for later.

"I remember coming to this place in high school with my family," she reminisced.

"My family did too."

"When you and I came here on our first date," she said, "I was pouring out my story of why I left Hidden Valley twelve years before, remember?"

"Then Logan showed up and—well, speak of the devil himself." Michael's gaze lifted to a place beyond her.

She looked over her shoulder and saw Logan approaching, with his cousin Summer following behind him.

Logan stopped at their table and rested a hand lightly on Jenessa's shoulder for a moment. "Hello, Jenessa. Michael."

She willed her heart to remain calm under his touch. She flicked a quick glance at Michael, whose lips had drawn into an irritated straight line. It was never a good time whenever Michael and Logan were in the same room. It was hard enough with them living in the same town. She never knew when they might cross paths.

"Hello, Logan." Jenessa smiled, hoping to keep things pleasant between the men. "Summer. Nice to see you again." The words felt stilted as they passed over her lips, uncomfortable in this awkward situation.

"Michael, this is Summer, Logan's cousin."

"Summer Monahan," the woman said.

"This is Detective Michael Baxter," Logan introduced, making it sound like they were friends.

"Hello," Michael replied graciously, offering the woman a polite smile before returning his gaze to Jenessa, his eyes asking her to relieve the uncomfortable situation.

Silence hung in the air for a few beats.

The courteous thing to do would have been to invite Logan and Summer to join them, but from the look on Michael's face, that wasn't even a remote possibility.

Fortunately, Summer broke the awkward moment. "Looks like the hostess is motioning that our table is ready. We should go, Logan."

He nodded.

"It was nice seeing you again, Jenessa," Summer said. "Nice to meet you, Michael." She took Logan by the arm and led him away.

Jenessa watched them go, noticing out of the corner of her eye that Michael slipped something into his jacket pocket. *What was it?*

"Do you want to go somewhere else?" he asked her.

"No, we were here first." She offered him a sweet smile, hoping to lift the mood.

He shot a quick glance over his shoulder. "You're right. Let's not allow him to ruin our lunch."

"He won't," she assured him. "Anyway, I'm sure he and Summer have plenty to talk about besides us."

Jenessa took a sip of water and sneaked a quick look past Michael, to the booth they had claimed.

"Do you know her?" Michael asked.

"From years ago. I remember talking to her at a couple of parties Logan took me to when we were in high school."

"She's your age? She looks older."

"She is older. She was just out of college at the time. UCLA, I think." She peeked at their table again. This time Logan caught her looking at him and grinned. An unexpected chill slithered down her arms and she swung her focus back to Michael. "She was recently married at the time, maybe, or just engaged. I can't remember."

"Engaged, huh?" His eyes were focused on the menu as he said it, like that was the only word he'd heard her say.

Jenessa recalled the bruise she saw on Summer's wrist earlier and how she had tried to cover it as soon as Jenessa caught sight of it. Her attention was once more pulled toward their table. "I wonder what her story is."

"You want to know what everyone's story is, Jenessa." Michael shook his head slightly, laying his menu down, then he reached across the table and took her hand. "How about we concentrate on the next chapter in *our* story instead?"

CHAPTER 3

A COUPLE OF DAYS LATER, as Jenessa sat at her desk that morning, she caught herself still thinking about the mysterious death at the lake. She hadn't heard back from Detective Provenza yet, but maybe by now Michael had looked into it for her as he had promised.

She phoned him.

"As a matter of fact, Provenza and I were just talking about it," Michael confirmed. "The dead body belonged to a college kid. The body was found floating in the lake near the rocks between the boathouse I pointed out and the Alexanders' place. Anyway, the medical examiner couldn't determine the cause of death, with nothing much to go on he ruled it accidental."

"Any potential suspects at the time?"

"No good leads. They had questioned his roommate and some friends at Whitfield College, Provenza said, as well as the people with lake houses nearby, but it sounded like the case went cold pretty fast."

"So George would have interviewed Grey Alexander then." The man certainly wouldn't have liked that. Logan's father was the richest man in town and owned most of it. Being questioned would have rankled him and he would have done his best to intimidate the unlucky officer.

"He didn't say specifically, but he must have." Michael paused. "Why all the interest in this old case?"

"It might make for a good story—especially if I investigate and find out it was more than an accident."

"More than an accident? You mean murder?"

"Exactly," she said emphatically. "As you well know, there are two main reasons someone murders another person—sex or money."

"Doubtful in this case. It's more probable that the kid fell into the lake and drowned because he was drunk, then the waves beat his dead body against the rocks. Anyway, that's what the ME determined was most likely the cause of death."

"So they found alcohol in his system?" she asked.

"Some."

"How old was he?"

The sound of papers rustling came across the line. Michael must have been searching through the file. "Says here he was twenty, a sophomore at Whitfield College."

"In good physical shape?"

"Six feet tall, a hundred and eighty pounds. Popular, good-looking kid, the notes say."

If there was a juicy story in there, she was going to find it. "Mind if I take a look at the file?"

"You know I can't let you do that. I've already given you all the info we're allowed to share with the press."

Michael was a by-the-book kind of cop, but Detective Provenza on the other hand...he was close to retirement and seemed to have a fondness for her, as much as he tried to hide it. Maybe she could sweet talk him into letting her take a peek.

"Thanks for the information, Michael. I really do appreciate it." But she needed more—a lot more.

"You're welcome. Wish I could give you the file, but you know the rules."

"Sure, rules." It wasn't that Jenessa was a rule breaker, but she had been known to bend a few on occasion, some so much so that they resembled pretzels.

Jenessa checked her watch. It was almost noon. Maybe if she dropped by the police station, she could ask Michael to lunch and run into Provenza. She grabbed her purse out of one of the deep desk drawers and headed toward the front door.

"Jenessa." Her editor called to her down the hall, just as her phone began to ring on her desk. She chose to answer her boss instead.

She stopped, backed up, and poked her head into his office. "Yes, Charles."

He stood behind his desk, bent over with his hands splayed out on it. He straightened when he heard her come in. "Got anything for the front page? I'm desperate for a big story, something that's going to create a huge organic buzz in this town." She sensed an undertone of worry coloring his words.

"A big fat gripping story?"

"Yes, real front page news. I hate to admit it, Jenessa, but we're losing readership. We need something with sizzle. You have anything like that?"

"Well, there is an idea I've been kicking around. Too early to talk about it, but I'll let you know when I have something concrete."

"That's good." His expression lifted a bit. "Don't wait too long." He crossed his arms and his gaze drifted out the window. "I've got to keep the readers engaged."

Charles' voice betrayed a tension that she had never heard in it before, and there was something in his eyes, an unfamiliar look of desperation. He was generally upbeat, especially since he had begun dating her bubbly best friend Ramey. Yes, the Herald was a small-town paper, but people in this burg had been loyal and loved reading about what was going on with their neighbors. Something at the newspaper must have changed.

"Is everything okay?" She took a few steps toward him, trying to catch his eye.

His attention slid sideways to her for a moment. "Don't spread it around, but since readership is down, money is tight."

From personal experience, Jenessa knew exactly what that meant—layoffs. She had been let go from the Sacramento paper a year ago because readership was dwindling. An uneasy feeling swept over her. Was her job at the Herald in jeopardy?

"Give me a few days to flesh this thing out, Charles, and I'll let you know." She left him staring out the window and continued down the hall, determined not to let flagging readership destroy the life she was building in Hidden Valley.

"Like I said, don't wait too long," he hollered after her.

"I'm going to lunch, Alice," Jenessa said as she passed the receptionist.

"Jenessa!" a man called.

Her gaze flew to the front entrance. From the way Logan strode toward her and the distressed look on his face, it was clear something was wrong.

"What's happened?" she asked.

"I need to talk to you. It's urgent."

"Sure, what's going on?"

Logan glanced around the reception area. "Can we step outside?"

Knowing Alice's penchant for gossip, Jenessa pulled open the heavy door and motioned for him to pass through first.

"Jenessa!" Alice exclaimed. "You have a phone call."

"You'll have to take a message," she replied over her shoulder, following Logan out to the sidewalk. "Tell me, what's wrong?"

"It's your aunt."

"Renee?"

"I was just at the hospital and—"

"The hospital? Why?"

"Summer's boy fractured his arm, but—"

"Oh no, that poor kid—what were you saying about my aunt?"

His eyes were filled with concern and she got an uneasy feeling.

"Listen, as I was leaving, I noticed the paramedics lifting her out of an ambulance on a gurney. I tried to call you."

"My cell is dead." Her head began spinning with worry. "So what happened to my aunt?" Her chest constricted at the grim possibilities and she almost couldn't breathe.

"I'm not sure. I tried to call you at the newspaper too."

The ringing phone she had ignored. "Sorry, I— Charles was calling me at the same time." She shook her head to clear the fog. "Was Aunt Renee in an accident?"

"I don't know, but I figured it must be serious if she was in an ambulance. I couldn't get ahold of you, so I raced over here from the hospital, hoping I could find you."

His perseverance and thoughtful concern was touching, but right now she had to concentrate on finding out what illness or injury had befallen her aunt. She drew in a sharp breath. "I've got to go, Logan. I need to see her."

"My car is right here." He motioned toward his red BMW, parked at the curb.

Jenessa gave him a nod and took a step toward the car, abruptly stopping at the thought of Michael.

"What is it?"

She looked at Logan and considered what she was doing. His persistent presence in her life was already wearing on Michael and affecting their relationship. "Maybe I should go get my own car."

"Don't be silly," Logan replied. "Mine is right here. It'll be faster."

The hospital was only a couple of miles away, but her car was sitting at home. He was right. She needed to check on her aunt as soon as possible. "Okay, okay. Let's go." Hopefully Michael would understand.

While Logan drove, Jenessa borrowed his cell phone to call her sister and Ramey. Neither were aware of Aunt Renee's apparent rush to the hospital and both agreed to meet Jenessa there.

She handed back the phone as Logan pulled up to the hospital entrance. She had considered calling Michael, but she wanted to see what was happening with her aunt first. She opened the car door. "Thanks for the lift, Logan."

"I'll park and meet you inside."

She wanted to say "No need" to avoid having to explain to Michael why Logan was at the hospital with her, but Logan had gone out of his way to track her down just to give her the news. She probably wouldn't even know yet if he hadn't done so. It would be rude to send him away like that—wouldn't it?

"Unless you don't want me to…"

"No, no, it's not that." She offered an apologetic smile. "You're a busy man. I don't want to keep you from something important."

He held her gaze for a moment, his expression serious. "There's nothing more important to me than you, Jenessa."

If she was going to build a life with Michael, she couldn't have Logan saying such things to her, tugging at her heartstrings like that.

She had loved Logan once—she had been so fully under his spell that there hadn't been anything she wouldn't have done for him. And she'd thought he loved her the same in return. But when she turned up pregnant, he turned tail and ran off to college to escape his responsibilities—something she was constantly reminded of by the absence of their child in her life. How could she get over that as long as she had no idea where their son was or if he was being raised in a good home?

Of course, that was almost thirteen years ago. And Logan was only eighteen at the time. People can grow up. And people can change too…can't they?

She slid out of the seat and turned back to him. "I'll see you inside."

CHAPTER 4

JENESSA RUSHED TO THE RECEPTION DESK in the emergency room of the Hidden Valley hospital and was informed by the formidably large nurse that the doctor was in with her aunt and that she could take a seat and wait for him to come out. Her first instinct was to press the nurse for more information, but the tone of the woman's voice told her it would be fruitless, so she reluctantly took a seat.

The large glass doors whooshed open and Logan strode in. He glanced around and, spotting Jenessa in the waiting area, made a beeline to her. "Any news?"

She bobbed her head toward the nurse. "The drill sergeant over there told me to cool my jets in one of these chairs."

"How about I give it a try?" Logan arched a brow and painted on a charming smile.

Jenessa gestured with a sweep of her hand. "Have at it."

He strolled over to the woman and leaned an arm on the counter. Jenessa couldn't hear what Logan was saying or how he was saying it, but from the softened expression on the nurse's face, even giving him a shy smile, he appeared to be working his magic on her.

"Well?" Jenessa asked once he returned.

Logan took the chair next to her. "The doctor's initial prognosis was a heart attack, but we won't know for sure until he finishes his examination and comes out to talk to you."

"How did you get that information?"

"Charm." Logan pumped his eyebrows, then stood. "I'd better go check on my cousin and her boy."

Jenessa pitched her chin toward a wide hallway that opened to the waiting area. "Looks like they're coming to find you."

Summer and her son approached. The boy, whose height reached just above his mother's shoulder, was wearing a red cast from his hand to just below his elbow.

"Hello, Jenessa," Summer greeted before switching her attention to Logan. "I thought you had left."

"I had," he nodded, "but an ambulance just brought Jenessa's aunt in, so here I am. Jenessa, this is Grayson."

"That looks painful," She told the kid. His blond hair and blue eyes made him the spitting image of his mother. And of Logan. If she hadn't met Summer, Jenessa's mind could easily have jumped to one of her scattered conclusions—the Alexander genepool was a strong one, for sure.

"Not too bad. I can take it," he replied, seemingly trying to be brave.

Logan glanced around. "Where's Lily?"

"Chet picked her up and took her home," Summer answered.

"Who is Lily?" Jenessa asked.

"Our daughter. She's six."

A perfect family, Jenessa thought. A boy and a girl. She wondered if Lily had the Alexander looks too, or if she more resembled her father, Chet.

Summer sat down in the chair next to Jenessa. "I hope your aunt is going to be okay."

"Thanks. Me too."

Summer patted Jenessa's hand. "How are you doing?"

"Anxious. I hate waiting." Jenessa sat back in her seat, her gaze traveling to the boy standing beside her. "What happened to your son's arm?"

"A spiral fracture," the boy answered before his mother could.

"Not a big deal," Summer said with a nervous chuckle. "You know boys, always breaking this or that."

Spiral fracture? Jenessa's eyes flicked up to Logan, who seemed oblivious to what she was thinking.

"How did it happen?" Jenessa asked.

Summer stood. "A little too much roughhousing, I'm afraid." Her focus went to her son. "I think it's time we get you home, Grayson." She turned to Jenessa. "We should get together and talk later."

"Sure," Jenessa replied with a slight nod.

"See ya, fella." Logan gave the boy's upper arm a soft, playful punch.

"Yeah, see ya." Grayson followed his mom. He glanced over his shoulder and tossed Logan a friendly grin and an awkward wave.

Jenessa waited for the two of them to cross through the large sliding glass doors before she spoke. "Does Grayson get hurt a lot?"

"I don't really know. I haven't seen them much since Summer moved away. Why do you ask?"

Maybe she was simply being overly suspicious. She tended to do that. Boys do get hurt horsing around and playing sports. "No reason." But then there was the bruise on Summer's wrist...

It's probably nothing.

Logan dipped his chin and raised his brows at her. "Come on. I know that tone."

"Jenessa!" Ramey exclaimed, rushing through the glass doors, her expressive blue eyes wide and her ruddy skin further flushed from the obvious sprint from the parking lot.

Sara followed close behind, looking just as concerned, her breathing a bit labored as well. "How is Aunt Renee?"

"We don't know anything yet," Jenessa replied.

Sara's eyes widened for a moment, appearing to be a little taken aback to see Logan at her sister's side. "Hello, Logan."

"Logan?" Ramey noticed Logan now and didn't mask her surprise.

"Hello, Sara, Ramey." He shoved his hands in his pants pockets and seemed suddenly uncomfortable—a look Jenessa had rarely seen him wear. "Maybe I should go." His head pitched toward the entrance as he said it, his eyes steady on Jenessa.

She wanted to reach out, put a hand on his arm to stop him, for he had been the one to track her down and bring her here—but she thought better of it.

"Where's Michael?" Sara asked, peering around.

"I haven't been able to reach him." Now that was a lie. Jenessa had meant to call him when she got to the hospital, but she had been distracted by Summer and Grayson…and Logan. "Let me try him again." She dug around in her purse and pulled out her phone. "I have no service. It must be dead."

Logan held his cell out. "Here, use mine." He knew perfectly well her phone was dead, but, aside from giving her a knowing look, he didn't call her on the lie.

"Thanks," Jenessa took it, avoiding his eyes. "Did you call Luke?" she asked her sister.

Sara had been dating Michael's cousin Luke for almost as long as Jenessa and Michael had been a couple. Having moved to Hidden Valley to take a job as a rookie patrolman in town, he seemed to be settling in to the small-town life.

"Not yet. He's on duty today," Sara answered. "I'll leave him a message when we find out what's what."

"Miss Jones?" The doctor stepped into the waiting area, drawing their attention.

"I'm Jenessa Jones." She gestured toward her sister. "This is Sara Jones."

"Doctor Takani," he introduced.

"How's our aunt?" Jenessa asked.

"She had a mild heart attack, but she's resting now," the doctor explained. "We're running some tests, but I think we're going to have to go in and clear the blockage, do an angioplasty and a stent, so the next one doesn't kill her."

"That sounds serious. Is she going to be all right?" Ramey asked, her brows knitting together with concern.

Jenessa draped a comforting arm around Ramey's shoulders. "Don't worry. I'm sure she'll be fine." Or at least she hoped she would. With both Jenessa's parents having already passed, losing Aunt Renee would be devastating. "She's a strong lady." Jenessa turned to the physician. "Right, Doc?"

"It could be much worse the next time." The doctor tucked the patient chart under his arm. "She's going to need to follow a strict diet and exercise plan. I think she'll be okay, but we'll know more after the surgery."

"When will that be?" Sara asked.

"As soon as I can schedule an operating room and a surgeon."

"Is there anything we can do?" Jenessa asked, feeling helpless and anxious.

"After the surgery, someone will need to take care of her for a few days," the doctor said.

"Maybe I can help," Logan said. "I'm happy to arrange for some in-home care while she's recuperating, on my dime of course."

"That's sweet, Logan," Jenessa laid her hand lightly on his forearm, "but no. We three can take turns until she's back on her feet. Can't we, girls?" She looked from Sara to Ramey, who both nodded their agreement.

"I'll make a chart," Ramey declared, "so we know who's on duty when. Someone will be with her at all times."

"I can take the first shift," Sara offered.

"Looks like you have things well in hand," the doctor commented.

"Can we see her?" Ramey asked.

"Well, I suppose you can go back and visit for a minute, but you'll have to keep it very short. She'll need to be prepped for surgery soon and she needs her rest. Room one sixty-four." He turned and wandered off down the hall.

"You two go ahead," Jenessa said to Ramey and Sara. "I really need to get ahold of Michael."

"Okay," Ramey replied, "but don't be long." She and Sara set off down the hall.

"I'll wait with you," Logan offered.

"That's not necessary." Michael would be furious at Logan doting on her—and maybe even at her for allowing it. She walked to a nearby payphone and dialed Michael's number, hoping Logan got the hint. It went to voicemail. He was probably in a meeting or something. She left him a message, briefly explaining what happened to her aunt and telling him what room she would be in.

She hung up the phone and turned to Logan. "Guess I'd better go see my aunt before the nurse shoos everyone out."

"I'll walk you down there."

"No, Logan," Jenessa let out a nervous laugh, anticipating Michael's imminent arrival, "you don't have to—"

"I want to poke my head in and say hello. I promise I won't stay long." His brows rose, asking for her approval.

"Okay, but only to say hello."

A playful smile curved on Logan's lips, reminding her of the teenage boy she once knew.

They found her aunt's room, stopping at the open door where they heard Ramey's voice emanating from the room.

"This must be it," Jenessa said.

CHAPTER 5

AUNT RENEE SAT, PROPPED UP SLIGHTLY with pillows, in a small, private hospital room, the sunshine diffused by gauzy sheers behind heavy, open draperies. Her eyelids were half-closed, but her expression seemed to brighten a tiny bit when she saw Jenessa step in, then it changed for a fleeting moment before her face relaxed again. Was it surprise at seeing Logan there that had widened her eyes? Or something else?

Jenessa slid past her sister and stepped to her aunt's bedside, while Logan hung back a little. She bent down and kissed her aunt on the cheek. Her skin was pale and she appeared weak, so uncharacteristic of her spirited aunt. "You gave us quite a scare."

"Myself included," Aunt Renee retorted, her voice frail.

"I can't stay," Logan said, his gaze flicking to Jenessa momentarily, then back to Aunt Renee. He took a slow step closer, standing near the foot of her bed. "I just wanted to say hello and see for myself that you were okay, Mrs. Giraldy."

"That was very kind of you, Logan." Her gaze traveled to Jenessa, as if she were trying to encourage her niece to say something to him.

"Yes, thank you," Jenessa offered to him. "Actually, it was Logan who let me know you were here."

"Is that so?" Aunt Renee's expression perked up a little. "And how did you know, Logan?"

He told her about his cousin's son and the injuries that brought him to the hospital, explaining that he happened to be there when the ambulance had delivered her.

"I see." Aunt Renee's head cocked slightly, her focus returning to Jenessa. "And where is Michael?"

"I'm right here." Michael stepped through the doorway and moved beside Logan, standing tall, asserting the few extra inches of height he had over him.

Logan straightened then and pulled his shoulders back.

"Sorry, but I just got Jenessa's voicemail—work, you know." Michael's warm brown eyes shifted to Jenessa, an apologetic smile raising the corners of his mouth. "How are you doing, Renee?"

"I'll be fine," Aunt Renee replied softly. "It's not a big deal. Just a little heart attack, the doctor said."

"Please take this seriously," Sara chided her aunt.

"Sara, I'll be fine." Aunt Renee laid a hand to her chest. "I just need a few days of rest."

"And surgery," Jenessa added. "The doctor said an angioplasty, I believe."

Aunt Renee closed her eyes as if she were about to drift off. "Oh, yeah...that."

"We'll be with you 'round the clock," Ramey assured her.

"Well, looks like you're in good hands," Logan said, slowly backing toward the door. "I think it's time I go."

"Thank you, Logan," Aunt Renee opened her eyes a slit, "for bringing Jenessa here."

Jenessa's spine stiffened, her gaze set on her aunt's pale face with her eyes closed again, avoiding Michael's glare. Had her aunt really just pointed out that inflammatory bit of information—on purpose?

Her neck muscles constricted, like someone had a chokehold on her throat. She could feel the heat of Michael's glare on the back of her head. She hadn't done anything wrong, so why did she feel like she had?

The echo of Logan's retreating footsteps seemed to fill the room as the atmosphere turned frigid. No one said a word.

"Visiting time is over," announced the stocky nurse as she bustled into the room. "We need to get the patient ready for surgery."

Jenessa gave her aunt another kiss on the check, as did Sara.

"When can we come back?" Ramey asked.

"Once she's out of surgery and the doctor feels she's up for a short visit." The nurse spread her arms out and herded them all toward the door like a mother hen with her chicks. "I'd call first to make sure. Might save you a trip."

"A trip?" Ramey gasped. "We're not leaving until she's out of surgery."

"I figured," the crusty nurse replied. "You can sit in the waiting area. Now, out you go."

"Take care," Michael called out over his shoulder to Aunt Renee as the group was hurried out the door. He took Jenessa's hand as they all traveled down the hallway.

"Why was Logan here again?" Michael asked as they reached the waiting room. His irritation was bubbling very near the surface.

"He was already at the hospital when the ambulance brought Aunt Renee in and thought I would want to know."

"Why was he already here?" Michael asked.

Jenessa explained about Logan's cousin's son. "Logan tried me on my cell phone but couldn't reach me, so he took a chance and popped in to the newspaper."

Michael took a deep, audible breath and blew it out. "He couldn't call the paper?"

"He did, but I was in a meeting with Charles."

"Hmm." He still wasn't convinced it was necessary. Logan seemed to take advantage of every opportunity to insert himself into Jenessa's life. "I'm glad he tracked you down—I understand this was serious—but why didn't you drive yourself over here? Why did you have to come with him?"

"I was desperate to get to my aunt and it was just faster. I walked to work today and I didn't want to have to go home to get my car. Please, Michael, don't make more out of this than it is."

And what exactly was it this was? "It's just that he's always around, always trying to save the day. I don't like it."

"This isn't the time to argue about Logan," Jenessa said. "Aunt Renee could have died."

"You're right, I'm sorry, it's just that..." He glanced toward Ramey and Sara, who were standing nearby. Obviously they couldn't help but overhear the conversation and appeared uncomfortable with the tension between him and Jenessa.

Sara stepped beside Jenessa. "We're happy you could be here, Michael," she said. "I'm sure our aunt appreciated it. I know we girls did, right Ramey?"

"Absolutely."

Were they trying to diffuse the uncomfortable situation, or take his attention away from pursuing this? He knew better than to air their personal laundry in public, but in his frustration he couldn't seem to contain himself.

"Yes, Michael," Jenessa added in a tight voice, meeting his gaze, "we do appreciate your dropping everything to be here, but you probably need to get back to work, don't you?"

Too late. He had embarrassed her—he could see it in her eyes. He was sorry for that, but he couldn't help it. Logan brought out the worst in him. Back in high school he never measured up to star-quarterback and heartthrob Logan Alexander, but now the tables were turned. It was Michael who had the girl that Logan wanted, and he had to admit, it gave him a bit of satisfaction.

"I do have to get going, but I hate to leave you like this." He wanted nothing more than to stay with her, not just in this crisis, but every day of his life. Lately, however, he felt her drifting away from him at times.

"I'll call you when she's out of surgery," Jenessa promised, giving him a little smile. "Don't worry about me, I'm fine on my own."

That was what he was afraid of.

~*~

The surgery seemed to go well, the doctor told them, but they wouldn't know for sure until Aunt Renee woke up. She was resting comfortably, but would be out for several more hours. The doctor asked the three women to let her sleep through the night and to come back in the morning.

An ominous feeling settled on Jenessa and she couldn't seem to shake it. Looking at Sara and Ramey, appearing relieved and happy, they didn't seem to share her fears.

She phoned Michael, as she had promised, and he came to the hospital to pick her up. As he drove her home, he held her hand, but they barely spoke two words. She was worried about her aunt. What if the heart attack had been worse? What if there was another one, more serious?

"Are you mad at me?" Michael asked, his voice soft, almost apologetic.

"It's not you," she muttered, pulling her hand out of his. "I was just thinking about my aunt. What if this heart attack had killed her?"

"But it didn't."

"But it could have, like the one that killed my father. Apparently heart disease runs in my family."

"I'm sure she'll be fine. Isn't that what her doctor said?"

"He couldn't possibly know that for sure." She crossed her arms and blinked back the tears that were trying to come to the surface, letting her gaze wander out through the windshield, staring at nothing in particular.

Her thoughts drifted to her parents. She had already lost both of them—one to a car accident, the other to a heart attack. Aunt Renee was the only parental figure she had left in her life.

What if she died too?

That terrifying thought brought a rush of tears that she could not hold back. An unexpected tightness in her chest sent tiny, painful pinpricks cascading down her arms. She rubbed her skin, then wiped her hands over her cheeks, shifting her body toward the passenger door. The last thing she wanted to do was talk.

Michael pulled his car to the curb in front of her house, then laid a hand over one of hers. "Is there anything I can do to make this better?"

She twisted in her seat to face him and shook her head no. He was a sweet man and she could see he only wanted to help, but what was there to do? He couldn't give her any guarantees about her aunt's health, no matter how much he may want to.

"I don't know what came over me." She ran her fingers under her eyes to clear away the last of the tears and pulled in a deep breath. "You're probably right, she'll be fine." Or at least Jenessa prayed she would.

Michael leaned over and gave her a soft kiss. "I love you, you know."

She opened the car door and looked back at him, nodding slightly. "I know. Thank you for being here for me."

~*~

Once inside her home, she flipped on the lights and dropped her purse on the entry table. She headed straight to her office at the back of the house. It had been her father's home office for years before he passed and left the house to her. Now, seated at his massive oak desk, Jenessa missed him. Their relationship had been strained, ever since Logan had gotten her pregnant, but with his death, her heart had softened and she wished he were still there.

A framed photo of her parents sat on the corner of the desk and she picked it up. Jenessa traced a finger lovingly over their faces, then clutched the picture to her chest, missing them more than she had in a very long time.

There too, on the desktop, was a framed picture of Aunt Renee when she was about thirty-five. The beautiful, vivacious blonde smiled broadly into the camera in the candid photo. Still clinging to the photo of her mom and dad, Jenessa picked up her aunt's picture too. "You can't die." Tears began to fall again. "Oh, God, please don't let her die."

CHAPTER 6

AFTER A FITFUL NIGHT'S SLEEP, Jenessa climbed out of bed and padded downstairs to the kitchen. She grabbed a bowl out of the cabinet and poured herself some cereal, wondering how her aunt had faired through the night. No emergency phone calls from the hospital gave her hope that all was well.

She phoned Ramey, who was already at work at The Sweet Spot, and then Sara, arranging to meet them at the hospital in an hour. After a quick shower, she threw on her clothes and a few dabs of makeup.

Though in a hurry, she stopped to check herself in the mirror. She looked tired. She leaned closer. Maybe a little highlighter would counteract those faint shadows under her pale eyes. She pulled her long dark hair up into a ponytail, applied a little mascara, slid a smear of berry lip-gloss over her lips, and called it good.

As soon as she backed her sports car out of the garage, her phone began to ring. She stopped in her driveway and dug around in her purse for it. "Hello," she greeted.

"Hey, Jenessa, it's Logan."

She had answered without checking the caller ID, expecting it to be Michael. Or the hospital. But not *him*. "Oh," her voice dropped, "good morning, Logan."

"Don't sound so disappointed."

"No, it's not that. I just thought it would be Michael." His was usually the first voice she heard most mornings, and after the spat they'd had the day before, and the sullen exchange in the car when he had dropped her off last night, she had hoped they could kiss and make up, so to speak. She wasn't about to tell Logan that part though. "What's up?"

"I thought I'd check to see how your aunt is doing."

"That's sweet." His thoughtful concern touched her. "I called the hospital a little while ago and the nurse said she had a good night."

"That's what I wanted to hear."

"I'm on my way to see her now, but there is something I'd like to discuss with you later. Can we talk sometime today?"

"Sure." He paused briefly. "About anything in particular?"

"A story I'm working on. How about later this morning?"

"I'm on my way to meet with some investors for a project I'm working on, but I'll be free this afternoon…say three o'clock at The Sweet Spot?"

After Michael's reaction to seeing her with Logan at the hospital yesterday, that probably wasn't the best place—too many prying eyes and the off chance Michael might stop in for a coffee. "How about Crane Park? The picnic tables by the tennis courts?"

"Three o'clock it is. I've got to run, but give your aunt my best."

~*~

Jenessa breezed through the large glass doors at the entrance to the hospital as they whooshed open. Her eyes widened and a smile spread across her lips seeing Michael waiting for her, leaning against the wall, arms crossed. He pushed off the moment he saw her, unfurling his arms to give her a hug.

"This is a pleasant surprise," she said, returning his embrace.

"I didn't like how things went yesterday." He hated it when they fought. "Am I forgiven?"

"Of course."

Michael put a couple of fingers gently under her chin and tilted her head back, then kissed her ever so briefly. Her lips were soft and full.

She let go of him and took a small step back. "But how did you know I'd be here?"

"Sara called me, said you girls were heading to the hospital. So after I dropped Jake off at school, I rushed over."

Jenessa's brows wrinkled into a frown and she cocked her head slightly. "Sara called you?"

"She thought I'd like to know and wasn't sure you'd call me after our fight yesterday."

"I wouldn't call it a fight. More like a little spat."

"Whatever it was, it's over. We've kissed and made up, so let's put it behind us. Why don't we go and see your aunt?"

~*~

By the time Jenessa and Michael reached Aunt Renee's room, they found Sara and Ramey already there, hovering over her from either side of the bed, speaking in quiet tones.

Ramey looked up at the sound of their footsteps entering the room. "The nurse said she's doing great."

Jenessa squeezed past her sister and moved to her aunt's bedside. "That's wonderful news." She leaned down and kissed her aunt's cheek, her appearance still pale and weak from the surgery. Her light green eyes had a grayish cast, her smoky brown eyeliner was bleeding below her eyes, and her honey-blond hair looked in need of a wash.

Her aunt was a beautiful woman, even in her late fifties, but today she looked like a much older version of herself.

"I want to go home," she muttered in a low, raspy voice.

"I know it's hard," Sara said in a patronizing way.

"You don't understand." Aunt Renee's voice took on a measure of strength. "The nurses come in and out at all hours of the night, and they're not quiet about it, let me tell you. I could hardly sleep a wink—thank goodness for pain meds. Then there are the awful smells." She sighed. "And that radiator there clanked on and off all night. And the food—oh, don't get me started, girls."

A snort erupted from Ramey while attempting to muffle a laugh. Jenessa threw a hand over her mouth to stop a chuckle too, lifting her eyes to Ramey across the bed.

"What's so funny?" Sara asked, turning and looking to Michael.

He shrugged and remained silent, apparently choosing to stay out of it.

Jenessa shook her head at Sara. "Nothing." Her aunt hadn't lost her spunk, she was going to be just fine. "Has the doctor been in?"

"Not yet this morning," Aunt Renee replied.

"Well, let's track him down," Jenessa declared to Ramey and Sara, "and find out when we can take her home."

~*~

Michael couldn't stay long at the hospital and headed off to work soon after. The girls waited hours for the doctor, until the nurse finally asked them to leave and let the patient get her rest.

Jenessa made a quick stop at the bank before going to the newspaper. There were several people in line ahead of her when she spotted Allison Reagan, a young woman with auburn hair who was the assistant bank manager. Jenessa waved and Allison walked over to her.

"Hi, Jenessa. Is there anything I can do for you?"

"No, I was just saying hello."

"I heard about your aunt. I'm so sorry."

"You heard? How?"

"Small town, you know. News travels fast around here. How's she doing?"

Before she could reply, Jenessa caught sight of Summer Monahan and her husband walking into the bank. Summer saw her too and came over, her husband following.

"Oh my gosh!" Summer exclaimed, her attention on Allison rather than Jenessa. "It's so good to see you." Summer reached out and gave Allison a hug.

Allison seemed stiff and awkward in her response.

"You two know each other?" Jenessa asked.

"We used to be best friends when we were in high school," Summer said, excitement glowing on her face. "I hate to say it, but we lost contact after that."

Jenessa glanced at Allison, expecting a warm smile for her old friend, but the woman looked hesitant instead.

"You remember Chet, don't you?" Summer asked Allison.

"Yes, I do." A wash of fear seemed to cast across Allison's expression as she replied.

"He's my husband now," Summer went on, as if she hadn't noticed, turning to Jenessa. "Chet, this is Jenessa Jones. She used to date Logan a long time ago."

Chet put out his hand and Jenessa shook it. "Nice to meet you," he said.

"Sorry," Allison cut in, "but I have some urgent business to take care of." She ran a shaky hand through her auburn hair. "Nice to see you again, Jenessa." Her gaze avoided anyone else's and she turned and rushed off. The sound of her heels clicking rhythmically on the tile floor faded as she disappeared behind a private door at the back of the bank.

What was wrong with Allison? Something set her off. She couldn't get away fast enough.

"Well, that was weird," Summer said, voicing Jenessa's thoughts while planting a hand on her hip. "She acted like I had two heads or something."

There was certainly something strange about Allison's reaction to Summer and Chet. According to what Summer had just said, they had been good friends years ago. Jenessa would have to find out what the problem was. Later. Right now she needed to make a deposit and get to work.

The bank manager approached. "Right on time, Chet. My office is over here." He motioned toward the back of the bank.

Chet and Summer turned to follow him.

Summer looked back for a moment. "We'll have lunch soon, okay?"

Jenessa nodded. *Yes, we will.*

Sitting at her desk in her cubicle, Jenessa checked her watch—two forty-five. It was almost time to meet Logan in the park. She clocked out with the receptionist and hurried to her car.

Crane Park sat in the center of town, not far from her old high school. As she passed the imposing brick building, memories flooded in, reminding her of the time she'd spent there. In her mind, she saw the wide masonry steps and sprawling lawn dotted with students interacting before and after class. She would often meet Logan, usually dressed in his letterman jacket, near the large circular fountain out front and he would take her hand and walk her to class.

She was starry-eyed back then, seventeen and totally in love with the handsome jock, dreaming of marrying him one day and living in a big house with lots of kids. She shook her head at the silly thoughts and kept driving. How different her life had turned out.

Not long after he had gotten her pregnant, she left Hidden Valley, and, for twelve years she'd had no desire to move back—until the day her father died the previous year, leaving the family home and his sports car to her.

Logan, on the other hand, went on with his life as planned after spilling the news of the pregnancy to their parents. He attended an ivy-league college, then returned and went to work in one of his father's many business ventures in town—the unexpected pregnancy not seeming to affect his life in the least.

From the day she returned to Hidden Valley, she had reconnected with her old high school friend Michael. He was no longer the gangly teen with braces and a face full of pimples. He had grown up and filled out, became a handsome specimen, and straight away she fell for him and his adorable little boy.

At first, running into Logan around town was uncomfortable because of their painful history, but the bitterness she had been nursing all these years was starting to dissipate the more time she spent with him, the more she saw how he had grown up into a caring, savvy, hardworking man.

Of all the things that surprised her about moving back to this quaint little town, the maturing of Logan Alexander was the biggest. Still, she was somewhat leery of his intentions.

Up ahead, the park came into view. It had been one of Jenessa's favorite places to spend time when she was a teenager, the site of many town activities. Today it was empty, except for an older couple playing tennis and a young mother pushing a small child in one of the swings.

Logan was already seated at one of the picnic tables when she pulled her MLK Roadster into one of the diagonal parking spaces. He appeared to be sending an email or a text on his cell phone while he waited for her.

She got out of her car and strode toward him.

He smiled and stood as soon as he noticed her approaching, sticking his phone in the pocket of his dress slacks. "Three o'clock on the dot."

"How did your meeting go?" she asked, trying to make small talk before diving into the real reason she had asked to meet him.

A slight crease formed between his brows. "Not as well as I would've liked, but I'm not giving up." Their eyes met. "I like a challenge."

Had he meant that last statement for her?

He sat back down on the bench, his back to the picnic table, and Jenessa sat beside him.

"How's your aunt doing?"

"Considerably better. I talked to the doctor a little while ago and he said she should be able to go home by this evening. My sister is sitting with her right now."

His expression brightened. "I'm glad to hear it." Then he paused and looked into her eyes. "You know I'd never turn down an invitation to get together with you, but I'm curious why you wanted to meet. Something about a story?"

"An old story—a cold case, really." Jenessa pulled a pen and small notepad out of her purse. She was tempted to mention it was the case of the death of the mayor's son, but held back.

"So the police are looking into a cold case?"

"Well, no, not yet, but if I can come up with some new evidence, a good reason for them to reopen it, then Detective Provenza said he'd take another look at it."

"Provenza, huh? What does Michael have to say about it?"

"Same as Provenza," she replied, not wanting to go any further. Logan didn't need to know about any friction there may be between her and Michael, though he might have sensed some at the hospital.

"I don't understand," Logan said. "Why are you looking into this case? Do you have a personal stake in it?"

CHAPTER 7

"NO, I DON'T HAVE A PERSONAL STAKE in this case, Logan. It's business. It's my job as a reporter to hunt down a good story, and I have a gut feeling there may be something more to this case."

"So what are we talking about?"

"A so-called accident that happened about twenty years—"

"So called?"

"Yes. At Jonas Lake, there was—"

"Wait, twenty years ago I would have only been eleven," Logan interrupted.

"I know, but your family may have been involved."

"My family?" His brows lowered and he cocked his head.

"Summer's mother is your father's sister, right?"

"Yeah."

"Well, there was a death up at Jonas Lake, and I think Summer's family, or at least their boathouse, may

61

have had some connection to it. I thought you might remember your relatives or someone else in town talking about it," she continued. "It had to have made the TV news. Do you have any recollection about it?"

"Twenty years ago, huh?" He rubbed his jaw, his eyes lifting skyward as he tried to think back and recall the event.

"Think, Logan."

"I'm trying." He brought his gaze back to her. "Did you check the newspaper's archives?"

"Of course, but I found very little in the way of real details." Knowing that Nick Evans' death had something to do with Grey Alexander's family he might have applied pressure on the paper's publisher at the time to squash any specific details of what happened, particularly where it concerned his family, considering he owned the newspaper.

"Please tell me you remember something." After all this time, finding any new evidence would be a challenge, but she was determined to keep digging. "Anything."

A mischievous grin tugged at his lips. "Anything, huh? Well, I do remember something very interesting."

"You do?" *Now we're getting somewhere.*

"I remember we used to play tennis over there," he gestured toward the courts. "And I remember this picnic table. It's where I first kissed you."

It was?

She shook her head. "That's not what I meant and you know it." His playfulness was annoying her.

"Just trying to lighten the mood. You're so serious."

"It's my job to be serious." And if she didn't come up with some attention-grabbing stories, she could lose that job.

"Okay, let me think." He set both elbows behind him on the edge of the table and leaned back. "I seem to vaguely recall something did happen about that time." He paused as he thought about it.

"We were at the lake for the weekend, or maybe the week, and I remember seeing some cop cars farther down the shore than where our house was. I wanted to run down there to see what was happening, but my father wouldn't let me. But I think I heard him tell my mom it was a drowning."

"Then what?"

"Later that day we drove back to town. I don't remember anything after that, I must have forgotten about it."

"How could you forget about something like that?"

"Hey, I was eleven, Jenessa. I was too busy playing little league baseball and Pop Warner football to care."

"And that's all you remember?"

He shrugged apologetically. "Maybe Summer can tell you more—she was older. And if her family was involved..."

Jenessa made a note on her pad. "I'll have to talk to her."

"Now that you mention it, though, right after that Summer was sent away to boarding school. I remember because it was her senior year and I thought how, if it were me, I would hate having to start a new school in my last year of high school."

"You think it was connected?"

"That I couldn't say. You'd have to ask her."

Jenessa checked her watch. "I've got to make a stop before I head to the hospital." She stood. "I really appreciate your trying to help me."

"You know," he hesitated and stood up from the bench, "if you want, I can ask my father about the incident next time he's allowed to call out, see what he remembers."

"I don't think so," she breathed a laugh, "your father hates me." That was an understatement. "I'd rather you ask your mother."

~*~

Jenessa pushed the door open to the police station, juggling a cardboard tray of coffees, and went straight to the reception desk. "Good afternoon, Ruby. Is Detective Provenza in?"

"You mean Detective Baxter?" Ruby winked.

"Today I'll take either one." Though Provenza was who she really wanted to speak with.

"Okay," the woman said slowly, her eyebrows wrinkling like that statement confused her. "Let me ring them for you." Ruby called the detectives' office and got the go ahead to send Jenessa back.

The door buzzed and Jenessa pulled it open and swept through. When she reached their office, the two detectives were seated at their desks, which faced each other.

"Hey, guys," she greeted as she stepped through the doorway. "I come bearing gifts." She set the coffees down on the edge of Provenza's desk. "There's a couple of Ramey's oatmeal raisin cookies in there too."

Michael stood with a smile. "This is a nice surprise." He came around his desk and kissed her lightly on the cheek before picking up one of the cups of coffee.

Provenza eyed her. "Is this a bribe of some sort?"

He knew her too well.

"Oh, I wouldn't call it a bribe. More like a thank you for the information you gave me on the accidental drowning."

Provenza took a sip. "Then you're welcome."

"I wondered," she glanced up at Michael, "if I might get a look at the old file."

"Not a chance." Michael sat back down in his chair, setting the cup of coffee on the desk. "We already went over this."

"Listen, guys, it's a cold case, and a twenty-year-old one at that. What could it hurt?"

Provenza twisted his lips as he considered her request. "The mayor was in here asking about it the other day. Seems his wife is in a lather with it coming up on the twentieth anniversary of the kid's death." He shifted his gaze to Michael. "Maybe some fresh eyes on it wouldn't be such a bad thing."

Michael shot a frown at his partner. "If anyone's going to take another look at this case, it's got to be us."

"But I can help, if you'll let me," she pleaded, her gaze bouncing from Provenza to Michael. "People might open up to me more so than if the police are questioning them."

"I thought you only wanted to satisfy your curiosity, Jenessa, not reopen this case and start digging all around in it." Michael's tone grew more irritated by the minute.

"At first, maybe," she replied, "but I have reason to believe it was more than an accident."

"What reason?" Michael asked.

Jenessa ignored his question, turning to his partner, remembering Provenza's earlier misgivings about drowning being the official cause of death. "Detective, you don't think it was an accident either, do you?"

"George, you can't seriously be considering her request." Michael's cell phone began to ring. He checked the screen. "I've got to take this." He put the phone to his ear. "Michael Baxter."

His solemn gaze shifted to Jenessa briefly as he listened to the caller.

"All right. I'll be right there."

"What is it?" she asked.

"That was Jake's school. He just threw up all over the place and they want me to come to get him."

"Poor little guy," Jenessa cooed sympathetically. She loved that boy and hated that he was sick—maybe it was her maternal instincts kicking in.

"Guess that means we won't be having dinner together tonight." Michael stood and slipped his phone in his pocket.

"Well, tonight's not good for me anyway. My aunt's coming home from the hospital in a while," she peered briefly at her watch, "so I'm headed over there after this. I think I should spend the evening with her, so you go take care of little Jake. Give him a kiss for me."

"I will." Michael grabbed his car keys from the desk.

"Thanks for stopping by, Miss Jones." Provenza raised his cup to her as if in gratitude for bringing the drinks. "I think we're done here."

Done? Was he shutting her down because of Michael's objections? Did he see this as the perfect time to get her to leave? "But, George—"

Provenza took a long swig of his coffee, ignoring her protest.

Now wasn't the time to argue with him, not in front of Michael, but they were definitely not done—oh no, not by a long shot.

"Here." Michael pulled the door open and held it for her, like he thought this would be the end of it. "Let me walk you out."

~*~

Jenessa hurried to the hospital, finding her sister already in their aunt's room, talking to the doctor about a strict diet and exercise plan. Aunt Renee was dressed, sitting in a wheelchair beside Sara, apparently ready to leave.

"Now, Mrs. Giraldy," he said in a firm, sober voice, "if you don't follow these instructions," he held out several sheets of paper, stapled together, "you can expect to find yourself right back in this place—only you won't be seeing me next time, you'll be seeing the coroner."

Aunt Renee sucked in a sharp breath, her eyes widening at the thought. "Yes, yes, I understand." She snatched the pages out of the doctor's hand. "I'll be a good girl and follow the plan, but it won't be any fun." She grimaced as she looked them over.

"You'll have to find your fun in other ways, Aunt Renee," Sara chimed in.

"All right," Aunt Renee conceded. "I get it."

"I'm glad to hear that," the doctor replied. "Maybe you'll find an exercise you enjoy."

"Something I enjoy?" Aunt Renee smiled to herself. "Well then, I guess I need a new man in my life. Sex is exercise, right?"

CHAPTER 8

"SEX?" JENESSA'S EYES flicked to Sara and met her quizzical gaze, a little giggle escaping her lips at their aunt's unexpected comment.

"Well...uh..." the man appeared a little embarrassed, "you'll have to work up to sex. Your heart's not strong enough for—"

Aunt Renee laughed. "I was just joking."

"Really?" The doctor's question dripped with sarcasm. He moved toward the door. "Well, you have been married three times." Apparently, he was quite familiar with her.

"You've got me there," Aunt Renee admitted as he walked out. "Girls, I think it's time you take me home."

~*~

Jenessa sat in the family room of her aunt's large Georgian-style home, keeping her company while Sara started dinner. She had offered to help, but her sister had declined, reminding Jenessa of what a bad cook she was.

"It's probably better for all of us if you leave it to me," Sara had said.

Jenessa couldn't agree more, but she didn't want to seem like she was shirking her share of the responsibilities. "Don't say I didn't offer."

"Your job right now is to entertain Aunt Renee," Sara shot back, "while I get supper on the table."

"I don't need to be entertained," their aunt grumbled. "I'm not a child."

Jenessa followed her into the family room. "This will give us a chance to visit." She helped her get comfortable on the sofa and took a seat beside her.

"Tell me, how are things with you and Michael? Good?"

"They're fine. He's tending to Jake, who came home sick from school today."

"Wouldn't you rather be helping him than sitting here with me?"

"Of course not. You just came home from having surgery."

"I appreciate that, Jenessa, but Sara is here and Ramey will be soon." Aunt Renee eyed her. "Are you sure everything is fine?"

"Yes, I'm sure. Why?"

"Just the way you said it."

"We're fine." How else could she say it?

"And Logan?"

"What about Logan?"

"I was a little surprised to see him with you at the hospital the day I had my heart attack."

"It was nothing." Was Aunt Renee trying to insinuate something was going on between Jenessa and Logan? "Why don't we change the subject? I know, maybe you can help me with a story I'm working on."

"All right, if I can."

"Do you recall anything about a drowning that occurred up at Jonas Lake about twenty years ago?"

"Twenty years ago? I don't understand. Why are you asking about something that happened so long ago?"

Jenessa explained a bit about the story she was working on and her suspicions that it might have been murder.

"Murder?" she echoed. "What makes you say that?"

"I can't tell you yet, but it was something Detective Provenza said. I wondered if you remembered anything that could help me."

"Well, let me think." Renee paused for a few moments. "Yes, I do remember that, now that you mention it. Haven't thought about it in years, but I seem to recall the town was all abuzz about it at the time, especially since it involved the Alexanders. You know how gossip spreads when it has anything to do with the town's number one family."

Jenessa nestled closer. "Tell me more."

"Seems to me there were some teenagers having a party at the boathouse that belonged to Grey Alexander's sister and her family. I think their daughter was one of the kids."

"Summer?"

"That's right. And I think the news said the drowned boy got drunk and fell into the lake."

"I couldn't find much about it when I researched the old newspapers. Even on the internet there was very little."

"Maybe Grey quashed the story," Aunt Renee suggested. "That would be something he could do."

"Yeah, maybe." Jenessa'd had that very thought, but did he have the power to suppress information on other media venues? "Did you know that Summer and her husband recently moved back to Hidden Valley?"

"No, I hadn't heard. Have you seen her?"

"A few times. I knew her before I moved away."

"I didn't realize that."

"Funny thing happened at the bank today. I was talking to Allison—"

"You mean Allison Reagan? The assistant manager?" Aunt Renee asked.

"Yes. I was talking with Allison when Summer and her husband came in. Allison got all weird, like she was suddenly afraid of something, or someone."

"That's odd. Allison and Summer were best friends in high school, as I remember it. I used to be friends with Allison's mother way back then."

"But not now?"

"No, over time we've drifted apart."

"It happens," Jenessa remarked, "like Allison and Summer seem to have."

"Too bad Allison never married," Aunt Renee said. "Nice girl. Went off to college, then came back and went to work at the bank. I seem to recall she had a serious boyfriend, but nothing came of it."

"Dinner's almost ready," Ramey called out from the kitchen. She had shown up after closing up the café and helped Sara get the meal on the table.

"Guess we'd better get going," Aunt Renee said. "Help me up?"

Jenessa assisted her aunt and walked her to the table.

"Steamed salmon and braised vegetables," Sara announced as she set a large oval platter of food in the center of the table.

"Is this what my future looks like?" Aunt Renee said, staring at the healthy dinner from her seat at the table. "No buttered rice pilaf or dinner rolls to go with it?"

Sara frowned at her. "Doctor's orders."

Aunt Renee flopped back against her chair. "Well, just shoot me now."

Jenessa huffed a laugh at her aunt's dramatic comment before taking the large serving spoon and scooping some vegetables onto her plate. "Healthy can taste good too. Give it a chance."

"That's right," Ramey agreed, spearing a piece of fish. "Hand me your plate."

Dinner conversation centered around Aunt Renee's health and her new diet and exercise program until she'd had enough. "Let's change the subject, please." She glanced around the table. "Sara, how is your young man these days?"

"Luke? He's, well, he's…"

Aunt Renee set her fork down. "Something wrong, dear?"

All movement and chatter around the table ceased.

Sara looked down at her plate. "Things are not going as well for us as they had been."

"What's wrong?" Ramey inquired with a worried expression.

"Seems we've hit a snag. We've talked about getting married—"

"That's wonderful," Ramey said, her face brightening.

Sara's gaze traveled to her aunt. "We *were* talking about it, until I told him I wanted children."

"What's wrong with that?" Jenessa asked.

Sara's eyes moistened. "He said he doesn't want any."

"No kids?" Jenessa shook her head. "That's tough to get past."

"It surprised me," Sara went on. "I honestly thought he'd be more like his cousin. Michael loves kids, and I adore the way he is with Jake."

"So do I." Jenessa smiled and took a bite, a vision of the two of them popping into her mind.

"Really." Sara's sarcastic tone surprised Jenessa.

"What are you trying to say?"

"If you adore them so much, why are you trying to screw everything up between you and Michael?" Sara asked.

Jenessa plunked her fork down onto her plate. "What are you talking about?"

"Logan."

Ramey jumped in. "What about Logan?"

"Yes, Sara," Aunt Renee set her fork down, "what about Logan?"

Jenessa's cheeks were on fire. How dare her sister say such a thing, and in such an accusatory tone? "What are you talking about?"

"The guy is always around," Sara replied. "Don't you think Michael sees it too? Like at the hospital?"

"Logan gave me a ride—that's all."

"You always have an excuse for him," Sara said. "How long do you think Michael is going to put up with it?"

Jenessa sat up straight, her back stiffening. "Why? Did he say something to you?"

Sara shook her head. "No, but I can see it on his face, in his eyes."

Had Jenessa missed it? Yes, Logan did seem to turn up here and there, but they were friends—Michael knew that, didn't he?

Jenessa's gaze moved to her aunt, whose expression showed she agreed with Sara.

Ramey? Her brows wrinkled and a nervous smile skipped across her lips, looking as puzzled by Sara's comment as Jenessa felt, which was of little comfort.

"I'm done." Jenessa picked up her plate and headed to the kitchen, feeling the need to end the conversation. She laid her dish in the bottom of the sink and ran water over it. The sound of rushing water was oddly comforting. A hand touched her back.

Aunt Renee had followed her, draping an arm around Jenessa's shoulder as she stood beside her. "Are you okay?" she asked in little more than a whisper.

Jenessa looked up from the sink, tossing a quick glance toward the dinner table. "I don't want to talk about it."

Aunt Renee followed her gaze. "Maybe later, then."

Jenessa nodded.

"I'm feeling rather tired, Jenessa. Why don't we go sit for a while in the family room," Aunt Renee said for the benefit of the others. "Sara and Ramey can clean up."

"But we made dinner," Sara protested.

Jenessa put her arm around her aunt's waist. "And it was delicious." She walked her aunt past the dinner table and into the other room.

"Thank you, girls," Aunt Renee added.

Jenessa helped her aunt to the sofa and sat close beside her. "Do you think I'm treating Michael badly?" she muttered quietly.

"No," Aunt Renee said with a light shake of her head, keeping her voice down. "I think you care for him and the two of you are good together."

Her aunt's words calmed her a bit. She thought they were good together too.

"But…"

The calm was only temporary.

"But what?" Jenessa cast a quick peek toward Sara and Ramey to make sure they weren't listening in.

Her aunt continued. "But you don't look at Michael the way you look at Logan."

"What do you mean?"

"You're happy when Michael is around—I can see that."

"Then what are you saying?"

"When Logan comes around, you light up."

"I do not." The words came out a little louder than Jenessa intended, seeing Ramey and Sara turn and look at them. Jenessa leaned her face closer to her aunt's and whispered, "I do not."

"Yes, you do," Aunt Renee whispered back.

"But I love Michael."

"I don't disagree, hon, but there's a spark in your eyes whenever Logan is near that just isn't there when you're with Michael."

"That can't be," Jenessa argued softly. She loved Michael and she loved his little boy.

Aunt Renee took Jenessa's hand and kept her voice low. "Oh, dear girl, you don't even realize it."

"Realize what?"

"That you're still in love with Logan."

"That's crazy."

"You can't help it, I'm afraid. Your brain is telling you that Michael is the better choice, but the heart wants what the heart wants."

CHAPTER 9

SITTING BESIDE HER AUNT on the sofa, staring straight into her eyes, Jenessa couldn't believe what her aunt was saying. "You seem to be rooting for Logan."

"No, dear, I'm rooting for you. I want nothing more than your happiness. I've watched you with Michael, who is a dear, sweet man, but—"

"He's more than that, Aunt Renee. He's loving and kind, strong and trustworthy, not to mention he's handsome and has abs you could bounce a quarter off of."

"All that is well and good, Jenessa, but does he make your heart jump every time you see him?"

"Of course he does." *Doesn't he?* She hadn't considered that before, but he must. Why wouldn't he?

"Are you sure?" Aunt Renee arched her brow.

"Why would I say that if it wasn't true?" *Why indeed?*

Aunt Renee patted Jenessa's hand. "I know that Michael is a good solid man. He's a great father and he'll make a wonderful husband, I'm sure, but are you going to be happy with him as long as Logan Alexander still has a grip on your heart?"

"Then you agree with Sara—I'm not treating Michael right. I'm a horrible person." She felt two inches tall at the thought.

Aunt Renee laughed lightly. "Oh, don't be so melodramatic. You're not a horrible person. You simply need to sort out your true feelings before someone's heart gets broken. And…"

"And what?" Clearly there was more her aunt wanted to say, although what could possibly be left unsaid Jenessa couldn't guess.

"Well, dear, I think that little boy of Michael's has more to do with it than you'd care to admit. So if you won't get honest for yourself or Michael, do it for that little boy Jake. He's already had one mother fly away from the nest."

~*~

As soon as Jenessa got home, she phoned Michael to see how Jake was doing. His stomach troubles seemed to have passed and he was fast asleep, Michael said. He asked about her aunt and they talked for a while about their days, but the conversation was forced—at least from Jenessa's side of things, so she finally announced it was getting late and she had to go.

"Good night, sweetheart," he said. "I love you."

"Love you, too," was her automatic reply. She meant it, though, didn't she? Not that long ago she would never have questioned it, but since Sara's terse comment and her private conversation with Aunt Renee, she had to wonder.

After changing into her pajamas, Jenessa stood before the bathroom sink, brushing her teeth. She paused and stared into the mirror, looking into her own eyes.

What spark had her aunt noticed there? She thought first of Michael. Then Logan. She saw no "spark" at the thought of Logan. Jenessa shrugged and finished brushing. Her aunt must have been seeing things.

Then Jenessa closed her eyes briefly and pictured Jake at school, feeling sick and throwing up, and her own stomach twisted with emotion for the boy. She opened her eyes and leaned closer to the mirror, reading her reflection for clues. She couldn't deny that Jake played a big part in her life...but it was more than that, wasn't it?

She flipped off the light and went to bed. She snuggled down and pulled the blankets around her shoulders, closing her eyes and hoping for sleep, hoping her mind would allow it. *There was no spark at the thought of Logan...but had there been one at the thought of Michael?* In the dark, her aunt's poetic phrase began to swirl through Jenessa's mind.

The heart wants what the heart wants.

She couldn't get those words out of her mind. Her aunt had to be wrong about her feelings for Michael. She would be crazy not to want to spend the rest of her life with him...and Jake. Maybe Aunt Renee was right about Jake, but she had to be wrong about Michael. He was a wonderful, handsome, sexy man. Adorable little boy aside, he was everything she had ever wanted. She was lucky to have them, to have *him*, in her life.

Still, there was the so-called spark. Aunt Renee seemed to see something in her that Jenessa couldn't, or wouldn't, see. Was Jenessa trying to deny her own truth? Was she simply trying to find a surrogate for her son…and for her lost love with Logan all those years ago?

The heart wants what the heart wants…

Her aunt's voice continued to float through her mind as she drifted off to sleep.

Jenessa woke the next morning, still thinking about what her aunt had said. "No more!" she hollered to her subconscious. She swung her legs over the side of the bed and hopped out. "I love Michael Baxter."

Once she was dressed and ready for the day, she popped into The Sweet Spot for a cup of coffee and one of Ramey's famous homemade energy bars.

Ramey stood behind the cash register, ringing up a customer. "Be right with you," she called out as soon as the brass bells tinkled on the door.

The customer moved aside and Jenessa stepped up to the counter. "Good morning, Ramey."

"Morning." Ramey flashed her usual bright smile. "What can I get you?"

Jenessa gave her order. "Sorry we didn't get an opportunity to chat much last night."

Ramey began filling the coffee request. "You and Aunt Renee were huddling like you were planning a bank heist or something."

Jenessa laughed. "No, nothing like that." But she couldn't tell her the truth either. "I was asking her if she remembered that old drowning at Jonas Lake, for my story."

"You didn't need to whisper if that's all it was."

"Okay, you got us. You were right, we were planning a bank heist."

Ramey sat the coffee on the counter with a small *thunk*, her smile gone. "Yeah, right." She moved to the bakery case and pulled out an energy bar, dropped it onto a small plate, and handed it to Jenessa. "If you don't want to tell me, just say so."

Jenessa gathered up her food and drink. "Someday I will."

The expression on Ramey's face softened. "Have it your way then. Someday." Her gaze moved beyond Jenessa. "Next."

~*~

The April air was crisp and clean, the sky a cloudless bright blue. It was a perfect day to walk. Jenessa parked her sports car at the newspaper and strolled a few blocks to the police station.

She waltzed up to Ruby, the receptionist, and asked if she could see Detective Baxter. She would be sure to make a mental note if her heart skipped a beat when she saw him.

"He's at the dentist—teeth cleaning, I think," the woman said, "but Detective Provenza is in if you'd like to see him."

"Yes, Ruby, Provenza will do." He might even be the better choice.

The receptionist called him, got his approval, and buzzed her through.

"Morning, George," Jenessa greeted from the doorway to his office.

"Detective Provenza," he muttered.

"What?"

"Morning, Detective Provenza."

"Sorry, I wasn't thinking." She entered and sat on the chair at the side of his desk. "I've been trying to find more information on that old drowning up at the lake, and I wondered if you've decided to let me take a look at the police file yet."

He leaned back in his chair. "I don't know. I already told you I'm not supposed to let civilians see it."

"Yes, I know, we've been over that ground before, but if I can find something that helps you solve this case, no one would have to know."

"I would know."

"The mayor's wife would be eternally grateful and the mayor himself would probably give you some kind of award."

"I don't need any award."

She rested an elbow on his desk and leaned toward him. "Listen, you're retiring soon, George. Don't you want this case solved before you turn in your gold shield?"

"So you're going to guarantee that if I let you look at the file, you'll solve the case?"

"Well, of course I can't guarantee it, but having someone else look at the facts certainly can't hurt—can it?"

"Baxter will be pissed."

"Then let's not tell him." She didn't normally like keeping things from Michael, but this was work and she had a story to write. Charles' ominous words rung in her ears. The Herald wouldn't be laying people off on her account.

"I guess a little peek wouldn't hurt." He went to the file cabinet and pulled the folder out. "You can take this to the conference room and read through it, but it has to stay here. And you'll have to be quick about it."

She agreed and he escorted her to the empty room. Once he was gone, she pulled out her phone and tapped on the camera icon. As fast as she could, she snapped a photo of each page in the file so she could take her time reading and rereading the information once she had left the station.

Within a few minutes, she returned the file back to Provenza, thanked him, and slipped out before Michael made it back from the dentist.

~*~

She hurried the few blocks back to her office in the two-story brick building that housed the Hidden Valley Herald and downloaded the photos to her computer. She sat for what seemed like hours studying each page, line by line, examining each photo, scrutinizing every detail.

One of the photos grabbed her attention. It was a picture of the deceased's top gum, the upper lip pulled up and out of the way to take the shot. There was a pattern of some sort indented into the skin. She enlarged the photo on her computer screen. The angled lines with a curved shape below them became more evident.

She crossed her arms and leaned back in her chair to think. What could have made that pattern?

The police report said the man's body had been found floating in the lake among a cropping of rocks not far off the lake's shore. It further described how it appeared that the body had been battering against the rocks as it bobbed in the water through the night.

But no rock, no matter how jagged, could have made that pattern on his gum—could it?

"Knock, knock," her editor Charles said as he stepped into her cubicle.

"Hello, Charles."

"I'm glad to hear your aunt is doing so well. Ramey said she almost seemed like her old self last night."

"Yes, spunky as ever."

"So, how's that big story coming?"

"That's what I'm working on right now." She gestured toward her computer screen.

"Where are you at with it?"

"I finally got Detective Provenza to let me have a peek at the police file on this old case. It was ruled an accident twenty years ago, but George always thought it was murder. He just couldn't prove it."

"And he can prove it now?"

"That's what I'm trying to help him do—hunt for something they missed way back then—then we'll have the exclusive on the story."

"Why do you think people in this town are going to care about a twenty-year-old murder?" Charles asked.

Jenessa tapped the end of her pen against the bulletin board beside her desk.

Charles pushed his glasses up on his nose and squinted as he read some of the phrases written on sticky notes plastered on the board. "Handsome college student. Teenagers drinking. Alexander family? Sex or money? Possible murder." He slid his gaze to Jenessa. "Intriguing notes. You think people will be interested because of the Alexanders?"

"Well, that and the fact that the victim was Mayor Evans' son."

"Now…that does change things."

"And if it was murder," Jenessa went on, "there's been a killer walking free in this town for twenty years. They'll care about that."

"You may be onto something." Charles stepped out of the cubicle. "Keep me posted."

Jenessa turned her attention back to the case. From the pages and pages of notes, she found Provenza and Michael's father had questioned a number of witnesses. Out of those interviews, she made her own list of people she might be able to talk to.

At the top of her list was Nick Evans' college roommate, a fraternity brother by the name of Mark Hemsworth. The detectives' notes said he'd had a fistfight with Nick two weeks prior to his death, but since they couldn't prove he had been at Jonas Lake, or that Nick's death had even been a murder, the police never pressed charges against him.

Still, if she could locate this Mark Hemsworth and talk to him, maybe he could give her something she could use.

CHAPTER 10

JENESSA TYPED NICK'S OLD FRATERNITY brother's name into the Google search bar—Mark Hemsworth—and was surprised by what she found. He was still living in Hidden Valley, teaching history at the local high school.

"That was easy."

It was just after twelve noon. Maybe he was on his lunch break. Jenessa phoned the school, had the secretary track him down, and he agreed to meet her if she could get there before his next class began.

When she drove up in front of the school, Mark Hemsworth was sitting on the raised concrete edging around the central circular fountain. For a second she had a déjà vu moment of her high school days, sitting in that very spot with Logan.

Giving her mind a mental shake, she willed herself back to the present. "Mr. Hemsworth?"

He nodded and rose to his feet.

She stuck out her hand and he shook it. "Jenessa Jones," she said.

"What's this about, Miss Jones?"

"I work for the Hidden Valley Herald and I wanted to ask you a few questions about the death of Nick Evans."

"Boy, I haven't heard that name in a long time. Why are you asking about his death now?"

Dare she tell him she has reason to believe Nick was murdered?

"Uh, well, I…" she stammered as she considered how to answer. Telling him might scare him off if he thought she was trying to point the finger at him.

"What?" he asked with a puzzled expression.

"I can't really say just yet, but I heard that you were an old friend of his, fraternity brothers."

His brow lowered and he crossed his arms. "You heard? From who?"

He seemed awfully defensive. "That's not important," she mumbled, hoping he wouldn't press the issue. "I was wondering if you could tell me about Nick and what you think might have happened to him."

Mark sat back down beside the fountain but didn't quite appear relaxed. "I thought the police decided it was an accidental drowning."

"They did, but I want to know about the man. Was he well liked? Did he have any enemies? That kind of thing."

He shrugged. "He was liked well enough, I guess."

"You don't sound so sure."

"College boys can sometimes be out of control, their hormones raging, only after what makes them feel good. Nick Evans was one of them."

"Really. How so?"

"Well…," he hesitated as if he were considering whether he should say or not. Finally, he proceeded. "Some of the guys in our fraternity liked to keep score of how many virgins they could cherry pick. Not all of us, but a small group of horndogs in our house."

"Cherry pick?"

"Yeah, that's what they called it. They had a whiteboard in the basement where they kept score. They all put in a hundred bucks and at the end of the semester the winner took the whole kitty."

Sex or money. Could he have been killed for one of those—or both?

"And Nick was one of these *horndogs?*"

"Yeah, one of the worst."

Had his father known what his son was up to?

"He liked the young ones," Mark went on, "the high school girls. He would brag about it, that they were the easiest ones to get to give it up."

"But you weren't one of those guys?"

"No, absolutely not."

Would he admit it if he was?

"According to the police report, you got in a fight with Nick right before he died—correct?"

"Not right before, and I certainly didn't drown him, Miss Jones."

"What was the fight about?"

"The creep was trying to put the moves on my little sister. She was a senior in high school and she came to visit me one weekend when we were having a party at our house. I caught him making out with her in one of the back rooms. I tore into him like I wanted to kill him, but I didn't. I might have, but some of the other guys broke it up."

There was mention of the fight in the police files, along with testimony from a few of the other fraternity brothers, but there weren't any details about the cause of it. Was it possible Mark Hemsworth had known Nick was going to be at Jonas Lake and had snuck up there to finish the job? "And that was the end of that?"

"Yep. Nick said he didn't know she was my sister and apologized all over himself. We were good after that."

"Friends?"

"Not exactly, but good enough."

"Is there anyone else you remember that might have wanted to kill him?"

He thought for a minute, his eyes raising to the right. "There was a high school guy I heard about—a football player, I think." His gaze returned to Jenessa. "Nick was doing his girlfriend and he bragged that the guy was so stupid he didn't even know it."

"You think the boyfriend might have found out?"

"Or someone else. Nick bragged he had more than one young girl under his spell and he had a place up at the lake where he was schooling them."

Jenessa's phone rang in her pocket. She pulled it out and saw it was Michael. She couldn't talk to him right now, so she hit *ignore* and stuffed it back in her jacket. "Schooling them?"

"That's what he liked to call it." Mr. Hemsworth checked his watch. "Sorry, but I need to get ready for my next class."

Jenessa handed him one of her business cards. "Please call me if you think of anything else. You've been a tremendous help."

~*~

"Hey, Jenessa, it's Michael. Call me when you can." He set the phone down on his desk after leaving her a message.

"No luck, huh?" Provenza asked between sips of coffee.

"Just voicemail. We keep missing each other."

"Too bad."

"Why did she stop by here again?" Michael asked.

Provenza shrugged, his eyes riveted to his computer screen.

"What's so interesting on your computer?"

"Not much. Just checking my Facebook page."

"Things have been pretty quiet in town," Michael said. "Maybe I could take Jenessa on a romantic getaway for a few days. Get my folks to watch Jake when they get back."

"Assuming she doesn't have to work. People do keep getting married and dying in this town, though hopefully not in immediate succession." Provenza chuckled at his own attempt at humor.

"I think she's probably given up on the notion of reopening that old drowning case," Michael said, ignoring his partner's cheeky remark, "and maybe someone else can do the obits and society pages for a few days."

"You think she's lost interest in the case?" Provenza asked.

"Why? You don't think so?"

Provenza shrugged, his gaze remaining on the computer screen. "Maybe."

~*~

When Jenessa returned to her car, she listened to the voicemail Michael had left her. She considered calling him back, but Ruby or George had probably told him she'd stopped by. He would want to know why.

She could say she just wanted to say hello and kiss his handsome face, that she missed seeing him—which was all true—but what if he mentioned the cold case? She didn't want to lie to him, and she didn't want him trying once more to dissuade her from pursuing it.

She pitched her phone into her oversized handbag and drove away from the school, thinking about the young women Nick Evans had supposedly been schooling. The police had interviewed residents around Jonas Lake, the ones near to where the body was found. One of those families was Summer's.

The interview pages showed the detectives had questioned James and Susan Walker, Summer's mom and dad. They had also talked to Summer. She would have been sixteen at the time. Could she have been one of Nick Evans' young conquests?

Summer had told Jenessa when they were at the hospital that she wanted to get together with her. Maybe now would be a good time. Jenessa phoned her and asked if she could stop by her house.

"Sure," Summer replied. "I'll have to pick up the kids from school later, but I'm free until then."

She gave Jenessa the address, and, before long, Jenessa was parked in front of the Monahan house, an attractive two-story in a new subdivision on the edge of town.

Summer opened the door and seemed genuinely happy to see her. "Please, come in." She stepped back as she pulled the door open so Jenessa could enter.

"This way." Summer gestured toward the formal living room.

Jenessa took a seat on the sofa and Summer joined her.

"Can I get you something to drink? Iced tea? Lemonade? Water?"

Jenessa appreciated the offer and, as much as a glass of cool iced tea sounded lovely, she really just wanted to get down to business. "No thanks, I'm good."

"So, what brings you by?"

Perfect.

Apparently Summer wanted to cut to the chase too. Jenessa liked that. "I'm writing a story about the death of Nick Evans," she said, jumping right in without preamble, "which happened about twenty years ago. Do you remember that?"

Summer's eyes grew wide and her hand flew to her chest. "Nick Evans? I do, but that was so long ago. Why now?"

A door closed in another part of the house, and Summer's head jerked in the direction of the noise. "Chet must be home." Her gaze returned to Jenessa, the expression on her face turning fretful, her eyes dancing nervously around the room.

Jenessa had wanted to talk to Summer alone, where she might be more open and forthcoming. But with Chet home, there was a decided shift in the atmosphere of the room.

CHAPTER 11

CHET MONAHAN WALKED INTO the room where Jenessa and Summer were sitting. "Hello," he greeted, his voice cordial. "I didn't know we had company."

"You remember Jenessa," his wife said nervously.

"Yes, we met at the bank, right?" He smiled at Jenessa, but there was something missing in the expression. While his lips spread wide, the sparkle of authenticity seemed to be lacking.

"That's right," Jenessa responded, forcing a polite smile. "Good to see you again, Chet." She'd faked the smile, might as well throw in a well-mannered lie too.

"Jenessa was just asking me about that drowning up at Jonas Lake a long time ago," Summer said. "Remember that?"

He nodded, then took a seat in a side chair. "Why now? After all these years?"

"I work for the Herald and I'm doing a story about it, hoping someone recalls some fact or detail that got missed."

"Was he a relative of yours or something?" Chet asked.

"No, nothing like that," Jenessa replied.

Chet scooted to the edge of the chair. "Are the cops reopening the case for some reason? Some new evidence or something?"

"I can't really say," Jenessa answered truthfully. She couldn't say there was new evidence because, to her knowledge, there wasn't any. But was Chet simply curious, or was he afraid of what a new investigation might find? "Were you up at the lake that night? The night Nick Evans died?"

Chet shot to his feet. "Of course not."

That wasn't the response she'd expected.

He rubbed a hand over his jaw, pitching a glance at his wife before sliding his gaze back to Jenessa. "I'm sorry, Miss Jones, but we don't know anything more now than we knew when the police questioned us twenty years ago."

Jenessa turned to the wife. "Summer?"

Chet moved beside her and rested his hand on Summer's shoulder.

"He's right." She looked down at her fingers, clasped together in her lap, before raising her uneasy gaze to Jenessa. "There's nothing we can add."

"Did you play football in high school, Chet?"

He folded his arms across his chest. "Linebacker. Why? What does that have to do with this?"

Had Chet been the clueless football player Nick had told his roommate about? The one whose girlfriend he'd been *schooling*. "Just wondered. You look like you've stayed in good shape." Did she dare to bring up Chet's juvenile record for fighting?

He relaxed his body somewhat, but his steely glare continued to cool the room. "Thank you, but like I already said, there's nothing more we can tell you." His eyes drifted toward the doorway, adding emphasis to his next words. "I think this interview is over."

For Summer's sake, Jenessa stopped the questioning and moved toward the door. "Thanks for your time—both of you."

Summer followed her and pulled the front door open. "I'll see you around town, I'm sure."

Jenessa stole a quick glance back at Chet, his arms again crossed and his eyes laser-focused on her. She nodded at Summer's comment and stepped out.

Something was going on here, but Jenessa wasn't sure what it was. These people knew more than they were saying—she could feel it—but it seemed like it was Chet who was controlling the situation.

She marched to her car. If only she could have spoken to Summer without her husband's imposing presence, maybe the conversation would have gone differently. She'd have to look for another opportunity to catch the woman alone.

She wondered if Logan knew how controlling his cousin's husband was. She'd have to bring it up the next time she ran into him.

~*~

As Jenessa drove away, she thought about the pages of notes she had photographed from the police file.

Hadn't one of them said Chet was up at the lake? She seemed to recall one of the interview pages saying he had gone to the lake early in the evening looking for Summer. Her parents had told him she had gone to a friend's cabin nearby—Allison Reagan—so he left.

She was sure she'd read in the report that when the detectives questioned Chet he'd said that when he didn't find Summer at home at the lake house, he had driven back to Hidden Valley. She had to know for sure. Jenessa pulled to the side of the road and scanned through the documents on her phone.

Bingo. There it was, just as she'd remembered it. The report also said Chet had friends who'd corroborated his story, saying they had gotten together to hang out at one of the boys' homes for the rest of the evening. Chet's own parents verified he was back home and in bed before ten o'clock.

So then why had he so adamantly denied being up at the lake that night?

Jenessa pulled into a parking spot in front of The Sweet Spot for an afternoon pick-me-up, something to give her the energy to pursue another person on her list.

With Allison Reagan's family having been on the police interview roster, not to mention her curious reaction to seeing Chet Monahan after all these years, she was someone Jenessa was anxious to talk to. Before going into the coffee shop, she phoned Allison at the bank and asked if she had a few minutes to meet with her.

"What is this about?" Allison asked.

"It's for an article I'm writing and I thought since you've lived in Hidden Valley for most of your life you could add something to the story."

"I'd be happy to. I'm due for a break anyway," Allison said.

"How about I buy you a cup of coffee at The Sweet Spot in ten minutes?"

"Sounds great. It'll give me a chance to get some fresh air."

When Jenessa entered the café, Sara was waiting on customers, which was unusual, because she generally preferred to run the business end while Ramey did the baking and running the front of the shop.

"I'll be right with you," Sara called out at the tinkling of the bells, not looking at whoever had entered. She continued making change for the man at the counter.

Jenessa didn't mind, though, because one last cinnamon roll in the bakery case caught her attention as she moved toward the register. The customer turned around to leave, coffee in hand, and almost bumped into a distracted Jenessa. He raised his cup and drew back to avoid a collision. His coffee sloshed, but he jumped back in time to avoid wearing it.

"Logan?" Jenessa gasped. "Oh, I'm so sorry." She grabbed a few napkins off the counter and dropped them to the floor, pushing them around with her shoe to clean up the spilled coffee. "Let me buy you another."

"No worries," he said, his eyes twinkling as he laughed. "My fourth cup today. Maybe someone's trying to tell me I've had too much."

"I really am sorry." A light warmth bloomed on her cheeks. "I missed lunch and that last cinnamon roll in the case was calling to me."

"I'm actually glad I ran into you—well, not literally," Logan began. "I wanted to talk—"

"Jenessa," a male voice said, interrupting him.

Logan and Jenessa turned in unison toward the sound of her name. It was Michael.

~*~

"Having coffee?" Michael asked, intentionally leaving off the word *together*.

His gaze traveled briefly to Logan and then back to Jenessa. It irritated him how Logan managed to find so many opportunities to be around her. He sucked in a deep breath, not wanting to get angry about it, not wanting to let Logan drive a wedge between them, but neither could he stand by, passively allowing Logan to insert himself further into Jenessa's life.

With great effort, Michael willed his voice to stay calm. "Hey, I've been trying to call you, Jenessa, but we seem to keep missing each other."

"I was just leaving," Logan said to Jenessa.

Michael noted that the man's gaze was not leaving hers, as if ignoring the fact that her boyfriend was standing right there.

"I'll call you," he muttered to her in a low tone, unfortunately not low enough to escape Michael's hearing. Then Logan was gone.

"Call you about what?" Michael asked, his lips feeling tight as he said it.

"I don't know," she shrugged. "He was about to tell me when you came in, so I have no idea. I guess he'll tell me some other time." She looked up at Michael and offered him a small smile. "I'm glad you stopped in. I haven't had a chance to call you back. I've been so busy with work and right now I'm—"

"I've missed you, Jenessa." He slipped his arms around her. "We've hardly spent two minutes together these past few days."

"Then take me out to dinner tonight," she suggested, giving him a squeeze before stepping out of his embrace. "It's Sara's turn to stay over with Aunt Renee, so I'm free."

"My folks are still out of town," Michael replied. "I'll have to see if I can find a sitter."

"No need, I'm available," Sara interrupted from behind the counter, apparently listening to their conversation. "It's actually Ramey's night with Aunt Renee, Jenessa, so I can watch Jake. He's such a sweet little guy."

"He is, but…" Jenessa wrinkled a brow, looking a little surprised, "I didn't think you—"

Sara waved a hand to quiet her sister, a smile spreading across her face. "I've got nothing else going on. It'll be fun. I haven't babysat since I was a teenager."

"What about Luke?" Jenessa asked.

Sara's smile faded. "Not seeing him tonight."

Michael turned back to Jenessa. "Well, there you have it. I'll pick you up at seven."

~*~

Michael got his coffee, and one for Provenza, and headed back to work.

As soon as he was gone, Allison Reagan arrived to meet with Jenessa. Sara filled their orders and, with coffee cups in hand, they took a small sunny table by the window.

"I appreciate you meeting me like this." Jenessa set her coffee down.

"Happy to help," Allison replied with an eager grin. "So, what's this story about?"

"The death of Nick Evans."

Allison's smile disappeared as her mouth went slack and the color began to drain from her face.

Jenessa hadn't expected that response. "You knew him, didn't you?"

"Why do you say that?" Her gray-green eyes danced nervously. She picked up her cup and took a drink.

"The expression on your face." Jenessa leaned forward. "I've obviously hit a sensitive spot."

"No, no," Allison gave her head a slight shake, "I'm just surprised is all, after all this time." Her gaze drifted out the window as she spoke. "I don't know what I can tell you. I don't remember much."

"You must have known Chet Monahan back then, being friends with Summer, I mean."

Her gaze slid quickly back to meet Jenessa's. "Yes, we all went to school together." When Allison reached for her cup of coffee, her hand was trembling.

"Logan Alexander told me Chet recently moved back here to manage the bank where you work, but you probably already knew that."

"My bank?" Allison's head tilted as she said it, her eyes widening with obvious surprise. Both hands clutched her coffee cup so tightly Jenessa feared it might explode under the pressure.

"That's right," Jenessa replied. "He was there today, remember?"

"He's going to manage the bank?" Her gaze flew out the window again as she nervously tucked a strand of her auburn hair behind her ear, releasing her grip on the cup. The realization seemed to shake her as the thought of it sank in. Finally, her gaze returned to Jenessa. "My bank?" Allison asked again, as if she couldn't quite believe it.

Apparently, the news of Chet taking over as manager of the bank hadn't been shared with anyone yet. Logan had said the employees didn't know, but Allison was, after all, the assistant manager. Shouldn't she have been let in on it?

"I'm sorry." Jenessa put a hand over one of Allison's to calm her. "I thought you knew."

Allison's bottom lip began to quiver and her eyes became moist.

"What's wrong? Is it Chet?" Had Jenessa struck a nerve?

The woman did not reply. Her gaze dropped to her coffee cup.

"You know, Allison, I get a bad feeling when I'm around Chet."

"Me too," she said in a pained voice that was barely more than a whisper.

Encouraged by the response, Jenessa continued. "The old police files showed he was violent as a teenager, getting in lots of fights. Do you remember him being violent?"

Allison clutched a napkin in her trembling hand and brought it her mouth. A sheen of sweat shimmered on her forehead as she nodded her response, her eyes still lowered.

This woman was terrified of Chet—that was clear—even after all these years, which only served to support Jenessa's nagging suspicion that Chet might be violent at home.

So, before the woman bolted to escape the uncomfortable conversation, Jenessa brought the discussion back to the reason for their meeting. "Is there anything you can tell me about the night Nick Evans died?"

She shook her head and glanced around at the other customers in the café. "Not here."

CHAPTER 12

THAT WAS GOOD. Allison wanted to talk about what really happened to Nick Evans, but something—or someone—had her spooked.

Allison tipped her cup and finished the last of her coffee. "I've got to get back to work." She grabbed her purse off the floor and stood. "We'll have to finish this another time."

If she gave Allison too much time, she might change her mind and back out. "How about after you get off work?"

"Maybe. Call me. We'll figure out a time that you can come by my apartment." Allison pulled a pen and business card out of her purse and scribbled her address on the back. "Sorry, but I've really got to go."

"Okay, I'll call you."

Allison hurried out the door and down the street.

"What was that all about?" Sara asked as she picked up the empty cup and began wiping the table with a damp cloth.

Jenessa snatched up the business card. "That woman knows something about Nick Evans' murder, but she was too afraid to say what."

"Murder? I thought he drowned."

"Shhh…keep that under your hat." Jenessa hadn't meant to let that slip. If talking about Nick's death made Allison shake like a leaf, maybe the woman had something to fear. "I need to do a little more digging before I can say what really happened."

"The town will want to know what you find out," Sara said as her gaze went beyond the window, in the direction that Allison went. "You know, she's not a bad-looking woman. I wonder why she never married."

"Not everyone wants that. Maybe her career is more important to her."

"Not me," Sara said, pulling her attention back to Jenessa. "I want a husband and kids and a house with a white picket fence."

"Since when?"

"Since I've been watching you and Ramey."

"I don't understand."

"Well, you have Michael and little Jake, and Ramey has Charles and Charlie, and I've got no one."

"What are you talking about? You have Luke."

Sara shook her head sadly and wiped at the table again. "He took a job in Colorado." When she looked up, sunlight from the window reflected in her glistening green eyes.

"I'm so sorry." Jenessa rose and put her arms around her sister. "I didn't know."

"I don't have the best luck picking men." Sara gave a nervous chuckle as she stepped back and ran her fingers under her eyes to clear away the tears. The bells on the door signaled a customer coming in, and Sara drew in a deep breath and plastered a smile on her face. "I'd better get back to work."

"We'll talk later," Jenessa muttered as her sister rushed to the cash register.

Jenessa had to agree with Sara—she really didn't have the best luck with men. She'd had a flurry of boyfriends in high school, then she had dated Logan Alexander for a short time while Jenessa was away from Hidden Valley, after he had returned from college. From what Ramey had told her, Sara had hoped she could build a life with him, but eventually Logan had ended the relationship, explaining he was still in love with Jenessa.

Reeling from their breakup, Sara quickly jumped into another relationship and they married within a matter of months. Sadly, that marriage ended in divorce after only a few years.

There were a number of men Sara had casually dated, but none of them serious contenders. Until last summer, that is, when Michael introduced her to his cousin Luke, shortly after he had moved to town. From the start, they had become inseparable. Jenessa had been thrilled that her little sister may have finally found long-term happiness.

She stood by the table for a moment, watching Sara as she waited on the customers. A genuinely friendly smile now lit up her pretty face, her honey-blond hair swinging happily above her shoulders as she flit from the cash register to the coffee machine to the bakery case.

In that moment, with all her heart, Jenessa wished for a good man for her sister, someone who would love Sara and give her that big house full of all the children she longed to have.

~*~

Jenessa went back to her office and logged on to her computer, adding a few more sticky notes to her bulletin board from her conversation with Allison. There was so much more that woman could tell her—she was sure of it—but she'd have to wait until they could speak again to find out what it was.

After typing up the day's obituaries and finishing a story about the Hidden Valley Garden Club's upcoming gala, she headed out. Before going home, she wanted to stop by Aunt Renee's house to see how she was doing.

"Hey, Ramey," Jenessa greeted as she traipsed down the wide center hall of the large Georgian manor and stepped into her aunt's kitchen.

A small pile of freshly sliced carrots and celery was heaped on a cutting board on the counter in front of Ramey. She wiped her hands on her apron and gave Jenessa a hug. "I didn't know you were coming by."

"I wanted to check in." Jenessa glanced into the family room. "Where's Aunt Renee?"

"Taking a nap."

"How's she doing today?"

"Getting her strength back and complaining about all the fresh veggies I'm making her eat." Ramey quirked the side of her mouth. "What are you up to?"

"I just came from the coffee shop."

Ramey picked up a large stainless steel knife and went back to preparing the vegetables. "Sara doing okay down there?"

"Yes, she's giving almost as fabulous service as you do."

"That's good. I was a little worried."

"Anything new with you?" Jenessa stole a carrot stick from Ramey's pile.

Ramey stopped chopping, a smile lighting up her eyes. "I think Charles is going to ask me to marry him."

"Oh, Ramey!" Jenessa flung her arms around her friend. "I'm so happy for you."

"Whoa, watch the sharp knife!" Ramey warned.

Jenessa gave her a quick squeeze and stepped back. "Charles is a great guy. You two are going to be so happy together. How is Charlie taking it?"

Charlie was Charles' twelve-year-old son and didn't seem to like the idea of someone replacing his mother—at least that was how he acted whenever Jenessa was around the three of them.

"Well, Charles hasn't proposed *yet*." Ramey returned to cutting up the vegetables. "I think he's waiting for Charlie to be okay with it before he does."

"His mom passed away about three years ago, didn't she?"

"Four," Ramey corrected. "It takes time."

"He'll come around, don't worry," Jenessa encouraged. "He'll come to love you like everyone else in town."

"You really think so?"

"What's not to love?" Jenessa stole another carrot

stick. "You're going to make a terrific mom. He'll see that."

"I hope he doesn't take too long. I'm already thirty-one and I'd like to have babies of my own before I get too old."

"I'm right there with you, sister." Jenessa popped the last bit of carrot into her mouth.

Ramey laughed.

"Speaking of people who want to have babies," Jenessa rested her hips against the counter, "did you know Sara and Luke split up?"

"Well, I knew they had hit a snag. He doesn't want kids. Remember, she mentioned it at dinner the other night?"

"Yes, but I figured they would work it out."

"Guess not," Ramey said, sliding the cut-up vegetables into a plastic container. "If she wants kids and he doesn't, that's a major deal breaker in my book."

"Hers too, apparently." Jenessa folded her arms across her chest. "She told me today that she was jealous of my having Michael and little Jake and you having Charles and Charlie."

"She said she was jealous?" Ramey raised her brows.

"Well…that was my word, not hers, but she did sound envious when she said it—I know that much."

"Hmm." With a frown, Ramey slammed her big knife hard into a large jicama, splitting it in two.

Jenessa expected more of a response to her statement, but Ramey only continued chopping up the vegetable. "What are you not telling me?"

Ramey lifted her eyes to meet Jenessa's. "Jealous just might be the right word for it."

"What makes you say that?"

Ramey's expression turned serious as she laid down the knife. "I never thought I'd have to tell you this, because Sara and Luke were together and it seemed like they were happy."

Her interest piqued, Jenessa slid onto a stool at the breakfast bar and faced her friend. "Tell me what?"

"When you left to have the baby, Sara missed you more than you know."

"I assumed she would, but it wasn't my fault. Mom and Dad sent me to Grandma's until the baby was born. I didn't have any choice."

"I know, but she was just a kid and it was hard losing her big sister. She idolized you."

There had to be more that Ramey was holding back. "And?"

"I already told you about her and Logan dating, years after you left—"

"Yeah."

"And how he broke her heart when he told her he was still in love with you."

"Yeah, I already know all that." It was old news—painful, yes, but old news nonetheless. "Why are you bringing that up now?"

"What I haven't told you," Ramey paused to measure her words, "was that right before you came back last year, I thought Sara and Michael might get together. She seemed to be a good match for him. He was single, she was single, and—"

"My Michael?"

"He wasn't your Michael back then. He wasn't anyone's. Josie had run off and left him and little Jake a year or so before, and he was lonely and totally available." She paused, as if waiting for a response, but Jenessa was still processing the idea, so Ramey continued. "He would come into The Sweet Spot just about every day for coffee. Whenever Sara was in the café, they'd talk and flirt a little. It was pretty cute to watch."

Sara? And Michael?

"I could tell Sara was beginning to look forward to him coming in, and I fully expected he would work up the nerve to ask her out. If he didn't, she told me, she was going to ask him."

"Did he ever ask her out?" Jenessa's pulse quickened, she had to know.

"No, he hadn't yet, but one day she came to work with this silly grin on her face. She told me she had finally decided that it was going be the day she would ask him out—she had waited long enough."

The muscles on the back of Jenessa's neck and shoulders began to tighten at the very thought of it. "And did she?"

CHAPTER 13

"YOU HAVE TO TELL ME, RAMEY." Blood began to pulse in Jenessa's temples and she rubbed them to alleviate the pain that was starting to build. "Did Sara ask Michael out?"

Ramey picked up the large knife and brought it down hard again on another large chunk of jicama. "No."

Jenessa's muscles began to relax. "Why not?"

Ramey looked up and caught Jenessa's gaze. "Because that was the day your father died."

Jenessa dropped her head into her hands. No wonder things were so strained between her and her sister for the first few weeks she was back in town. She thought Sara was still pining for Logan, not realizing it was because Jenessa had swooped in and taken all hopes of Michael from her too.

Luke had been Jenessa's reprieve, unwittingly, but now he was gone.

She raised her head to find Ramey's admonishing stare on her. "I didn't know," Jenessa shrugged. "You have to believe me."

She'd truly had no idea, and something sour began twisting in the pit of her stomach at the thought of it.

"Now you do."

She loved her baby sister. She would never sacrifice Sara's happiness for her own. "What can I do to make it up to her?"

"First," Ramey gave a defenseless cauliflower a couple of loud chops on the cutting board, "don't let her know I told you this."

Jenessa nodded. She didn't want to have that awkward conversation either. "And second?"

"Second," Ramey gave the vegetable another good whack. "Stop hogging all the good men."

The muscles in Jenessa's neck tensed again, at the accusation. "What do you mean by that?"

"The two most eligible bachelors in this town are both madly in love with you, Jenessa—you know that." Ramey wagged the knife at her as she said it. "Do those boys—and this family—a favor and cut one of them loose."

"Well, I...I..." she stammered. Her genuinely sweet friend wasn't normally that bold or direct. Jenessa tried to think of a clever comeback, but nothing came to her. Apparently, she had only been thinking of herself. A sour taste rushed up from her stomach and burned her throat at the very thought of it, making her unable to reply.

Ramey continued to take out her irritation on the

poor cauliflower. "Don't act like you don't know what I mean."

~*~

Ramey had given Jenessa some hard things to think about. How was she going to make it up to her sister? Maybe she'd feel better after talking to Aunt Renee. She didn't have to wait long before her aunt got up from her nap and came downstairs. They visited in the family room while Ramey continued to prepare dinner.

After a time, Jenessa peeked at her wristwatch. "I'd better go home and get ready. I have a quick stop to make first, and then Michael's coming at seven to take me to dinner."

Ramey joined them in the family room. "The food will be ready soon."

Aunt Renee leaned back against the sofa. "Is Sara joining us?"

"Not tonight," Jenessa said. "She offered to babysit Jake while Michael and I went out."

"Sara, babysitting? Willingly?" Aunt Renee smiled like a Cheshire cat. "Well, what do you know about that? Sounds like your sister is finally experiencing some maternal instincts."

Jenessa met Ramey's knowing gaze, recalling their earlier conversation.

"I've really got to go." Jenessa gave her aunt a kiss on the cheek and rose from the sofa. "I'll be back after my date. It's my turn to spend the night."

"I'll walk you out." Ramey hooked her arm around Jenessa's. When they reached the front door, Ramey held it open for her. "Remember what I told you—cut one of them loose, please."

~*~

Jenessa phoned Allison to see if she could stop by her place to finish their conversation. Allison agreed.

"Thanks for seeing me," Jenessa said as they sat on a sofa in the apartment that Allison shared with her sister, Kelly.

"Sorry you had to come here to talk. I was afraid to say anything in the café. You know—big ears."

"I get it." Jenessa nodded. "Now that we're alone, I hope you'll tell me everything you remember about Nick Evans and the night he died."

"I'll do my best." Allison looked at her watch. "My sister and I are having dinner with the parents in about an hour, so we don't have much time."

"Then I'll get right to it." Jenessa pulled her notepad and pen out of her purse. "I'd heard you and Summer Monahan—well, Summer Walker back then— were best friends."

"That's right. My folks had a cabin not far from her family's."

Jenessa recalled what Nick's old roommate had said about the sex games his fraternity brothers had played back then, but she wanted to hear it from Allison. "How did you and Summer know Nick?"

Allison blushed, her gaze dropping for a moment before she answered. "We were...uh, well...we were sleeping with him."

"Both of you?"

Allison nodded, lowering her eyes again, as if she were ashamed to admit it.

"And you both knew about the other?"

"Yes. I know that must sound strange to you, but it was supposed to be casual, no strings attached. Everyone was doing it, or so I was told."

"How did you meet him?"

"We had met Nick at a frat party. Summer had an older friend who was going and she invited us along. The beer was flowing pretty freely and somehow we both ended up in a room with him, maybe a bedroom, I can't remember—could have been a storage room for all I know—and Nick was drinking with us, and flirting with us. It was crazy. He was so hot—the face, the body, the voice—oh my gosh, he was *so* sexy. We were only sixteen and we couldn't believe this gorgeous college guy was hitting on us."

"So, that was at the frat house?"

Allison nodded.

"What happened at the lake?"

"We were such stupid teenage girls. I look back now and can't believe what idiots we were."

"What do you mean?"

"He convinced us it would be the most exciting thing we would ever do, and best of all there would be no strings attached. Friends with benefits, he called it. Summer was all for it, but I was more hesitant. We were still virgins, but Summer had Chet and they had gone pretty far, just not all the way, she'd told me. I hadn't done more than kiss a boy, but Nick promised he would be gentle and teach me the fine art of being a woman."

What a scumbag.

"I had no idea how addicting sex could be. Once we started sleeping with him—well, no one actually slept— we couldn't get enough. It was like being addicted to a drug, we couldn't wait to be with him again. We would have done anything for him—well, me, not Summer. I was totally in love with him."

"But not Summer?" Jenessa asked.

"No, she was dating Chet at the time, so it was just fun for her."

"And Chet didn't know?"

"No, he was clueless about the whole thing."

"How long did that go on?"

"A couple of months," Allison said.

"Do you think Chet ever found out?"

Allison froze, her gaze fell to the floor and stayed there.

"Allison?" Jenessa squeezed the woman's hand. "What is it?"

"That night, the night Nick died, it was all so horrible."

The apartment door opened and Allison's younger sister walked in, tall and beautiful with long chestnut hair. "Hey, Allison."

Jenessa stood. "Hello, I'm Jenessa. You must be Kelly."

"I am. It's nice to meet you. A friend of Allison's?"

Allison rose abruptly. "Thanks for stopping by Jenessa. We'll have to get together again real soon." She took Jenessa by the arm. "Let me walk you to the door."

~*~

Jenessa arrived home, still shocked by the way Allison had shut down and ushered her out of the apartment once her sister came home. Obviously, she didn't want her little sister to know what she had done. She figured Kelly would have been only ten or eleven years old at the time, by the look of her now.

On the drive home, Jenessa phoned Allison's folks in hopes of setting a time to talk with them regarding what they remembered about that fateful night, but they did not prove very cooperative. Mrs. Reagan had been brusque, refusing to allow an interview. "We told the police all we knew at the time. My husband and I were quite upset by what happened. There's no need to stir it all up again," she had said.

Running short on time to get ready for her date, Jenessa dropped her purse on the entry table and sprinted up the stairs to change into her favorite little black dress and freshen up her makeup, looking forward to Michael's arrival.

At six forty-five, the doorbell rang.

Jenessa checked her watch. "He's early." She slipped into her spiked heels and hurried down the stairs, trying not to twist an ankle on her way down. Without hesitation, she flung open the front door.

"Hello, Jenessa."

She froze for a moment. "Logan." She glanced past him, to the street, to see if Michael had pulled up. He wouldn't be happy if he found Logan at her house.

"You look surprised." A pleased smile made his eyes sparkle.

"I wasn't expecting you." If Michael were to show up, there could be trouble.

Logan's intent gaze scanned the length of her body like she were a shiny new Ferrari. "Wow! You look gorgeous. Where are you going?"

"Out." She refused to go into detail.

His gaze drifted up to her eyes. "I got your text saying you needed to talk to me. I was on my way home and saw your car, so..." He frowned and cocked his head. "Is this a bad time?"

"I meant we could talk on the phone," she replied. As long as he was there, however, she might as well talk to him. "Come in." She grabbed his arm and pulled him into the entry, hoping to make this quick, before Michael appeared. She pushed the door almost closed, purposely leaving it slightly ajar. Surely Michael wouldn't think anything was going on between them if the door was open and they were only standing in the entry, just in case he arrived before Logan left.

"What did you want to talk to me about?" He looked handsome in his tailored navy blue suit and gold tie. The colors brought out the intensity of his brilliant blue eyes, as if they needed any help.

She drew a deep breath and gathered her thoughts. "Maybe it's better I tell you this in person anyway, rather than over the phone."

"Now you really have my attention. What is it?"

"I hope I'm wrong, but…"

"Tell me."

"I have reason to believe that Chet has been abusing Summer, and maybe even the children."

"What?" Logan's eyes narrowed with the question. "What reason?"

"I've seen bruises on Summer, haven't you?"

"I hadn't noticed."

Men can be so clueless. "What about the spiral fracture of Grayson's wrist?"

"Summer said he was just horsing around. You don't believe her?"

"It could be as simple as that, but then, at the hospital, she whispered to me that she wanted to get together and talk."

"About what?" Logan asked.

"She didn't say, but she seemed serious, like she wanted it to be in private."

"Private doesn't mean abuse."

"True, but I was at their house earlier today. She and I were sitting in the living room, chatting. She was relaxed and friendly, but the minute Chet walked in, her whole demeanor changed. She became like a nervous little rabbit. She was clearly afraid to speak freely in front of him, Logan."

"Are you sure it wasn't just that overactive imagination you're famous for?" He quirked one side of his mouth as his brow lifted.

"It wasn't my imagination. I wish it were. She was about to say something to me, but when he put his hand on her shoulder, she clammed up. I saw fear in her eyes, Logan—real fear."

"I can't go on assumptions. For something this serious, I have to know for certain, because if that guy is laying a hand on my family, you might as well call the coroner because his life is over."

"Well, she's not the only one afraid of him."

"What do you mean?" Logan put his hand on her shoulder. "Are you—"

"Not me. Allison Reagan." Jenessa was fully aware of his touch. "She works at your bank and—"

"Yeah, I know Allison—the assistant manager, right?"

"Yes." She glanced at his hand and he pulled it back. "I was talking to her, and when I mentioned Chet, she started shaking like a leaf."

"But why?"

"I don't know, but there's something..." she fumbled for the right word, "something sinister about that man."

Logan crossed his arms and shifted his weight. "Sinister?"

"Wrong, bad, evil, wicked—take your pick."

"I never got that sense from him," Logan said, "but if there's even the slightest chance you're right, we have to do something."

"I'll try to get Summer alone and talk to her," Jenessa said, "but if she won't open up to me, perhaps she will to you."

"And maybe I can get Grayson alone—throw the football around or something, see if he'll tell me anything." Logan shook his head slightly. "I hate this."

She touched his arm, an instinctive gesture to comfort him. "I can't bear the thought that Chet might be hurting those kids."

Before she could pull back, Logan covered her hand with his and held it there. "Me too." His eyes became sad. "I never told you, but when I was a kid, my father..." His voice trailed off for a moment, then he seemed to catch himself before he finished his thought. His fingers wound around her hand and he gave it a gentle squeeze. "I appreciate your letting me know. You didn't have to do that."

The warmth of his hand caused a ripple of tingles to spread up her arm. She looked up into his eyes, a hint of pain lingering there, his face inches away. "Yes, I did."

His gaze locked on hers, her hand still encased in his, neither saying a word until he broke the heavy silence. "While I'm here, I should tell you that the private investigator I hired has been working to track down our baby."

Our baby. "He has?" She felt her heart lift, lightened by finally not having to carry the weight of the search alone.

"I need you to understand that I want to find him as much as you do." His voice was thick with emotion. His gaze still riveted to hers, he lifted her hand to his lips and brushed a whisper of a kiss against the back of it.

Feeling his lips against her skin sent a rush of warmth through her. "Any luck?" was all she managed to squeak out.

She pulled her hand back, but Logan continued to hold her gaze. "He thinks he'll have some news in the next week or so."

Her heart was hammering wickedly inside her chest. She wasn't sure if it was because the child she had been longing for might finally be found or because of the man standing before her, promising to make it happen. "Oh, Logan—"

A knock at the door broke the electricity sizzling between them. Jenessa took a startled step back. The door swung open and she saw Michael standing in the doorway.

"Am I interrupting something?" His voice was serious, his eyes shifting between Jenessa and Logan with obvious suspicion.

She could only imagine the expressions he caught on their faces.

"Interrupting?" she repeated, trying to collect herself. "No, not at all." She snuck a quick glance Logan's way, seeing a shadow of disappointment in his eyes. She shared his feeling, but didn't dare let Michael see it in her.

She painted a smile on her face as she explained. "Logan just stopped by to give me some information for a story I'm working on."

"Oh yeah?" Michael didn't look convinced. "What story?"

"About Logan's cousin, Summer, and her family moving back to Hidden Valley. Her husband is going to be managing the bank. Oh, no," she paused, turning to Logan, "I wasn't supposed to let that out, was I?"

"Not a big deal," Logan replied. "I just didn't want it getting back to the employees before the official announcement."

She turned back to Michael, who looked aggravated she and Logan shared a secret. "You remember meeting Summer at the restaurant the other day, don't you, Michael?"

He nodded slowly, his stare fastened on Logan.

Logan backed up toward the front door, edging around Michael. "Well, I guess I'd better be going."

Jenessa scooted behind Michael too, holding the door open for Logan. She looked up into his wistful eyes, wishing they'd had more time to talk—about their little boy, about Summer, about...but no. "I appreciate your stopping by."

"No problem." Logan looked at her, then glanced around the edge of the door at Michael. "Anytime."

She watched as Logan stepped off her porch and onto the walkway before closing the door. *If only they'd had more time.*

Judging by the expression Michael wore, he was thinking the exact opposite. "What's really going on, Jenessa?"

CHAPTER 14

THE FRONT DOOR WAS SHUT, but Michael's question still hovered in the air between them. "Why was Logan really here?"

"I don't know what you mean." Jenessa walked past him to grab her purse off the entry table.

"When I opened the door I sensed something," Michael said, "like I'd caught you with your hand in the cookie jar."

Michael was very perceptive. Too perceptive. The atmosphere in the room *had* shifted when he walked in, but what could she say? How could she explain it without hurting him?

"I honestly did not know he was stopping by." Which was true. "Do you really think I would invite him in if I had something to hide—knowing you were on your way here? And leaving the door open?" She explained how she had left a message asking for some information, fully expecting he would simply call her back. "He saw my car out front and stopped to talk to me, rather than pick up the phone. That's all."

Michael glanced toward the door. "That guy takes full advantage of any occasion he gets to be with you. I don't like it, Jenessa. I don't like it at all."

He was right. Logan was in love with her, and he never hid that fact from anyone. It was always there, right between her and Michael, pulling at her heartstrings. Logan had been her first love, and she had been his—crazy, passionately in love. There was no denying it. And they had created, and lost, a son together. Would she ever be able to move past it and make a life with Michael and his son?

She relented. "I know—and I'm sorry for that—but I didn't want to be rude. Should I have told him he couldn't come in, that he should go away and telephone me instead?" She breathed a laugh. "That'd be kind of silly."

Michael stared at her, like a cop, as if he were studying her expression, her body language, wondering if she were being truthful. Could he see right through her, into her heart?

"I don't want to fight," he said with resignation, pulling her into his arms, her body pressed against his. "Let's forget about Logan. Please." His warm brown eyes searched hers, like he was getting ready to kiss her. "We'll go and have a nice dinner, just the two of us."

~*~

Michael took Jenessa to a fine steakhouse on the edge of town. Once inside the restaurant, they approached the hostess station and he told the young woman they had reservations.

After checking the book, she pulled a couple of menus from the cabinet. "Right this way, Mr. Baxter." The hostess led them to their table.

The place had crisp, white-linen tablecloths, and fine crystal stemware that sparkled in the warm glow of candlelight flickering on each table. Michael hoped the ambience wouldn't be an instant giveaway for Jenessa.

As they followed the hostess, Michael fumbled with the little velvet box in his jacket pocket.

"Here we are," the hostess said, laying the menus at each setting.

When Michael had made the reservations, he had asked specifically for this table—the one near the bank of windows that overlooked a garden, lit with decorative lights, in full view of the stunning waterfall feature. "Perfect." He pulled out a chair for Jenessa.

She smiled at him, then took her seat. "This is beautiful, Michael."

He sat too, unfurling the linen napkin and draping it over one knee. "I thought we could use a special night out. Seems like we keep missing each other lately."

"I'm sorry," she said, picking up her menu. "Work has been crazy. Lots of stories to write, then the scare with Aunt Renee."

"How is she doing?" Michael scanned his menu.

"Better. Ramey has her on a pretty strict diet and once she's feeling stronger we're going to take her out walking after dinner. The evenings are becoming warmer, so it should be nice."

"It was a close call. I'm glad to hear she's doing well." He recalled it was Logan who broke the news to Jenessa and whisked her to the hospital so she could be by her aunt's side. It should have been him, not Logan. He felt anger rising just thinking of the man.

Not tonight! He pushed thoughts of Logan out of his mind so he could concentrate on his time with Jenessa. He loved her and she loved him. She had told him so, on more than one occasion. He fingered the small box in his pocket again.

"I haven't been able to spend as much time with her as Ramey has, but I hope things will change once my workload lightens up."

"Any stories I'd be interested in?" he asked.

Jenessa looked up from her menu. "I told you about the story I'm doing on Summer's husband, Chet."

"Yeah, I got that. Anything else?"

"Well, I hate to mention this, but there is something I think I've stumbled upon."

"What's that?"

"In gathering information about the Monahans, I got this gut feeling that there's something not right about Chet."

"How so?"

"I could be totally wrong about the guy, but I think he may be abusing his wife and kids."

Michael set his menu down. This was serious. If there was a man in town hurting his wife or his kids, he'd definitely do something about it—but he'd need proof. Not just a gut feeling. "Do you have any evidence?"

Jenessa explained what she'd seen—the bruise on Summer, the spiral fracture of Grayson's arm, the intimidation of Summer when Jenessa was trying to interview her. "And Allison Reagan, at the bank, is scared to death of the guy. She didn't say so, but I could see it on her face at the very mention of his name."

As much as Michael would like to throw a man like that in jail, he knew he'd need more than what Jenessa gave him to do anything about it. "Unless Summer files a complaint or the kids tell an adult or the police, there's nothing we can do."

"That's what I was afraid of." She sat back in her chair. "I'm going to try to get Summer alone this week and see if I can get the truth out of her."

A middle-aged male waiter approached their table. "Good evening, I'm Peter. I'll be taking care of you this evening. Are we ready to order?"

They gave him their dinner selections and he spun off to another table. Before long, he returned with their food, which they enjoyed, along with good conversation.

"How's Jake doing?" Jenessa asked, finishing her meal. "I haven't seen him since we went to the lake."

"He lost another tooth this week." Michael set his napkin on the table. "The tooth fairy has been very busy lately."

"I love that little guy," she said with a smile.

"Me too." He felt the little box in his pocket. Was now the time to bring it out?

"I wonder if I'll ever see my son." Jenessa took her last sip of wine from the crystal goblet.

"Your son?" *Why would she bring that up now?*

She pushed her empty plate away and crossed her forearms on the table. "Why do you say it like that? You know I had to give up my baby boy."

"Yes, but you don't really talk about him. I assumed you'd moved on, knowing he was being raised by someone else."

"I've tried to move on, Michael, but you don't know how hard it is. He's in my heart, and he's never been out of my mind—not one day. A mother can't just give birth and forget her child. I want to find him. I need to find him, know he's okay, that he's happy."

"Why didn't you tell me this before? I would have understood."

"Would you have? Knowing he was also Logan's son?"

Logan's son. Perfect. She had to point that out.

Yes, Michael had known Logan was the father, but he had put it out of his mind, believing Jenessa had left the baby—and the man—in her past. She'd been a teenager at the time she gave him up for adoption.

"Does Logan know you've been trying to find the boy?" he asked, feeling a slight throbbing at the base of his head.

She nodded, watching him, as if she were waiting for his reaction to her answer.

"I wish you would have told me. I thought our relationship was deep enough that you could tell me anything. I love you, Jenessa."

"Then I should probably tell you that when Logan was at my house earlier, he told me he had hired a private investigator to find our son."

The waiter appeared at their table. "Did you leave room for dessert?"

"No," Jenessa told him, "not tonight." They both went silent as the man removed the plates and left.

Michael crossed his arms over his chest, his jaw tightening. "I didn't know Logan was looking for him." He paused and stared at her for a moment. "Did you?"

CHAPTER 15

"WE WERE HAVING SUCH A NICE DINNER, Michael. Let's not ruin the evening by talking about Logan."

"You didn't answer my question." Michael sat stone-faced, waiting for a response. "Did you know?"

"Yes," she replied, "I knew. There, is that what you wanted to hear? Logan told me a few weeks ago that he was going to hire a private eye to try to find the child. Last night I found out for certain."

"And you didn't think to tell me?"

"I didn't think it mattered, not until the man came up with something concrete."

"So you and Logan talk behind my back regularly?"

"Behind your back?" She stiffened at the accusation. "I'm not trying to hide anything, Michael, but I do speak with Logan from time to time. This is a small town, so we run into each other sometimes. His family owns the newspaper I work for, so he comes in to meet with Charles once in a while and he stops by my desk to say hello." Her lips felt tight as she defended herself. "Do I have to report to you every time I talk to him?"

Michael leaned forward. "Please lower your voice." His tone was firm but hushed.

Jenessa glanced around, seeing every eye in the restaurant was on her. She hadn't realized she had raised her voice. "I'm sorry." Her gaze dropped to her lap, embarrassed.

"I think it's time I take you home." He pulled a number of twenty-dollar bills out of his wallet and stuffed them into the black leather folder the waiter had slipped onto the corner of the table. "Jake is probably running Sara ragged and I'd better save her."

Jenessa simply nodded, not wanting to add to her humiliation.

~*~

Michael drove Jenessa to her aunt's house in silence. It was her turn to spend the night there. He pulled into the driveway and put the car in park.

Jenessa turned to him. "You don't have to get out."

He would have if she hadn't stopped him. He was always the gentleman, always opened her door and walked her from the car to the house. It was who he was.

"This evening didn't go the way I had expected," she said.

"For me either." His dark eyes appeared sad, void of their usual warmth.

She wanted to make it right between them again. "Can I have a do-over?"

A little smile spread across his lips and his eyes brightened. "Of course."

"Sunday night?"

He nodded. "I'll try to find a sitter." He leaned over and kissed her softly. "Sunday then."

~*~

As Michael drove home, he fumbled once more with the little velvet box in his coat pocket. He had been so close to pulling it out, presenting it to Jenessa. Her words echoed in his mind—the evening definitely did not go the way he had expected. They would try it again Sunday night and he would bring the tiny box.

She was perfect for him, and little Jake had become quite attached to her. Michael had told her he loved her and she had returned his sentiments. These last few months together had been amazing—if only Logan Alexander wasn't constantly worming his way in between them.

And now he was giving her hope of finding the child she had given up for adoption, as if Logan suddenly cared about the boy. Was he simply using it as a ploy to get close to Jenessa, or was there a chance his investigator could locate the child? Either way, where would it lead?

A car horn blared long and hard behind Michael, and he realized he had been sitting at the stop sign, lost in thought. He waved an apologetic hand in the air, pushed his foot down on the gas pedal, and headed for home.

Sara's little blue compact sat at the curb when he pulled into the driveway of his 1940s bungalow. Most of the interior lights were on, a welcome sight after the evening he'd just had.

Michael stepped into the living room, but it was empty, the house quiet. He crept down the hallway, finding Jake's door standing slightly ajar, a sliver of soft white light glowing from the bedroom. As he came closer, he heard a faint voice.

Slowly pushing the door open, he found Sara sitting on the side of Jake's bed, leaning back against the headboard. Jake was snuggled against her as she quietly read to him from the book laying open on her lap. His eyelids were half shut, trying not to fall asleep, but he was losing the battle.

Sara looked up when Michael filled the doorway and put a finger to her lips to warn him not to speak. She tucked a stray lock of golden hair behind her ear and continued with her reading.

Michael crossed his arms and leaned against the doorjamb, happy to oblige. An unexpected wave of gratitude washed over him at seeing his son so content in Sara's care. He'd have to remember to thank her.

As he waited at the door, he visualized Jenessa reading to Jake and putting him to bed. The boy needed a loving mother and all that having one entailed.

Sara read a few more sentences, occasionally checking his sleepy face. When she seemed certain Jake had drifted off, she gingerly removed herself from beside him. She pulled the blankets up around his shoulders, kissed him on the forehead, and turned the light out before joining Michael in the hall.

She motioned for Michael to follow her and they tiptoed toward the kitchen. "I wasn't expecting you home so soon."

"I wasn't expecting it either." Michael pulled out a chair at the table and dropped into it.

"You look like you could use something to drink."

"No, I'm good."

She came to the table with a bottle of water and sat. "Something happen?"

Michael looked at her, not sure how much he should divulge.

"Sorry, I didn't mean to be so nosey." She offered a small smile and a shrug as she unscrewed the bottle top. "Habit, I guess."

"We just called it an early night—no big deal, only Logan getting between us again."

"That seems to happen a lot." She took a sip of water.

"I think so too," he agreed, "but Jenessa doesn't see it. Or if she does she isn't doing enough to stop it."

"Want me to talk to her?" Sara raised her brows, her soft green eyes full of question. "Maybe I can help."

"No, she'd only think you were meddling and I was tattling. I'll handle it." That was all he needed, for Jenessa to think he was to talking to her sister about their issues. "Let's talk about something else. How did it go with Jake tonight?"

She smiled. "Oh, we had a ball. He's a great kid. I'd love to have a little boy like him someday." A hint of sadness passed through her eyes and they became moist. "Too bad Luke didn't agree."

Michael knew his cousin had taken a job in another state, had broken up with Sara, but he wasn't sure why. "What happened?" he questioned, hoping he wouldn't regret having asked.

"My maternal instincts are kicking in, Michael, and my biological clock is ticking."

"I see." He wasn't sure what else to say.

"Basically, I wanted kids and he didn't." With tears spilling over, she managed to squeak out the rest. "He said, 'No need to continue dating if we can't agree on this, Sara. I love you, but we just want different things.' What could I reply to that?"

Compassion welled up in him. The urge to wrap his arms around her and give her a hug was strong, but he restrained himself.

She pulled a napkin from the holder in the middle of the table and wiped her eyes. "I thought he was more like you, Michael—that he would love to have a family—but I was so wrong. How could I have been so wrong?" The tears began to flow again.

Without thinking this time, he reached across the table and took her hand. "It'll be okay. There's a great guy out there waiting for someone like you."

"Someone like me?" She huffed a laugh, dabbing under her eyes. "What does that even mean?"

He pulled his hand back, suddenly aware of what he'd done. "I just meant, well—you're pretty and you're smart. You care about other people."

She sniffled. "I do?"

"When your mom died, for instance, you didn't hesitate to jump in and help Ramey run The Sweet Spot."

"Well, that's true."

"You help your aunt whenever she needs you. You were quick to offer to watch Jake when I needed a sitter—and I saw you with him, how you cared for him. I was impressed."

"Yeah, but I'm not as pretty or as smart as Jenessa."

"Sure you are."

"But she's way more accomplished than I am. She graduated from the university, when I barely got my Associates degree at the community college."

"Don't sell yourself short, Sara. You manage the finances of a very successful business. That's no small feat."

"Wow," she said, considering his comments. Her pensive expression turned into a smile. "You make me sound like a great catch, Michael."

"You are. Any man would be lucky to have you."

CHAPTER 16

"YOU REALLY THINK SO? That any man would be lucky to have me?" Sara repeated Michael's words. "I never thought of myself that way."

"You should." Michael checked his watch and got up from his chair. "It's getting late. I'd better let you go."

"Thanks for the pep talk." Sara stood. "I'm happy to return the favor, you know. Call me any time you want to talk." She went to the counter to retrieve her purse. "With Jenessa busy investigating that old drowning for the paper, she probably isn't spending nearly enough time with you and Jake."

Sara started toward the living room, but Michael tugged her arm to stop her. "What did you say?"

"The old drowning—I'm sure she must have told you—about the college kid that died up at Jonas Lake years ago?"

Yes, they had talked about it. He had given her information he'd gotten from Provenza to satisfy her curiosity, but as far as he knew she had dropped it after he and Provenza both told her she couldn't look at the police file. So, why was she keeping it from him?

"Sure, that's right." He released her arm. "Detective Provenza and my father worked the case and I gave her some details for her story. Sorry, it's been a long day."

"No problem." Sara patted his arm, showing she understood. "Like I said, call me anytime. With Luke gone, I'm totally available."

~*~

When Jenessa walked into her aunt's house, she found Ramey and Aunt Renee sitting in the family room, drinking tea and watching television.

"You're back early." Ramey set her cup down on the end table, muted the TV, and straightened in the overstuffed side chair. "Everything okay?"

"What makes you ask that?" Jenessa questioned, feeling a little defensive.

"The time, for one thing," Ramey replied. "It's not even nine."

"Not to mention the melancholy look on your face," Aunt Renee added. "Come, sit down." She patted the sofa cushion beside her. "Tell us all about it."

Jenessa kicked off her high heels and lumbered to the sofa, sinking down beside her aunt. "It wasn't a big deal, just a little spat."

Aunt Renee took her hand. "What was it about? If you don't mind my asking."

"The usual," Jenessa mumbled.

Ramey scooted to the edge of the chair. "Logan?"

"How did you know?" Jenessa asked, surprised by Ramey's perception.

"Lucky guess. He seems to be the reason for friction between you and Michael pretty regularly lately."

Jenessa felt the urge to deny it, but she held her tongue. Was it that apparent?

Ramey gave her a knowing grin. "Am I right or am I right?"

Jenessa shrugged, an embarrassed rush of heat spreading up her neck to her cheeks. She didn't know it had been so obvious to those close to her. "Can't hide anything from you."

Aunt Renee shifted in her seat to face Jenessa. "What did Logan do this time?"

Jenessa explained how he had been at her house when Michael arrived to pick her up. "Logan told me he's been working with a private investigator to find the baby we gave up for adoption."

"Well," Aunt Renee said, "I wondered how long it would take that boy to grow up and want to know his son."

"You did?" Jenessa hadn't thought that Logan ever gave the baby a second thought until very recently, maybe even as a way to get back into her good graces.

"Certainly," her aunt replied. "Any decent man would want to know, but they wouldn't all have the means to find out."

"Fortunately, Logan does," Ramey added.

"And he is a decent man," Jenessa concurred, she had seen the marked difference in him between now and when he was a teenager.

"Especially since his father was sent away," Ramey said, "he's really stepped up."

Jenessa couldn't argue with her statement. Logan was impressing even his father's board of directors with his running of the Alexander companies. It was Michael who was not impressed by Logan's tactics. "Yes, yes, but with all that being said, the truth is that Michael is not thrilled that Logan is looking for our child."

Aunt Renee huffed. "Well, that's crazy. If any man should understand that, Michael should."

"You would think so...but no," Jenessa gave her head a light shake. "He thinks Logan is only doing it to win me back."

"So he's jealous," Ramey said. "Does he have reason to be?"

"No, of course not," Jenessa quickly shot back. Maybe too quickly. Then her gaze moved to her aunt, who raised a suspicious brow at her, but said nothing. Jenessa swallowed, reading her aunt's expression. "Let's find a new subject of conversation, okay?"

"All right," Aunt Renee agreed. "Tell us, how is your story coming? The one about the mayor's son that drowned."

"The mayor's son drowned?" Ramey gasped. "Oh, poor Alex. He and Charles are golfing buddies. How come I didn't hear about this?"

"Not Alex," Aunt Renee said. "Nick. Twenty years ago."

"Oh." Ramey slumped back in her chair. "You scared me for a minute."

"You would have been about eleven when it happened," Jenessa said. "Maybe you remember hearing about it on the news."

"No, not really."

"Did you know Kelly Reagan back then? You would have been about the same age as her."

"Kelly Reagan?" Ramey thought for a moment. "Yeah, I remember her. We weren't really friends, just in the same grade in school. She would have graduated high school with us if she hadn't switched to the Catholic school around the eighth grade," Ramey recalled. "Why are you asking about her?"

"It happened near her family's cabin, and I get the feeling they're somehow connected to Nick Evans' drowning," Jenessa replied.

"Oh dear," Aunt Renee muttered, her teacup clinking against the saucer.

Ramey sat up straight. "How?"

"I don't want to say just yet. I'm still investigating, but—"

"Is Michael helping you with that investigation?" Ramey interrupted.

"No," Jenessa answered. "He refused to share the police file with me, so I'm doing it on my own." It was probably better not to let anyone know Detective Provenza had given her access to it.

"You mean you're doing it behind his back," Ramey clarified.

"I'm doing it because Charles—your Charles—gave me an order to come up with a big story or else."

"Or else what?" Aunt Renee asked.

Charles probably wouldn't want the newspaper's financial woes spread all over town, so Jenessa kept what he had told her to herself. "Let's just say, it wouldn't be pretty."

Jenessa caught the concerned look being shared between Ramey and her aunt. "Don't worry, it's not what you think." She rose from the sofa, tugging at the short hemline of her little black dress as she stood. "I'm going up to bed. This inquisition is exhausting." She took a few steps.

"Not so fast." Ramey got up. "I'm heading home now and it's your turn to help Aunt Renee take her medication and change into her pajamas."

"Don't talk about me like I'm not here," Aunt Renee grumbled.

Ramey flashed her a patronizing smile. "Just giving Jenessa some instructions."

"I'm not an invalid, girls." With some effort, Aunt Renee got herself up from the sofa. "You don't need to treat me like I'm ninety years old." She hooked her arm through Jenessa's. "Now, help me up the stairs."

~*~

The next morning, around ten o'clock, Sara came to Aunt Renee's to relieve Jenessa. When she walked in, Jenessa was in the kitchen, making herself a cup of coffee at her aunt's Keurig machine.

"Good morning," Jenessa greeted as her sister approached. "How'd it go with Jake last night?"

"Couldn't have gone better," Sara replied. "He's a sweet little boy." She moved to the refrigerator and retrieved a bottle of orange juice. "How was your dinner?"

"Michael didn't tell you?" Jenessa had suspected that Michael might have mentioned something since he had come home so early.

"Tell me what?"

If he had, Sara wasn't saying.

"Oh nothing," Jenessa said with a wave of her hand.

"Was he supposed to tell me something?" Sara pressed.

"We just had a little disagreement, that's all. It was nothing really." Jenessa set her unfinished coffee in the sink, avoiding her sister's gaze. "Well, I'm off to work. Aunt Renee is upstairs in her bedroom, reading." Jenessa gathered up her purse and jacket and went down the hallway toward the front door. "Call me if you need anything," she said before she closed it.

With her car still at her house, she walked the few blocks into town. Prior to going in to the paper, she stopped by the bank to see if she could speak with Allison again. The woman had been on the verge of saying something—maybe something important—when her sister had walked in and she completely shut down.

When Jenessa entered the bank, Allison was sitting at her desk in a glass-enclosed cubicle, talking on the telephone. She motioned to Jenessa to come to her, then hung up the phone and stepped out.

"Good morning, Jenessa. How can I help you?" Allison smiled. Around her neck hung a school ring on a gold chain of medium length, an odd choice for a necklace, Jenessa thought.

Her gaze rose to meet Allison's. "I wondered when we could finish the conversation we started yesterday. You were about to say something when Kelly came in."

"No, I think we were done."

Not by a long shot.

"I'd love to buy you lunch today, if you're free."

"Sorry, I'm having lunch with my dad today."

Didn't she just have dinner with him last night?

"You two must be very close," Jenessa said, her gaze momentarily slipping down to the ring hanging around her neck. "I wish I'd had that with my father."

"We're not that close," Allison said, "just some business to discuss."

"I couldn't help but notice the ring you're wearing." Jenessa waved a finger toward it. "From your high school?"

Allison touched it. "No, it's from Notre Dame. I went to college there. So did my father and grandfather." She tipped it up and glanced at it, a smile spreading on her lips.

"My dad went there too." Jenessa caught a glimpse of the intricate design.

"Really?" Allison brought her hand down. "Wow, small world."

"But I don't remember him having a school ring." Jenessa gave her a friendly smile and touched her arm, hoping to endear herself. "I guess we have more in common than we thought."

"Guess so."

"Well, I'll let you go for now, you probably have a lot of work to do," Jenessa said, "but I'd still like to get together with you sometime soon, have some fun, a little girl talk." There was something about Allison that made Jenessa think she could use a friend.

Jenessa backed toward the glass doors. "I'll call you."

Allison gave her the slightest nod. That was all Jenessa needed to confirm she was open for a follow up.

Once Jenessa reached the sidewalk, she pulled out her cell and phoned Summer. If she couldn't talk to Allison right now, maybe Summer was available.

Summer answered and sounded happy to hear from Jenessa. She was hanging out at a nearby baseball field while her son had a Saturday morning practice, or rather, while his team had practice. In spite of his injured arm he still wanted to go, Summer had said, even if all he could do was watch. "Why don't you stop by?" she asked. "I'd love the company."

Jenessa felt encouraged at the possibility that they could have a private conversation this time. Hopefully she would open up without Chet there to put a damper on things. When Jenessa reached the ballfield, she found Summer seated on the bleachers with her young daughter, Lily, beside her. Her spirits dimmed at not finding the woman alone.

Summer greeted Jenessa the moment she saw her climbing the benches. They exchanged small talk for a few minutes before Summer suggested Lily go and have fun on the nearby play equipment. She and Jenessa followed her to the little playground and talked while the girl climbed on the bright blue jungle gym and slid down the sunny yellow slide.

"Sorry about the other day," Summer said. "I didn't want to get into things about Nick Evans in front of Chet."

"Sure, I can understand that. I spoke to Allison the other day about Nick."

Summer's head snapped toward her, her eyes rounding for a moment, then she looked away, across the playground. "What did she say?"

Jenessa explained what Allison had divulged about their unusual relationship with him. "Was that the truth?"

CHAPTER 17

A NERVOUS LAUGH SLIPPED through Summer's lips. "Yes, Allison's description of our relationship with Nick was pretty close." Summer looked briefly at Jenessa, then turned back to the playground. "We were crazy stupid teenagers, had no idea what we were doing or how things would end up. I wish Nick had never come into our lives."

"Why is that?"

"Maybe he'd still be alive."

"You think your sex games had something to do with his death?"

Summer didn't answer for a long time, her eyes fixed on her daughter. "Lily! Be careful!" She glanced at Jenessa. "Kids can be so careless."

"Especially sixteen-year-old girls?"

"Yeah, those too," Summer admitted with a wan smile, her gaze still focused on Lily.

"The night Nick died, did you see anyone around the boathouse?"

"No, I was inside, freshening up in the bathroom while I waited for Allison to come by."

"I thought Nick would have been the one waiting for Allison."

"Well, normally, yes." The corners of Summer's mouth lifted into an impish grin as she cut another sidelong glance at Jenessa. "But he didn't want to be with Allison anymore. He said he only wanted me."

"I thought it was no strings attached."

"It started out that way," Summer turned to Jenessa, "but Nick said he was falling for me. He wanted to duck out before she got there and wanted me to tell her. He thought she'd handle it better coming from me."

What a chicken.

"Was the feeling mutual?" Jenessa asked.

"I thought so at the time, but heck, I was only sixteen. What did I know?" Summer's attention returned to her daughter. "I had been going out with Chet for a few months, but when Nick came along," her eyes flicked to Jenessa, "how could I not fall for this gorgeous college guy?"

"So he liked you better than Allison," Jenessa restated. Summer was thinner and prettier than Allison now, so it was likely this was the case back then too. "Did you ever tell Allison what Nick said?"

"No." Summer gave her head a slight shake. "I never got the chance."

"Oh?"

"She never showed up to the boathouse like I'd expected. After waiting a couple of hours, I went back to our lake house."

"And you never heard anyone outside of the boathouse?" If there had been a scuffle, surely she would have heard something.

"No, I didn't." Summers' reply was curt, her focus on Lily. "I was in the bathroom. Check the police report, that's exactly what I told them."

"Well, I'm not privy to the police report, Summer."

"Oh, sorry, I just assumed…"

Jenessa shook her head. "Do you think Chet could have known about Nick?"

"Chet?" Summer crossed her arms and pitched a quick look at her. "Oh no, I don't think so."

Her answer may have been *no*, but there was something in her voice that seemed unconvinced.

"But you don't know for sure, do you?"

"I know that if he had, he certainly wouldn't have kept quiet about it," Summer said. "That's not Chet's way."

"What do you mean? Was he aggressive? Confrontational?"

Summer looked to her daughter again, as if to make sure she was okay and still out of earshot. "Let's just say he was pretty quick-tempered."

"His police record says he got in a number of fights when he was a teenager."

"I guess." She shrugged, seeming evasive.

"And after Nick's death, how did Chet act?"

"I couldn't say. With the police questioning all of us, my parents were quick to send me off to boarding school to avoid the gossip in town."

"Did your parents know about you and Nick?"

"They never said it outright, but I think they suspected something."

"Did anyone suspect Chet of being responsible for Nick's death?"

"The police suspected everyone. But Chet specifically? I don't know. I had cut off all ties with him when I went away to boarding school. I didn't see him again until my sophomore year at UCLA, when he transferred there."

"Did he know you were going to that college?" Had he kept track of her, stalked her?

"He said he didn't." Summer cocked her head, her brows lowering into a frown. "Why?"

"Just wondered." It seemed awfully coincidental.

She continued standing beside Summer, watching Lily play, not saying a word for a few minutes. She needed to ask if he had been abusing her, without scaring her off. "So," Jenessa eventually ventured in, "has Chet always been violent?"

Summer spun toward Jenessa, and surprise sparked in her eyes. She held Jenessa's gaze, but didn't say anything at first, as if she were considering her reply. Finally she spoke. "I don't care to talk about it."

"When someone has an anger problem, he doesn't just get over it. Unless he's had professional help—"

Summer's eyes filled with sadness.

Jenessa could see she had struck a nerve. "He hasn't gotten any help, has he?"

"He tries to keep it under control, but…" She bit on her bottom lip.

"Be honest with me, Summer, is he abusing you?"

"Why would you ask that?" she snapped, her eyes growing wide.

"I know you didn't want me to see it, but I noticed the bruise on your arm last week."

Summer rubbed her wrist at the mention of it. "I didn't realize."

"So, is he?" Jenessa pushed.

"I don't want to talk about it." Her attention shifted back to her daughter, her lips pressed firmly together. "Lily, wait your turn!"

What was it going to take to get her to open up?

"If he's hurting you or your kids, you have to speak up, get some help. If not for yourself, at least for your children."

Summer's gaze was fixed on her daughter, her arms wrapped tightly over her chest.

"If you're afraid of the town gossiping, at least tell your family—your mom or your dad, even Logan. You know that he and I have been friends for a long time. I'm positive he'd help you." Jenessa waited for a response, but there was none. "You know I'm right."

Summer chewed her lower lip, like she wanted to say something but couldn't, afraid to let the truth out, her gaze still cast toward her daughter.

"He's hurting you, isn't he?"

Summer nodded, her eyes moist. Her gaze fell to the ground for a moment, then traveled to her daughter again. "Yes," she finally admitted, her voice barely a whisper. She took a deep breath before continuing. "Not very often, though. And he's always really sorry. Honest."

I'll bet.

When Summer brought her focus back to Jenessa, there was an uneasiness in her eyes. "There have been a few times when he's been physical, but I'm only talking about a grab or a shove. Mostly he gets verbally abusive when he's really angry."

Jenessa's blood began to pulse faster at Summer's admission. "That's still abuse."

Tears rushed into Summer's eyes. "I know." She swiped at her cheeks.

Jenessa had to ask about the children, almost afraid of what the answer would be, but she needed to know. "What about the kids?"

Summer looked away. "Chet never really bonded with them."

The statement puzzled Jenessa. How could that be? Was he a sociopath?

Summer ran her fingers over her cheeks to clear the tears that had spilled.

"And he's hurt them too?" Jenessa questioned. Anger began to rise in her at the very thought.

"He's never laid a hand on Lily," Summer said as she looked toward the playground again. "He's strict with Grayson, though. Teenage boys, you know." She shrugged then ran her hands up and down her arms, as if she felt a sudden chill.

"Strict? You mean strict like child abuse." The words escaped Jenessa's lips in an almost imperceptible murmur. "Teenagers are still considered children in the eyes of the law, Summer. Besides, Grayson can't be more than eleven or twelve. Hardly a teenager yet."

Sadness and compassion for Grayson rushed over her like a tidal wave. And for Lily too. Even if Chet had

160

not laid a hand on her—yet—she still had to bear witness to the abuse of her mother and brother. The effect is the same. Maybe worse. A little girl would feel guilty at being the only one spared. Like survivor's remorse. Jenessa steadied her breathing then spoke. "You can't let it continue."

Summer's eyes came to meet Jenessa's, tearful and apologetic. "I know it sounds horrible, but you have to understand, Chet was abused by his father when he was a kid. He's worked hard to keep his temper under control, but there are times when he loses it. It's not his fault. He can't help himself."

That's no excuse!

Jenessa reined in her rage, for Summer's sake, and for her own—she wasn't finished asking questions. She couldn't have her shutting down now. "Grayson's spiral fracture?"

Summer whipped her gaze back toward the play area, pausing before she answered. Her voice was cool and even, and she was seemingly unable to face Jenessa. "It was an accident."

~*~

Jenessa propped her elbows on her desk at the newspaper, staring at her computer screen, still fuming from her discussion with Summer. How could she write about the next phase of her investigative report without exposing the woman to ridicule and town gossip? She began typing her notes from today's interview, playing over in her mind what Summer had said.

It was an accident? That's all she had to say? Was she just protecting her husband—or was it something else?

Lost in angry thoughts, Jenessa startled when the phone on her desk rang. She took a deep calming breath and answered it.

"Listen closely," the muffled voice said. "Stop digging around in Nick Evans' death. You're opening a can of worms you're going to regret."

What? Jenessa bolted to her feet. "Who is this?"

There was a click, then the line went dead.

She stood there for a moment, in shock. Her heart beat so hard in her chest that it hurt. She pulled in a deep breath and forced herself to calm down. She replaced the receiver and dropped into her chair.

Who was that?

It was difficult to say if it were a man's or a woman's voice. Medium tenor, muffled with something, maybe even altered.

The threat shook her, but it also told her she was onto something—something big.

She grabbed for the phone to call Michael, but she paused, hesitated, knowing exactly what he would say. She'd been careful to look into this story without his help—or, as Ramey had put it, behind his back. If she told him about this menacing call, he would order her to drop the story—she was certain of it.

But there was no way she could do that. Not only was Charles depending on her for a big story—her job could be on the line. Being laid off in Sacramento had devastated her, and the last thing she wanted was to be forced to leave her home in Hidden Valley to find a job at a newspaper elsewhere. She had put down roots here—the people she cared about were here.

Maybe she should make George Provenza aware of the threat somehow, without Michael knowing. Then again, he was Michael's partner and George would probably feel obligated to tell him. No, she would keep the phone call to herself—for now.

For all she knew, it could have simply been a prank call anyway, couldn't it?

"Hey, Jenessa," Charles called out.

She jumped at the sound, expelling a sharp, quick gasp. "Don't sneak up on a girl." She swiveled in her chair and faced her boss, who was standing in her doorway.

"You okay?" he asked. "You look like you saw a ghost or something."

"No ghost, just a creepy caller."

Charles cocked his head. "Come again?"

"This story I'm working on." She crossed her legs and leaned back in her chair. "Someone just called me and told me to back off. But don't worry, it's no big deal," she said, doing her best to cover how much it rattled her.

His brows rose and his eyes lit up with anticipation. "That must mean you're onto something—something big."

"Exactly."

CHAPTER 18

CHARLES McALLISTER TOOK A SEAT in the chair beside Jenessa's desk. "This story seems to be heating up. Tell me what you've got so far."

She ran down the facts she had uncovered and what she still hoped to learn. "I wasn't sure it was going to turn into anything, but that phone call confirmed it. Detective Provenza and I aren't the only ones who don't think it was an accidental drowning."

"Sounds like someone doesn't like you digging around in something that was put to rest a long time ago."

"Provenza said he never felt right about it being ruled an accident, but he couldn't prove it."

"What does Michael think?" Charles asked.

She hesitated. Should she tell him?

"Jenessa?" he said slowly, drawing out her name like her father used to do, raising the final syllable in a question.

"Well," she paused, "he doesn't know I'm still digging into the story."

"Is that wise? I'd think you'd want his help."

"Once I have enough evidence that proves it was a crime, I'll bring him into it, Charles, I promise."

With his hands on his knees, he pushed off to stand. "We're running out of time, Jenessa. I need something with sizzle I can run in the next few days."

"I got that."

"I need buzz, Jenessa!" he exclaimed, shaking his fist as he said it.

"And I'll give it to you, Charles. Don't worry." She put on her bravest face. "I'll have something big you can print."

~*~

After Charles left her office, his words about Michael echoed in her mind. She hadn't been completely truthful with him, which could backfire on her. Trust was an easy thing to lose and she was walking a fine line there.

She hoped Michael would understand, she simply had to pursue this story, and having him try to stop her was the last thing she needed right now. But when he found out what she'd done—and he eventually would—would he be angry with her? Hurt that she'd gone behind his back? Was this story worth the rift it would most certainly cause between them?

Both Ramey and Charles were right, she needed to do what she should have done earlier—she would tell him. So she gathered her things and headed for the door.

On her way out, she stopped at the reception desk. "Alice, I'm going over to the police station if anyone is looking for me."

The elderly woman looked up from her magazine. "Say hello to that handsome detective of yours."

"Sure thing."

Jenessa pushed through the door and stepped out into the glorious spring afternoon. She paused on the sidewalk and drew in a deep breath of fresh air, enjoying the mild temperature and the sunshine on her face—if only Michael would be as welcoming.

She hadn't walked but a block when her cell phone began to ring. It was Michael. She stared at it for a moment, thinking. This was something she needed to do in person. She might lose her courage if she didn't talk to him face to face. She hit ignore and kept walking.

Before long, the phone beeped that she had a message. Perhaps she should listen to it. Maybe he was calling to tell her he was going off somewhere. She stopped and played the voicemail.

All he said was, "Call me back." Or at least that's all she thought he said. The end-of-message beep didn't come, nor did the computerized voice saying she had no more messages. Noises like paper moving around was what she heard, and Detective Provenza's voice in the background.

Michael had forgotten to hang up the call—that must be it. She pressed the button to start the message over, listening carefully this time.

"Were you able to reach her?" she heard Provenza ask.

"No, just voicemail," Michael replied.

"Don't worry. It'll all work out."

"I don't know," Michael said, his voice seeming to be coming from across the room. "I came so close to taking Josie back," his voice grew louder, as he must have been walking back toward his desk, "but I chose Jenessa." His voice sounded raw and dejected. "Now she's slipping away, George. I can feel it."

He came close to taking Josie back? His ex-wife? Shock tore through her, so much so that she almost missed the rest of what he had said.

"If she slips away," she heard George respond, "then it wasn't meant to be."

Jenessa couldn't listen to any more of it. She hit the *end* button and shoved the phone in her purse. She couldn't talk to Michael about the case after what she'd just heard. She turned and walked away from the police station…going where? Anywhere but where Michael was at this very moment, that's where.

Before she knew it, she found herself in front of The Sweet Spot. She paced back and forth, not sure she wanted to go in and be around people in her current frame of mind.

He came close to taking Josie back. The words played on a continuous loop in her head.

Josie had come to visit a number of months ago, for little Jake's sixth birthday, and Jenessa had suspected she was trying to win Michael back, but he kept denying it. The woman had stayed at his house, but he swore she had slept in their son's room.

Of course he would say that, but could Josie have climbed into Michael's bed at least one of those nights? He would never have admitted it, not if he wanted to save his relationship with Jenessa. But did it happen? Is that why he almost took her back? Having her in his house, in his bed, felt like old times?

"Jenessa?" Ramey held the glass door open. "Do you want to come in?"

She stopped pacing. "I can't."

"Then why are you here?"

She told Ramey what she had heard Michael say. "I can't get it out of my head."

"Come in. We'll talk about it."

With Ramey holding the door, several customers exited the café. Jenessa's gaze fell to the sidewalk and she turned away as she waited for them to go out of earshot.

"I'd better go," she muttered, still eyeing the concrete below.

"Where?"

"Thanks, Ramey," said the next person leaving café, a female voice Jenessa recognized.

She lifted her head to see the woman. "Allison?"

"Hello, Jenessa."

This must have been where Allison had lunch with her father. "Do you have a few minutes to talk now?"

Allison raked a hand through her hair as her gaze shifted to the street, where cars were parked, customers of the nearby businesses. Was she looking for someone?

"I'm free if you are," Jenessa said, trying to pull the woman's attention back.

Allison nodded as her gaze slid back to Jenessa. "Sure, I'm free. The bank closed at noon."

"Why don't we walk?"

Ramey quietly stepped back inside her shop and closed the door.

Allison shrugged. "Why not."

The two women set off down the sidewalk, Jenessa taking the curb side. The walkway was congested with people ducking in and out of the shops, others simply strolling to enjoy the mild, sunny Saturday. She waited for Allison to say something, so when she didn't, Jenessa jumped in. "Beautiful day, isn't it?"

Allison glanced toward the sky and put her hand up to shade her eyes. "I hadn't noticed." She seemed distracted.

"I was hoping you could tell me more about what happened at the lake the night Nick Evans died," Jenessa said.

"I don't know what else there is to tell."

A few blocks ahead was Crane Park. Perhaps Jenessa could get Allison to sit down on one of the park benches and open up. "Did you ever play tennis at Crane Park?"

"Crane Park?" Allison's gaze drifted off in the direction of the park. "Sure, lots of times. What about you?"

"Yes, Logan and I played there, back in high school."

"Logan Alexander?" Allison seemed a little surprised. "I didn't know you two were friends."

"More than friends, back then. You know him through Summer?"

"Not really. He was just a kid when Summer and I were friends, but I've had my eye on him the last few years. I mean, really, what woman hasn't?"

Could Allison be attracted to Logan? She was five years his senior, but still, some men like older women. "Would you like me to introduce you to him?"

"Oh, no," Allison let out a nervous giggle, as though she were a schoolgirl, her gray-green eyes crinkling at the corners. "We've already met. His family owns the bank, so he's my boss, technically." She turned a little toward Jenessa as they walked. "I get all nervous and tingling when he comes into the bank. He's such a good-looking man, don't you think?"

"Uh, yeah, he's very good looking." Put on the spot, Jenessa couldn't help but admit she was finding him increasingly irresistible as well.

"Those brilliant blue eyes," Allison sighed. She had barely gotten the words out when someone barreling out of one of the shops bumped into her.

"Oh, sorry," the man apologized. "I didn't see—"

"Chet?" Allison gasped.

"Hold on a second," he said into his phone. He took a closer look at her. "Allison? Please forgive my clumsiness, I didn't see you there." He held out his phone as if that was his excuse, then put it back up to his ear as he hurried away and continued talking.

Allison's lips tightened as her eyes danced about nervously.

Jenessa took her by the arm. "Let's keep walking."

Allison remained stony silent for the next few minutes until they reached the park. "I hate that man." Tears were pooling in her eyes. She dropped down onto a park bench, her gaze glued to the ground.

Those were strong and unexpected words. She had seen Allison's fearful reaction in the bank when Chet and Summer had walked in, which had puzzled Jenessa at the time, and now she wore that same pained expression.

Jenessa sat down beside her and rested an arm on the back of the bench. "Why do you say that?"

Allison lifted her moist eyes to Jenessa. "You want to know what happened the night Nick died? Well, I'll tell you."

CHAPTER 19

AN UNEXPECTED GIDDINESS danced in Jenessa's chest. This was exactly what she had been waiting for, a detailed, first-person account of what really happened to Nick Evans. Was it an accident? Or was it murder? Allison was finally about to tell her.

"You already know that Summer and I were both sleeping with Nick." Pink bloomed on Allison's cheeks at the admission.

Jenessa nodded, anxiously waiting for more details.

"That night, we had arranged for Summer to go first. At around eight thirty, it was supposed to be my turn. I was so excited to be with him, I started for the boathouse a little early. I knew our times together meant absolutely nothing to him, but I was totally in love with the guy." Allison cupped the ring she wore on a chain around her neck. "Pretty stupid, huh?"

"Where boys are concerned, I've learned that most teenage girls are pretty stupid," Jenessa huffed, thinking about her own youthful indiscretions.

Fondling the ring seemed to calm Allison when she was nervous or upset. An odd habit. Or did it have special meaning?

"Sorry, I didn't mean to break your train of thought. Please, go on."

"Well," Allison continued, "I told my parents I was going over to Summer's, whose lake house was not that far from ours, although I was really going to the boathouse. I took the path through the wooded area that's between her lake house and the boathouse. When I was getting close, I saw Nick and Chet arguing and fighting, so I stepped back behind a tree and peeked around it."

"Then what?"

"From what I saw, I assumed Chet must have caught Nick coming out of the boathouse and questioned him about what he was doing there. I couldn't hear what they were saying, but I'm sure they were quarreling over Summer."

"Did you see Summer at all?"

"No. She said later that she was showering or something inside the boathouse and wasn't aware of what was going on outside."

"And you believed her?" Jenessa asked.

"I had no reason not to."

So Allison never knew Nick was going to dump her. "Okay, then what happened?"

"Chet knocked Nick to the ground and punched him over and over again until Nick quit fighting back and stopped moving."

"So Chet murdered Nick," Jenessa muttered under her breath.

"That's what it looked like to me." Allison must have heard her anyway.

"Did you see him throw Nick's body in the water?"

"No. I was too scared to stick around. I took a step back, behind the tree, so he wouldn't see me. A twig snapped under my foot, and Chet must have heard it because his head whipped in my direction. I was afraid he'd come after me and beat me to death too for witnessing what he'd done."

"So, what did you do?"

"I tiptoed a few yards away, as quietly as I could, then ran through the trees, back to our cabin. It was getting pretty dark by that time, but as I got closer, I saw someone at the back door, through the screen, about to step out. The porch light wasn't on, so I couldn't tell who it was. One of my parents, I assumed, so I skirted around to the side of the house and waited until I was sure the coast was clear. I snuck back inside and crept to my bedroom without anyone noticing me."

"Wasn't your family at home? Wouldn't they have seen you?"

"No, they were in the living room, at the front of the cabin. I could hear the television blaring." Allison wrapped her arms around her abdomen, as if to comfort herself. "I've never been so terrified in my life. I just knew I couldn't tell anyone what I had seen. I couldn't risk Chet coming after me."

Jenessa draped her arm gently around Allison's shoulders. "I know you're still scared, but I need you to come with me to the police station and tell them what you saw. It's time to make things right, Allison."

"But what if Chet comes after me? After all, I'm the only witness."

"When you tell the police what you saw, I'd think Chet would be arrested. Then you won't have to worry."

"But no, then he'll probably get out on bail, and I'm sure he could figure out where I live."

"Do you want him getting away with killing Nick?" *Not to mention what he is doing to his family now…*

"No," Allison replied softly, her shoulders drooping.

"You want him walking the streets as a free man after what he did?"

"No, of course not." Her voice gained strength.

"Don't you think that after all this time, Nick's family deserves to know the truth of what happened?"

Allison sniffled as she nodded.

"The police will make sure you're safe." Jenessa thought of Michael. If anyone could protect her, it was him. Strong, devoted, the rescuer of damsels in distress—that was Michael in a nutshell.

Allison pulled in a long breath and lifted her eyes upward, toward the bright blue sky peeking through the canopy of leaves above them. "It actually feels good to have gotten that off my chest, to finally tell someone after all these years."

Jenessa couldn't even imagine what it had been like for Allison, keeping such a horrifying secret for so long.

Allison stood from the bench, her purse in hand. Pulling her shoulders back, she straightened, closed her eyes, and drew in another deep breath. When she opened them, she looked directly at Jenessa. "I feel like I've had a huge weight lifted from my shoulders." She even smiled a little. "I'm ready to go to the police station now."

~*~

While Jenessa and Allison marched to the station, Jenessa phoned Detective Provenza and asked if he and Michael could meet her there.

"What's going on?" Provenza asked.

"You know that Nick Evans case I've been chasing?"

"Yeah…" he muttered suspiciously.

"I think I just broke it wide open. I've got Allison Reagan with me and we're headed down to the station."

"I remember that name from the interviews. She works at the bank now, right?"

"That's the one," Jenessa confirmed. "In the interview notes, Allison said she didn't see anything."

"I remember."

"She was a terrified teenager, but the truth is that she actually did witness what happened that night, and I've convinced her to put it all down in writing."

"Well, I'll be darned, Miss Jones. Good job." Provenza sounded genuinely pleased he'd let her peek at the files. "Michael's gone home for the day, but then you probably already know that."

"Uh, yeah, that's right. I was so excited I forgot." They had been missing each other lately and, truthfully, she had lost track of his schedule. "Can you find him and get him down to the station?"

"Sure. He won't want to miss out on this."

Jenessa knew Michael wouldn't be happy about it either—at least the part about her going around him to pursue this case.

"I really meant it when I said good job, Jenessa."

"Thanks, George."

~*~

"The detectives will be waiting for us," Jenessa told Allison as she dropped her phone into her purse while they walked. "Don't be nervous. Just tell them what you saw."

"I can do that."

They approached the entrance to the police station. Jenessa swung the heavy glass door open and held it for Allison to enter first.

Allison paused in the doorway and glanced back at Jenessa, like maybe she had changed her mind.

"You can do this," Jenessa said, hoping to instill some confidence.

Allison nodded and straightened her shoulders. "I'm ready."

Jenessa strode to the reception desk and told Ruby they were there to see Detective Provenza.

The woman called Provenza's office, then set the receiver back in its cradle. "Looks like Detective Provenza is on another line. Why don't you take a seat over there," she lifted her chin toward the chairs, "and I'll let him know you're here when he gets off."

"Thanks, Ruby." Jenessa moved to the waiting area and Allison followed her, each taking a seat. "It shouldn't be long."

A few minutes later, Michael ambled through the front door with Jake and Sara. He seemed to be laughing at something Sara said, then swept Jake up in his arms.

"Daddy's got to work," Michael said to the boy, apparently not noticing Jenessa sitting nearby. "Go with Sara and we'll do something fun tonight."

Jenessa rose from the seat and hurried to them, leaving Allison in the waiting area. The movement caught Michael's attention and he turned his head in her direction, his lips almost smiling. "I didn't see you there." He set Jake down and the boy ran to her, flinging his arms around her waist.

"Hi, Jenessa!" Jake squealed.

She crouched down to his level and put her arms around him. "Hey, Jake." She grunted as she gave him a good squeeze. "Having a fun day?" Her gaze rose to Sara, wondering why she had come with the fellas.

Sara stepped closer, appearing to read the question in Jenessa's eyes. "Michael and Jake were at the café when he got the call from Detective Provenza, so I offered to watch Jake."

"That was nice of you." Jenessa felt oddly jealous, which surprised her.

"Follow me back to my office," he said to Sara, "and I'll get my extra house key for you."

"What about me?" Jenessa asked.

Michael glanced at the waiting area. "You and your friend can wait right here and Provenza and I will be out in a minute."

Jenessa planted her hands on her hips as irritation danced up her neck. She'd often been let back to the detectives' office, so why did Michael tell her to wait? It must have been because of Allison. Or was it because of Sara?

No, she was being silly.

Sure, their relationship had been pretty bumpy the last week or so, but he wouldn't really be giving her the brush off, would he? She gave herself a mental shake to rid her mind of that unsettling thought, but it didn't seem to want to leave her. Rather, Ramey's voice played in her head, recounting how there had almost been something between Michael and Sara before Jenessa came back to town.

Once he and the others had walked away, Allison came and joined Jenessa. "What a nice-looking family," Allison commented as she watched Michael hold the door to the back offices open for Jake and Sara. "I always thought I'd have that one day."

"They're not a family," Jenessa was quick to correct.

"If you say so."

CHAPTER 20

MICHAEL OPENED THE DOOR TO THE BACK offices for Jenessa and Allison. "Ladies."

His jaw appeared tight as he spoke, his tone as if they were strangers. Had Detective Provenza told him what she had been up to? He had to have. Otherwise how would George have explained to Michael why she and Allison Reagan needed to meet with them right now?

Jenessa peered up at Michael as she slipped through the doorway, followed by Allison. He did not meet her gaze, but seemed to avoid her. He called to the receptionist, "Ruby, hold our calls," before closing the door.

"Hello, Miss Jones," Detective Provenza greeted, getting up from his desk. "And you must be Allison Reagan."

"I am."

"Michael, why don't we take Miss Reagan into the conference room to talk to her?" Provenza directed. "Jenessa, you know you can't be in on this part."

Yes, she knew that, but she had hoped she could at least observe the interrogation from behind the two-way mirror. "The observation room?" she asked, her eyebrows lifted with hope.

"Not this time," Michael said. "We have to do this by the book. You'll have to wait out front and we'll talk after the interview."

Jenessa wanted to plead her case, but it was evident from the expression on his face that he was angry with her. She turned to Provenza. "George? Please? For my story."

"I'd like to say yes," he snuck a quick look at Michael's stern expression, "but you'd better go wait out front."

"But, George—"

"We sincerely do appreciate all you've done." He looked over at Michael. "Don't we?"

Michael gave a slight nod and an irritated grunt, his eyes focused on his partner.

"See, he agrees." Provenza gave her an apologetic smile. "Now maybe we can catch the SOB that killed that boy."

Jenessa rested her hand on Allison's shoulder. The woman's brows were knit into a frown, as if she were nervous to tell the police all she'd seen that night. Or was it Chet she was afraid of?

"Don't worry, Allison." Jenessa patted her shoulder lightly. "Just tell them what you told me. They'll take care of the rest."

Allison nodded. She stood up straight and squared her shoulders. "I will."

"Thank you, Jenessa." Michael's voice and his expression softened a bit. "You must have put a lot of time and effort into investigating this case and convincing Ms. Reagan to come in."

"You're welcome." She mustered up a small smile. "I did. It's my job."

They all filed out of the detectives' office. Jenessa went to the left and the rest of them headed down the hall to the right.

After a little more than an hour, with Jenessa still seated in the reception area, Allison came through the door, followed by the two detectives. She wore an expression of relief at having two decades of weight lifted off her shoulders.

Jenessa stood from her chair, proud of Allison for giving her testimony in the face of fear. She cautiously strolled toward them. "So, what's next?"

"We'll bring Chet Monahan in for questioning," Provenza said.

"What about me?" Allison asked, uncertainty quivering in her voice. "Who's going to protect me when Chet leaves here?"

"I can see if the captain will approve having a uniform watch your place," Provenza suggested.

Michael crossed his arms and shifted his weight. "Do you really think he'll be a threat after all this time?"

"I don't want to take the chance," Allison replied, with fear etching creases around her eyes. "I saw him beat a man to death. Why wouldn't he come after me for turning him in? You don't think he would try to stop me from testifying against him when it goes to trial?"

"Ms. Reagan," Michael said, "I think you've been watching too many crime dramas on television."

Provenza shot a frown at Michael before turning back to Allison. "We'll do our best," he said to her, "but you call us if he makes any kind of threat against you."

Allison turned to Jenessa, her face pinching into an angry expression. "But you promised me the police would protect me if I came forward."

Knowing what Jenessa did about Chet's history of violence, she didn't believe they should totally rule out the threat. "What if you stay with your parents for a while?"

"If the police won't protect me," Allison pitched Michael a seething glare, "I guess my father will have to."

~*~

Allison had stomped out of the police station when she left. Jenessa had been sure Michael and Detective Provenza would have offered her some kind of protection in exchange for coming forward. She had tried to argue the point with them, but in the end they said it was up to their captain. They promised to put in a request, but Hidden Valley simply didn't have the financial resources of a bigger city and they doubted he would go for it, unless she could prove she really was in physical danger.

"Do what you can," Jenessa said.

"Of course we will." Michael was clearly angry with her. She could see it in his eyes—or maybe it was disappointment—she couldn't tell. Whatever it was, it had cut a wide swath between them.

In the early months of their relationship, they were almost always in sync, personally and professionally. But lately, there seemed to be one misstep after another. Would they ever be able to return to their comfortable rhythm again?

As she walked back to the newspaper, she phoned her editor and told him she needed him to hold the press, she had a huge breaking story for the front page of the Sunday morning edition.

"This is the big story you've been begging for, Charles."

"It has to be something the whole town will be talking about," he said.

"Oh, they'll be talking about this for a long time."

"You don't know what this means to me, Jenessa, and to the paper. Things are looking a bit dire around here. Great job!"

"Don't congratulate me yet. Wait until after you've read the story."

"I knew you'd come through for us."

Yes, she could be counted on, but Charles had no idea what this story could cost her.

~*~

Michael and Detective Provenza drove to the Monahan home, looking for Chet.

"I had a gut feeling that boy didn't accidentally drown," Provenza said as he drove.

"Then why didn't you continue with the investigation?" Michael asked. "Instead, you let Jenessa pursue it."

"Never in all those twenty years did I ever forget about it, but I had done all I could. Your father and I had interviewed everyone involved or that lived in the vicinity. We pored over what little physical evidence there was, time and time again, but nothing."

"I wish you'd told me she was looking deeper into the case, rather than finding out, after the fact, that my girlfriend was chasing a cold case behind my back."

"You know how she is, Baxter, gets her teeth into something and won't let go." Provenza pulled the car to the curb in front of the Monahans' upscale house. "Hell, it's one of her best qualities."

Michael wasn't so sure he agreed.

Provenza turned the engine off. "Now get your mind off that girl and back onto this case."

The two climbed out of the car and marched to the front door. Michael rang the doorbell and they waited. No answer. He pushed the button again.

Eventually, the front door opened and standing there was a boy with wavy blond hair that Michael judged to be about junior high age.

"Is your dad home, young man?" Detective Provenza asked.

Before the boy could reply, Summer appeared behind him. "Can I help you?"

"We're looking for your husband, ma'am," Provenza said.

"Grayson," Summer put her hand on the boy's shoulder, "go get your dad, please. He's in the backyard."

The boy spun away and disappeared into the house.

"What's this about?" she asked.

"We need to talk to your husband," Michael replied.

"Regarding?"

"It's best if we wait until your husband is here."

"Would you like to come in?" she offered, totally unaware of what was coming.

CHAPTER 21

SUMMER STEPPED ASIDE and let the detectives into her home. The entry was formal and spacious, with travertine tile and a sweeping staircase. It was the kind of house Michael knew he could never afford on a small-town detective's salary, but there was something cozy and comfortable about his small bungalow that he preferred over this expensive home. Any woman he married would have to prefer it too.

She stood in the entry with them as they waited for her husband to join them, crossing her arms, then uncrossing them, shifting her weight from one side to the other, looking uncomfortable at the awkward silence. "I don't know what could be keeping him. I'll go check." She left Michael and Provenza alone in the entry, waiting.

As if out of nowhere, a little girl, about six, with curly brown hair and big brown eyes, appeared. "Hi, I'm Lily."

Provenza seemed startled by the child, but Michael bent down on one knee to speak with her. "Hi, I'm Detective Baxter," he put a hand to his chest before holding it out to his partner, "and this old guy is Detective Provenza."

Lily giggled. "I like your white hair," she said to Provenza. "It's like Santa Claus's."

"Oh really?" Provenza didn't seem to like the comparison.

Michael stood. "That was a compliment," he mumbled to his partner.

Just then, Chet, dressed in shorts and a worn-out t-shirt, stalked toward them, carrying a white hand towel that had seen better days. Summer and Grayson trailed behind him. "Sorry to keep you waiting. I was getting the pool ready for the season." He wiped his hands on the towel. "Now, what can I do for you?"

Michael looked at the little girl, and then the boy, knowing it would be better not to do this in front of them. "Mrs. Monahan, do you think you could take the children somewhere else so we can talk to your husband in private?"

"Grayson," Summer said, her gaze focused on Michael, "would you please take your sister upstairs?" Apparently she wanted to stay and hear what they had to say.

"But, Mom—"

"Grayson," she said with force, "do as I asked."

He grumbled under his breath and frowned. "Come on, Lily."

Once the children were out of earshot, Chet questioned the detectives. "What is this all about?"

"Has something happened?" Summer asked.

Detective Provenza's gaze shifted to her, then back to Chet. "Chester Monahan, we need you to come down to the station with us for questioning in the murder of Nicholas Evans."

"What?" Summer gasped.

Provenza continued. "As a person of interest, we'll need to take you in."

Michael gripped Chet by his upper left arm, forcing him to take a step toward the door.

"No!" Summer shrieked. "What are you doing?"

"This is crazy!" Chet shouted as he pulled back, out of Michael's hold. "I didn't kill anyone!"

Provenza stepped in front of the man and glared into his face. "We didn't say that. We said person of interest, but thanks for the tip." He looked to Michael briefly then back to Chet. "Now, you can come voluntarily, or we can arrest you for obstructing our investigation."

Chet's expression turned stone cold. "I know my rights. You can't make me answer your questions."

"Not true." Michael quickly stepped behind Chet, firmly gripped his shoulder with one hand, and clamped his other around Chet's right wrist, pulling it behind him.

Chet twisted and turned, trying to pull free. "Get off me!" He swung at Michael with his free fist, connecting with his jaw.

The blow caught Michael off guard. The shooting pain made him stagger back for a moment, then he regained his balance and charged Chet, taking him to the floor. They struggled for a few seconds, until Michael rolled him over roughly, pinned him face down with his knee, yanked both his hands behind his back, and secured them with handcuffs.

"You're under arrest for assaulting a police officer." Michael dragged him to his feet, then proceeded to read him his rights.

An angry scowl twisted Chet's features. "You're making a big mistake." He turned toward his wife and shook his head, his voice seething with fury and desperation. "I did not kill anyone. You have to believe me."

Summer said nothing in response, appearing too stunned to speak.

"We have evidence to the contrary," Michael said, still holding on to Chet by the arm. "Now, let's go."

"What evidence?" Chet asked.

"An eye witness," Provenza declared, holding the door open.

"After all these years?" Summer slumped down onto a cushioned bench in the entry. "Who is it?"

"You'll find out soon enough." Michael wasn't about to say it was Allison, knowing how she feared that Chet would retaliate against her. His eyes flicked to Provenza, who returned a slight nod of agreement, acknowledging he had the same thought. "I said, let's go."

"Summer, call Logan," Chet ordered as Michael pulled him through the doorway. "Have him get me a good lawyer."

~*~

Michael hadn't wanted Jenessa present when they brought Chet Monahan in, but yet there she was, camera in hand as she stood on the sidewalk outside of the Monahans' home. She had a job to do, just like he did—and he would have to understand. Charles was counting on her.

The ornate front door opened. Detective Provenza stepped out first, followed by Michael leading Chet by his cuffed arm. Jenessa shot a few photos, one of which would certainly make the front page.

Michael tossed her a harsh glare as he marched the suspect past her.

Her gaze flew back to Chet's distraught family. Summer and the children were standing in the doorway crying. Jenessa raised her camera, considering a shot, but lowered it. She couldn't do that to them.

At the sight of this mother, with her arms around her panic-stricken kids, trying to hold them back as they called out for their father, Jenessa wondered what Summer must be feeling. She had told Jenessa that her husband could get violent when provoked, so, for all these years, had she secretly known that Chet was the person who had killed her lover? Or at the very least suspected?

The children quit struggling once their dad was away from the house, now standing stoically. Summer kissed Grayson on the top of his head and ran her hand lightly over his hair.

The sound of someone opening the back door to the police car drew Jenessa's attention. Michael put his hand on Chet's shoulder. "Watch your head," he warned and helped him in.

Jenessa snapped a picture of Chet, an angry yet forlorn expression on his face, as he sat, waiting to be taken to the police station. When the car pulled away, he turned and stared right at her, his eyes dark and brooding.

She watched, from her position on the sidewalk, as the car drove off and disappeared around the corner. When she turned back to the house, the door was shut. Should she go up and knock? See if there was anything she could do for Summer and her family?

Maybe now was not the best time for that. Summer was probably phoning Logan to get a lawyer to meet her husband at the station. Later, Jenessa might call to check on her, once Summer had time to make arrangements and get her bearings again.

~*~

Now that the case was officially open again, Michael and Provenza would certainly be interrogating Chet aggressively and drilling down hard into the investigation. The DA would want all the ammunition he could get to make sure he won the case and that Chet's conviction was assured before he would issue an arrest warrant for murder.

With the tenuous way things stood between her and Michael, she wasn't so sure he would give her the inside scoop on whatever they uncovered. A cloak of sadness covered her as she thought of how much their relationship was going awry. Tears threatened to fill her eyes, and blinked them back.

She didn't have the luxury of dwelling on her personal life right now. She had to concentrate on the job at hand. Charles would be counting on her for follow-up stories to Chet's arrest and the truth of what really happened to the mayor's son. She'd have to come up with a way to obtain that information.

Perhaps George Provenza would help her, as she had helped him. He had wanted to solve this case so badly that he'd kept it on his radar for the last twenty years. Maybe out of gratitude he'd grant her access to the details before any other news outlet got them.

Would they also interrogate Summer again, in light of the new facts Allison had given the police? Probably not, for now she was married to the prime suspect and they could not force her to testify against her husband. And with Summer being an Alexander, the family would likely close ranks around her and the children.

Jenessa had gone back to the newspaper after the arrest and was hard at work in her cramped cubicle, her fingers clicking over the keyboard as she put her story together. Between the interviews and the imminent arrest for murder, it was shaping up into a juicy piece.

Sex, Lies, and Murder would be the headline. How could the townspeople not be talking about it?

She thought of Mayor Evans and his family. Had Michael or Provenza informed them of what was happening with the case? Did they know yet that Nick had not accidentally drowned but had, in fact, been murdered? She could only imagine the shock and horror of his family members if they had to learn about it in the Sunday paper.

She rested her hand on the receiver of her desk phone. Should she attempt to call the mayor? No, she thought better of it and pulled her hand back. Surely the detectives would have let the parents know. Maybe she should call George to ask…

The phone rang. She checked her watch—six o'clock. The office was quiet as a tomb. Most of the employees would have already gone home. The receptionist must have put the call through before leaving for the day. Jenessa almost let it go to voicemail—she had to finish the story—but maybe it was important.

"Hello, Jenessa Jones," she answered.

"I warned you to stop digging," a gruff voice growled, almost indiscernibly.

"I'm sorry?" She sat up straight in her chair. The voice was familiar. The same muffled voice that had issued her a warning earlier in the day.

"Stop digging around in this story," the voice grumbled.

"Who is this?"

Apparently, whoever was on the other end of the line was not aware of the recent arrest. It probably wouldn't be prudent for her to mention it.

"You have no idea about the destruction you're about to unleash. Drop it or you'll wish you had."

"I can't do that," she said, "but if you'll—"

Click. The caller hung up and all that remained was a dial tone.

A chill shimmied down her back. She stood up and peered over the walls of her cubicle. Most of the lights had been turned off—the receptionist must have done it on her way out. It didn't appear there was anyone else there, and it gave her an eerie feeling.

"Charles?" she called out, but there was no answer.

He would be expecting her story soon, so he must be coming back to give it a once over and get it into the paper for the morning's edition, right? The printers had to still be there, didn't they? Her cell phone rang and she jumped.

CHAPTER 22

JENESSA DUG HER CELL OUT of her purse, relieved to find it was Logan calling. "Hello."

"Hey, Jenessa." His voice sounded more serious than usual. "You have a few minutes to talk?"

Should she tell him about the threatening phone calls? She should tell someone, but not now. She had to get her article finished in time for the morning paper. "Can I call you back? I'm down at the Herald, just finishing up a story, and I'm really under a deadline here."

"I'd rather we talk in person," he said. "How about if I came there?"

She was curious as to what this was about, but she didn't have time to ask. By now he surely would have already spoken to his cousin regarding her husband's arrest and he probably wanted her take on what happened. But what more could she tell him?

"All right, Logan. Give me thirty minutes to finish up and I'll meet you out front."

~*~

When Jenessa left the newspaper, she found Logan getting out of his car, parked at the curb. "Perfect timing," she called to him.

As he approached, the serious expression on his face gave her pause. Was he angry with her because of Chet's arrest? Had there been a new development in this case?

She stood under the overhead light that illuminated the entry to the newspaper. "Everything okay?" she asked, not really wanting to know.

He drew close to her. "I have some bad news."

"About Chet Monahan?"

"No, about our baby."

Her chest tightened. It felt like a giant hand had grabbed her heart and squeezed, hard. "Our baby?" Taking a deep breath, she willed her body to relax. "What do you mean?"

"Remember, the other night at your house, I talked to you about the private investigator I hired to find him."

She nodded. How could she forget?

Since that night, though, her focus had been mainly on the Nick Evans case. *Wait, he said he had bad news.* "What did he find?" She grabbed the lapel of his jacket, an ominous feeling spreading over her. "Tell me, Logan."

His hand covered hers. "He thought he was close. He promised me he'd have something concrete by this afternoon—"

"But?" She was desperate to know.

"The lead didn't pan out, I guess." He put an arm around her shoulders. "I was really hoping…"

"I didn't know he was so close to finding him." Jenessa felt a little dizzy as the realization of it hit her, and she rested her head against his shoulder. "He's going to continue looking, isn't he? He has to keep looking."

"I'm willing to pay him whatever it costs to keep searching for the child, but my guy said he's at a dead-end. He thought this last lead would be the one, but it wasn't."

A tsunami of disappointment washed over her and she leaned into him and cried. With her face buried in his chest, he held her and rubbed his hand over her back to console her.

Finally, the sobs subsided enough that she could speak. "I'm sorry to be such a cry baby, it's just that—"

"I know," he murmured, still cradling her against his chest. "I know."

She wiped the tears from her cheeks and took a deep breath, enjoying the comfort of his embrace. "You must think I'm an emotional basket case."

"No." He lifted a couple of fingers under her chin and gently tipped up her jaw until their eyes met, holding her gaze, wet with disappointed tears. His eyes glistened as well. He lowered his lips to meet hers and he kissed her tenderly, sweetly.

Heat spread through her core and she was surprised by the way her body responded to his gentle touch. Without thinking of the consequences, she had kissed him back and wanted more. With a fistful of Logan's shirt in her hand, she pulled him closer and kissed him hard.

He wrapped her up in his arms, and his tongue parted her lips. He kissed her deeply, his mouth moist and urgent. Finally, when their lips parted, he rested his cheek against her temple.

She closed her eyes and snuggled against his body.

"I love you, Jenessa," he whispered with so much emotion that he might as well have been shouting it. "I always will."

Michael's face materialized before her mind's eye and she pulled back. "I have to go."

"No, don't. Please."

"I have to." She spun away from him and stepped into the street, heading toward her car, which was parked on the other side of it.

"Jenessa!" Logan screamed.

As if in slow motion, his footsteps pounded on the pavement and the sound of a car's motor raced toward them. She felt her body being pushed forward and she crashed to the asphalt, pain shooting down her legs as she scraped her knees. The palms of her hands burned from trying to break her fall.

She whipped her head around, seeing Logan's body bounce off the hood of a dark compact car, then slam against the passenger side of the windshield, sliding to the pavement as the driver sped away. The crash and rumble of the impact was terrifying. From her position on the ground, she couldn't see who was driving, and there was no time to get a license plate number.

Jenessa dragged herself up and ran to him, dropping down beside his body as it laid motionless in the street.

"Help us!" she shrieked, looking around, but the streets were dark and empty.

She choked down a sob—there was no time for crying. She had to keep a clear head. With trembling hands, she quickly pulled out her cell phone and managed to dial nine-one-one.

~*~

By the time Michael arrived on the scene of the accident, a couple of officers had the area cordoned off with yellow tape, and Detective Provenza was standing beside the ambulance, speaking to Jenessa, a blanket draped around her shoulders, and her editor, Charles McAllister. The paramedics were loading a man into the rear of their vehicle, and he looked a lot like Logan Alexander.

Just great.

Michael strode over to Jenessa and the other men, hoping to get some answers. He put a hand on her shoulder. "Are you okay?"

"I'm fine, except for a few scrapes." She held out one leg to show her bloody knee.

"Looks painful," Michael said.

She turned toward the ambulance as one of the EMTs closed the back door. "It's Logan I'm worried about."

Logan. That's all he needed. Now Logan would be playing the sympathy card. He looked beyond her, not seeing Logan moving. "What the hell happened here?" *And why was she with Logan? Again.*

She pulled back around and met his gaze.

"Someone ran him down."

"Didn't they radio you?" Provenza asked. "It's a hit-and-run."

"Yeah, yeah, I got that." That wasn't what Michael was asking. "How bad is he hurt?"

"They're not sure," Jenessa said. "He's unconscious and probably has internal injuries." Tears filled her eyes as she watched the ambulance drive away. "He saved my life."

Michael groaned inwardly. Now Logan was playing her rescuer. "How?"

"The car was coming straight for me and he pushed me out of the way. He took the hit instead of me."

"Any idea why?" Provenza asked.

"Why what?" Her attention shifted to him. "Why he took my place?"

"No, why the car was aiming for you?" Provenza questioned. "Anyone you pissed off lately?"

Her gaze lowered to the ground and she slid her foot from side to side on the pavement, as if there were something she didn't want to say.

"What are you not telling us, Jenessa?" Michael pressed.

"Okay." She raised her eyes to him. "I've gotten a couple of calls warning me to back off this story about Nick Evans."

"Why didn't you say something?" Michael was hurt. The woman he loved didn't trust him enough to tell him she was being threatened.

"Sounds like you guys have this under control," Charles cut in. "I've got work to do, so I'll leave you to it. Jenessa, this will make for a sensational first-person story, but more so, I'm glad you're okay." He turned and walked away.

"Thanks, Charles," she called after him.

"Answer my question," Michael pressed.

She eyed him for a moment. "Because I knew you'd tell me to drop the story…and I couldn't."

"Why not?"

"I can't say."

"Listen, Miss Jones," Provenza said, "if there's something you know about the Evans case, you need to come clean."

"It's not about the case," she lowered her voice, "it's about the newspaper."

"What about the newspaper?" Michael demanded. Was that why she was meeting with Logan? His family owned the newspaper, after all.

"I can't say—it's confidential, but I assure you it has nothing to do with the case or what happened here tonight."

Michael softened his tone. "Are you sure you're okay?" He truly was concerned for her welfare, especially if someone were trying to kill her.

"I'm fine," she said. "Don't worry."

How could he not worry about her? He took it as his personal mission to protect the people he loved.

"Then let's go down to the station," Provenza said, "and you can tell us all about this threatening call and what you've really uncovered about the Nick Evans murder."

"I'm happy to talk to you, George, but first I need to go to the hospital to see how Logan is doing." Jenessa slipped off the blanket and handed it to him.

"If you're in danger—" Michael began.

"I'll let you know when I'm leaving the hospital." Jenessa pushed up on her tiptoes and kissed him on the cheek. "Don't worry."

As she started to walk away, Michael grabbed her arm to stop her. "What were you doing with Logan, here on this deserted street?"

She tugged her arm away. "We were talking."

"About what?" Michael wasn't sure he would like her answer, but he had to know.

"Something personal." She began to walk to her car. "You and I will talk about it later. I have to go."

"No, come back," Michael called out.

"I have to go, Michael." She slid behind the wheel, started the engine, and drove off.

Something personal, huh? Between her and Logan?

Now Michael knew he wasn't going to like the answer.

CHAPTER 23

MICHAEL AND PROVENZA STAYED at the site of the hit-and-run until the CSI unit was finished going over the scene. Provenza called in a bulletin to be on the lookout for a car matching the description he had gotten from Jenessa, one with front-end, passenger-side damage with a possible broken windshield.

"We should head to the hospital too, Baxter, see when Mr. Alexander might be conscious and up to talking to us," Provenza said when the CSIs were packing up.

As much as Michael hated to go to see his nemesis, it was his job. "I left Jake with Jenessa's sister this afternoon. I'll have to let her know I'm going to be a little longer than planned."

"Heck of a thing, Logan jumping in front of that car to save someone else," Provenza said as they took off walking toward their cruiser.

Michael did not reply. As much as he was grateful that Jenessa wasn't hit, he was tired of Logan always trying to steal the spotlight and draw her attention toward him. His partner was right, though, he did pick a heck of a way to do it this time. Oh sure, he probably wasn't thinking of that when he saved her life, but the outcome would be the same—Logan Alexander, the town hero.

Jenessa's hero.

Provenza paused before opening the car door. "You okay?" He must have seen something in Michael's face. Or was it the low growl of exasperation that emanated from his throat?

Michael opened his door. "I just wish I knew what was going on between those two."

"Logan and Jenessa?"

Michael nodded. "I can feel her pulling away, George, and I don't know what to do about it."

"If she's meant to be with someone else, the only thing you can do is let her go."

"Do you think I should have taken Josie back?" Michael climbed into the car.

Provenza slid behind the wheel. "That's not for me to say."

"I need some help here, George. Give me something I can use."

"I can tell you this much, I've lived long enough to know that if Jenessa is not *the one*, there's another great gal out there for you, just around the corner."

His partner's words did nothing to allay Michael's fears. "I wish I could believe you." He loved Jenessa, but he could feel her starting to slip through his fingers.

Provenza's eyes darted toward him, his lips pinched tightly together as he started the engine. "Enough already."

"I just meant—"

"Listen, Baxter," Provenza's tone revealing his irritation, "I need you to put your personal issues on the backburner for now. That's an order." He checked the mirrors, then pulled away from the curb. "I've waited too long to solve this case to let your girl problems get in the way. Got it?"

"Yes, sir." Michael gave him a mock salute. If only he could do as ordered.

~*~

Jenessa sat in the small, crowded waiting area of the emergency room at the hospital while a medical team worked on Logan. She hoped to hear something, but not being immediate family, the doctors put her off.

She phoned Ramey, who was with her aunt, and told her what had happened. "Don't burden Aunt Renee with this. I'll let you know when I find out more."

Ramey promised and told her not to worry.

Jenessa got up and paced back and forth. Not knowing how badly Logan was injured made it hard to wait. It could have been her in there. It should have been her. She should have told Michael about the threatening calls right away. She should have been more careful.

When was someone going to tell her something?

A pretty blond nurse stepped behind the check-in desk, taking over from the previous shift. Jenessa recognized her as the granddaughter of Alice, the receptionist at the newspaper. The young woman had come in to visit her grandmother a few times, dropping off flowers or home-baked treats for her and the staff. Maybe she could get some information out of this nurse, if she could remember her name. *Leanne? Loreen? No, Lanae.*

Jenessa strode up to the counter. "Hello, Lanae. Remember me? From the newspaper?"

The young woman looked at her for a moment. "Oh, yes. You're one of the reporters, right?"

"That's right. Your grandmother talks about you all the time, you know. She's so proud of you."

"Well, thanks." The nurse smiled. "What can I do for you?"

"I wanted to check on a friend of mine."

"The name?"

"Logan Alexander."

"For a story in your paper?"

"No, Lanae, we're friends. Well, more than friends."

"I thought my grandma told me you were dating that handsome police detective."

"I am, but Logan and I go way back. I was with him when he got hit by the car. As a matter of fact, it would have been me in that exam room if he hadn't pushed me out of the way."

The woman's eyes popped wide. "Oh wow!"

"So you can understand, I have to know how he is."

The nurse glanced around. "I'm not supposed to give out information to anyone that's not family," she bit her bottom lip, "especially to a reporter."

"But I'm like family."

A frown bloomed on Lanae's brow as she cocked her head. "How is that?"

Jenessa wanted to say she was the mother of his child, but she couldn't. That juicy tidbit of information would be all over town by morning. Their parents had kept it hush-hush by sending her away to have the baby.

"I just meant we've stayed really close since high school. And for goodness sake, the man just saved my life—how much closer can you get?"

The woman stared at her for a long time, apparently trying to decide what to do. Finally, her gaze shifted to the computer screen and she typed something on the keyboard. "He's been put in room two fifteen," she whispered. "He has a concussion, two broken ribs, and quite a bit of bruising from the impact. They're checking for internal injuries and should know soon."

"Thank you," Jenessa whispered back.

"You can't let anyone know you got this from me."

Jenessa nodded. "Can you call his mother, Elizabeth Alexander—hopefully she's in the country— and his cousin, Summer Monahan?"

"Sure. Give me their numbers."

The nurse grabbed a note pad and pen from the counter and scribbled their names and numbers down as Jenessa read them off from the contacts in her cell phone.

"Thanks, Lanae." She turned away and walked toward the elevator. Now, to find room two fifteen and sneak into it without being stopped.

Jenessa boarded the elevator and went to the second floor. When the doors glided open, no one was at the nurses' station. She crept down the hall a short way, finding Logan's room. Putting her ear to the door, she heard nothing—no voices, no television, no moaning—a good sign.

She pushed the door partly open and slipped inside. The room was dimly lit with a small table lamp on the nightstand and pale moonlight from the window. Logan lay flat on his back, IV tubes connected to his arm. His eyes were closed. Was he unconscious? In a coma? Hopefully, he was only sleeping.

She moved to the foot of the bed. The right side of his face was scraped, and around his right eye was black and blue. His abdomen was tightly wrapped and his right leg was on top of the blankets, secured in a stabilizing device.

The sound of his moan brought tears rushing to her eyes. This was her fault. He was in pain because of her stubbornness. She had to make it right, but how?

"Logan?" She tiptoed to the right side of his bed and touched his hand.

His eyes fluttered open and her heart leapt.

"Jenessa." His voice was weak. He closed his eyes again, but gave her fingers a light squeeze.

"You're going to be fine, Logan. I just know it," she lied, but what else could she say?

The corners of his lips lifted into a little smile.

"What were you thinking? Jumping in front of that car."

Still grasping her fingers, he pulled her hand to his lips and kissed it. "I was thinking of you." His eyes slowly opened again and his gaze locked on hers, his sleepy blue eyes as mesmerizing as ever.

"I love you," he said and her heart melted. "You should know that by now."

He had said those words to her numerous times— sometimes to toy with her, sometimes to make Michael mad—but never had she reacted so strongly to them. This time she knew he meant it. He had willingly put his life on the line for her.

"You saved my life, you know. I'll be forever grateful."

"You're welcome." He gently kissed her hand again and the feel of his warm lips on her skin brought back memories of the passionate kiss they shared right before the accident.

She pulled her hand back. "I guess you think I owe you now."

"Yes, I do."

She wasn't expecting that.

"I'll take my payment right here." He tapped his index finger to his lips. "Like the kiss you gave me earlier."

"Then we're even?" That was an easy exchange.

"What kiss earlier?" Summer waltzed through the doorway.

Jenessa whipped around to face her, heat rushing to her cheeks. "He's hallucinating." She looked back at Logan, over her shoulder, and pitched him a frown, hoping to quiet him.

"Who's hallucinating?" Michael asked, stepping into the room behind Summer.

"It's the meds, I guess," Logan covered, as Summer came around to the other side of the bed.

Michael crossed his arms and planted himself at the foot of the bed. "So, now's not a good time to ask you about the accident then?"

"Accident?" Jenessa questioned. "It was on purpose, Michael. Attempted murder."

"Attempted murder?" Summer laid a protective hand on Logan's shoulder. "But why?"

Provenza squeezed in next to Michael. "That's what we're trying to find out. What can you tell us, Mr. Alexander?"

"Are you up to talking, Logan?" Summer asked.

"What on earth is going on in here?" A tall, gray-haired nurse exclaimed as she joined the crowded room. "This patient has not been cleared for company. Any of you immediate family?"

Summer raised her hand. "I'm his cousin."

"You can stay," the nurse said, making her way around the bed to the hanging IV bag. "The rest of you will have to vacate."

"We're the police, ma'am," Provenza said.

She turned and looked him in the eye. "I know who you are, George. You went fishing with my husband, Bob, a couple of weeks ago."

"Gertie?" Provenza asked, his eyes widening. "You look different in those scrubs and with your hair pulled up in that tight bun."

"Police or not," the nurse said, "this patient isn't finished with his tests and the doctor doesn't want him to have visitors yet. So out you go, all of you except this young woman."

"Thank you, Gertie," Summer said.

"All right, Baxter, you heard the lady." Provenza started moving toward the door. "Let's move out."

Michael followed him to the hallway.

As Jenessa turned to leave, Logan caught her hand. "We need to talk."

"I'll be back in the morning." She leaned down, pushed his blond waves back, and kissed his forehead. "I promise."

"Okay then," Summer said, looking surprised by the exchange.

Jenessa started for the door. Michael was standing there, looking in. Had he heard what Logan said? Had he seen her kiss him good-bye?

"What was that about?" Michael asked when Jenessa stepped out into the corridor.

"What?" she replied, trying to keep her response innocent.

"You bent over and kissed him. I saw you."

"I kissed him on the forehead, like you would a sick child."

He eyed her for a moment, like he wasn't sure he believed her. "It's late. I have to call Sara, check on Jake."

"Sara is with Jake again?" A prick of jealously surprised her.

"Still. She's been great, stepping in to help." His gaze continued to study her. "Can we talk later?"

"Sure, but do you mind if we make it tomorrow?"

Michael turned and marched away without another word. He looked hurt, like she had done something to betray him, but she wasn't ready to discuss her feelings. She wasn't even sure what they were. And this was definitely not the time or the place. Her feelings were changing, that much she knew, but she couldn't quite put into words how. Should she trust her head or follow her heart?

As she stood there, watching Michael walk away, Aunt Renee's words echoed in her mind. *The heart wants what the heart wants.*

She leaned her back against the wall, not sure where to go from here. Home? Aunt Renee's? She had told Michael and Provenza she would go back to the station and give them a report about the threatening caller. But at this hour she was sure they had gone home from here.

That's where she wanted to be—home, tucked safely in her own bed. But would it be safe to go to her house alone, knowing someone had just tried to kill her? Before she could decide, a doctor and a male nurse walked past, pushing a gurney, going into Logan's room.

In less than a minute, Summer came out. "You're still here?"

"Yeah, trying to decide my next move."

"Want to get a cup of coffee with me?"

Jenessa nodded and pushed off the wall. They strolled down the hall to the cafeteria. "How's Logan doing?"

"They're prepping him for some tests. MRI or CT scan or something like that."

~*~

After getting their coffees, Jenessa and Summer settled at a small square table in a private corner, sitting perpendicular to one another.

"You still care for Logan, don't you?" Summer ripped open a packet of sugar and stirred it into her coffee.

"What makes you ask that?" Jenessa took a sip from her cup, her eyes still on Summer as she considered her answer.

"It's plain as day on your face."

"It is?" Jenessa's hand went to her cheek. She hadn't thought it was that obvious. Sure, lately she had felt drawn to Logan more than she had since her return to Hidden Valley, but she was with Michael. Everyone knew it.

"So I'm right, aren't I?" Summer arched a questioning brow at her.

Jenessa's eyes lowered to her cup. "It's complicated."

"Isn't it always." It was a statement, more than a question. Summer sat back in her chair. "Men," she muttered with a sigh of exasperation.

Jenessa's gaze raised to meet Summer's. Dark circles under her eyes made her look tired. "How are you holding up?"

"You mean with my husband's arrest?"

Jenessa nodded and took a sip of coffee.

Summer's head shook slowly. "Chet didn't do this—I just know it. He couldn't have."

"What do you mean?" Did she know something she wasn't saying?

"It's not in him. I know he has a temper, but murder?"

"According to what I'd heard, he went ballistic after

finding out about you and Nick, that he exploded, lost control."

"What you heard?" Summer sat back. "From who?"

"I can't say, but it'll all come out soon enough."

"After twenty years, someone has suddenly decided to start talking about that night? Why now? What changed?"

"Maybe your family moving back to town triggered something," Jenessa offered.

"Hmm, maybe." Summer took a drink of her coffee as she considered the possibility. "It was a horrendous time in our lives—the questions, the accusations, the upheaval in our families. Allison Reagan and I were sent away to escape it all, once the police said we were free to leave. Did you know that?"

"I did hear that."

"From Logan?"

"No, from Allison," Jenessa replied.

"I'd forgotten you knew her." Summer leaned an elbow on the table and took another sip. "Now it's going to begin all over again."

"I'm sorry for that." The words seemed hollow. Jenessa rested a hand on Summer's arm. "You said before that you thought your parents might have known what you and Nick were up to, but you weren't sure."

Summer shot Jenessa a wide-eyed look. "Well, if they didn't know already, I suppose there's probably no hiding it now."

"And Allison's folks?"

"Maybe." Summer shrugged, her gaze falling to her coffee cup, stirring it mindlessly. "You'll have to ask her."

Summer looked uncomfortable with the probing questions, but Jenessa needed to keep pressing, she had to know. With all the woman was going through with her husband, though, perhaps she should do her the kindness of changing the subject, for now. "I hope Logan was able to recommend a good lawyer for Chet, before the hit-and-run."

Summer nodded and turned away, a pained expression on her face. She had a lot to deal with right now. When her gaze returned, her eyes were moist. "It's been hard on the kids, and it's only going to get worse."

"Where are they now?"

"The three of us are staying with my mom and dad for the time being, trying to shelter Grayson and Lily from having to endure town gossip." She sighed. "But I guess it's inevitable. They have to go back to school on Monday and kids will be saying awful things to them, hurtful things. You know how cruel children can be."

"Maybe you can homeschool them the rest of the year, even into the summer if they miss too much school. If the trial goes on through the fall and winter, well, see how it goes then."

Summer's eyes turned glassy and intense, anxiety and fear seeming to turn them from blue to gray.

"Did I say something wrong?" Jenessa asked.

Tears flooded Summer's eyes and spilled over. She wiped her fingers over her cheeks, but said nothing.

"Summer?"

"I don't have that much time, Jenessa. I'm dying."

CHAPTER 24

"DYING?" A TREMOR OF SHOCK rattled Jenessa, rendering her speechless. All she could do was mutter an "Oh, Summer."

Then Summer dropped her face into her hands, her long golden waves falling forward, her shoulders shuddering as she cried.

A heavy sadness settled on Jenessa, for she was helpless to do anything for her. Summer's revelation was the last thing she had expected. Having to go through her husband's arrest was bad enough, but that on top of this? "I'm so sorry. Do you want to talk about it?"

Summer grabbed a couple of napkins and wiped under her eyes. "It's melanoma," she finally said, drawing a deep breath. "It has spread throughout my lymphatic system. I guess too many summers lying out in the sun at the lake." She offered a weak smile, then let out a low, breathy laugh, like she was blaming herself for the disease. "I waited too long to go to the doctor. I didn't notice the moles changing shape until it was too late."

"What do the doctors say?"

"The cancer has been pretty aggressive. They told me I only have a few months to live, six at most, and that's if I agree to continue treatment, but I don't want to spend what time I have left feeling horrible."

"Does Logan know?"

Summer slumped back in her chair, wiping her hand over her cheek again. "Yeah, he's been great. I've always been able to count on him."

Count on Logan?

"That's why he offered Chet the bank job, so we could move closer to my family."

"You look so healthy. I never would have guessed..."

"Thank goodness for makeup, right?" She pulled a compact out of her purse and flipped it open, checking her mascara in the mirror. "I'm so vain, Jenessa."

"Don't say that. You just want to look good, like every other woman on the planet."

"No, I really am vain." She snapped the compact shut. "One of the worst things is that I've lost my hair with all the chemo I had. This," she grabbed a handful of thick locks, "this is a wig."

"I couldn't tell—honest."

"That's sweet." Summer leaned forward and crossed her forearms on the table. "The chemo was making me so nauseous—throwing up all the time—and it wasn't really helping. I decided to stop it. I didn't want to spend these last few months with my family feeling sick to my stomach every day."

"If there's anything I can do…"

A shadow of darkness drifted through her eyes and the corners of her mouth turned down. "I don't think there's anything anyone can do." Clearly, she had been dealing with her illness, procedures, and a myriad of doctors for a while and it was wearing on her. "What I hate most is that my babies will grow up without their mother or father."

With the possibility of Chet being sent to prison and the certainty of Summer passing away, what would happen to their children? Her parents were getting up in age, but they would most likely be the ones to take them in. Jenessa hoped not, especially if they were anything like Summer's ruthless uncle, Grey Alexander, Logan's father. After all, they were closely related.

Hopefully she had other ideas for her children. It wouldn't be Chet's parents she would turn to—Jenessa was sure of that—not after how Summer had described Chet having been abused by his father throughout his childhood. Something inside Jenessa wanted to ask— call it motherly instinct—but it seemed better to let Summer tell her in her own time, if she wanted Jenessa to know at all.

"I hated the thought of leaving the kids with Chet when I died, but now that he's been arrested, maybe I won't have to worry about that. I'm sure you know the police are looking at him for Nick's murder—"

Jenessa nodded.

"So if they make it stick, I won't have to worry about him having our kids. That's the one positive thing in this whole tragic situation, if you can call it that."

"I'm sure it'll be hard for them, Summer, but like I said, if there's anything I can do to help, just ask."

Summer patted Jenessa's hand. "You're so kind to offer. No wonder Logan is so taken with you."

"I mean it." Jenessa couldn't wait any longer and she jumped in. "Have you decided who you want to raise them?"

"Yes." She nodded. "I have someone in mind." But she gave no names and Jenessa didn't think she should press.

Summer's cell phone rang on the table and she picked it up. "It's my mother." She swiveled out of her chair and got to her feet. "I need to take this. I'll talk to you again soon, Jenessa." She answered the phone call as she walked toward the exit.

Jenessa stayed at the table, finishing her coffee, trying to make sense of the shocking news. She had hoped she and Summer would become better friends, but now that would never happen. The woman's life was crumbling into a tragic heap, leaving behind her loved ones to pick up the pieces.

After her cup was empty, Jenessa checked her watch. It was after nine o'clock. The hour was getting late for her to visit Logan again, besides he was probably still having tests done.

She had promised Detective Provenza a written statement about the hit-and-run, but certainly he was home by now. Would Michael be expecting it tonight?

Michael.

They really did seem to be missing each other lately, her zigging when he zagged. He looked exasperated that she had continued to pursue this case without telling him, frustrated that she hadn't told him of the threatening phone calls, hurt that she was spending time with Logan Alexander.

She couldn't blame him. She would feel the same way if the shoe was on the other foot, wouldn't she? Months ago she had declared her love for him, so why was she pulling back?

Ramey's terse directive echoed in her head. *Cut one of them loose.*

~*~

It was late and she was tired. It had been one of the most taxing days she could remember in a long time. A soothing soak in a hot bath sounded heavenly as she walked down the hospital corridor toward the exit. The drama with Michael and Logan could wait until tomorrow. So could her statement.

The night air had turned cool by the time she stepped out of the hospital and headed for the parking lot. She pulled up short, frozen in her tracks, chill bumps rose on her arms. The thought struck her that the person who had tried to run her down earlier was still out there somewhere. She scanned the parking lot. Could he or she be watching her right now? Waiting for another opportunity?

She slipped her hand into her purse and clutched a slender can of mace. She rolled her shoulders to relax them before starting for her car. Her gaze flicked back and forth between the vehicles until she reached her own. As she pushed the unlock button on her key fob, the lights flashed and her car emitted a couple of quick beeps. Before opening the door she peeked inside her sports car. All clear.

She slid behind the wheel, tugged the door shut, and locked it. Drawing a deep breath, she started the engine.

The sound of a couple of quick taps on her window startled her and she jumped in her seat. Where was that mace? She felt in her purse on the seat beside her and dragged it out, holding it to her side, finger on the spray button, turning to see who had rapped on the window. It was a middle-aged man in blue scrubs, a man she did not recognize, and he looked like he was breathing rapidly. But was it from exertion or agitation?

She dropped the window a few inches, a firm grip on the mace.

"You left your phone in the cafeteria."

She lowered the window a few more inches when he held it out to her. "Thank you," she said, as the man passed it through the opening. "I appreciate you going out of your way to return it to me." She felt silly, but still a little apprehensive, being alone with a strange man in a dark and almost empty parking lot.

"You're welcome." He gave her a casual wave as he turned and walked back toward the hospital entrance.

She immediately shut the window, backed out of the space, and headed to Aunt Renee's house for the night, where, hopefully, she would be safe.

~*~

When Jenessa arrived at her aunt's house, it was about ten o'clock and she had already gone to bed, but

Ramey was in the kitchen preparing a vegetable frittata for breakfast the next morning.

"Can I get you a cup of coffee, Jenessa?"

"Only if it's decaf." Jenessa perched on a stool at the granite breakfast bar. "How's Aunt Renee doing?"

"Better." Ramey grabbed a cup from the cupboard and stuck the flavor insert into the Keurig. "She was tired, so she went to bed about an hour ago. She seems to be getting her strength back." She handed the coffee to Jenessa.

"I'm glad to hear that," Jenessa said, taking the cup from her. "Thanks." She took a sip. "Did you hear what happened to Logan tonight?"

"I did. How's he doing?"

"You did? How?"

"Sara was here. She brought Jake by to swim. Something about a car accident?"

"More like attempted murder."

"What?" Ramey gasped, her blue eyes growing round as her jaw went slack. "Oh my gosh. What happened?"

Jenessa told her the whole story about how someone had tried to run her down, how Logan had pushed her out of the way at the last moment, and that he had been hit by the speeding car. "He could have been killed."

"So you're saying you stepped into the street without looking? That's not like you." Ramey eyed Jenessa, who had gone silent. "Jenessa?"

"I was upset, I wasn't thinking. Logan and I had been talking, then I turned to go to my car, which was across the street."

"You were upset? Why?" Ramey pressed.

"It was nothing."

"Tell me." Ramey wasn't going to let it drop.

Jenessa looked down at the warm cup in her hands. "Because we kissed."

"You kissed? Way to bury the lead." Ramey huffed a breath. "Tell me all about it, and don't leave out any of the details."

CHAPTER 25

"LOGAN AND I WERE STANDING outside of the newspaper, talking about searching for our son, and Logan had said his private detective had a promising lead, but that he hit a dead-end, the last dead-end. I was so upset, I started to cry, and Logan put his arms around me. Before I knew it, his lips were on mine."

"Like a soft peck?" Ramey asked, as she stuck the frittata in the refrigerator.

"No, open mouth, tongue—the full nine yards."

"Oh my." Ramey raked a hand through her red curls. "Did you, for one second, consider Michael?"

"That was the problem. When Logan kissed me, I swear every nerve ending in my body came alive. I haven't felt that way since..." Jenessa hesitated, her mind going back in time.

"Since when?" Ramey urged.

"Since I was seventeen." She recalled how she felt the impetuous night Logan had gotten her pregnant.

"I see. And Michael doesn't kiss you like that?"

"Oh, don't get me wrong, Michael is a great kisser—but no, I don't get that every-cell-of-my-being-crying-out-for-more kind of feeling when we kiss."

"Boy, that's something that could flip your world upside down," Ramey said. "I still don't understand how that kiss made you dash recklessly across the street."

"Because when our lips finally parted, I did think of Michael, how hurt he would be if he knew I'd kissed another man—and not just kissed him, but *thoroughly* kissed him—and enjoyed it. I'm a terrible person, aren't I, Ramey?"

"Of course not. Don't be silly. You're a wonderful person, Jenessa. You're just being pulled in two different directions by two very desirable guys, and you don't seem to be able to make up your mind which one you're in love with. I think you're afraid you'll hurt someone's feelings. And," Ramey continued, "this is not just about the men in your life…it is about the boys too. Namely Michael's boy, Jake, and the boy you and Logan gave away."

"That's pretty insightful, Ramey." Jenessa took another drink. "Why does love have to be so complicated?"

"I don't know, but it is sometimes." Ramey took a stool next to Jenessa. "It's up to you, my friend, to uncomplicate it. Like I told you before, you need to cut one of them loose. It's only fair."

Jenessa swiveled in her seat and looked at Ramey. "I know, and you are right—but which one?" She slid off the stool and took her cup of coffee to the sofa in the adjacent family room.

"That's for you to decide." Ramey followed and sat beside her. "You never said how Logan is doing, after the accident."

"A few broken ribs, bruises, maybe a concussion, possibly internal injuries…I don't know exactly. They were running tests when I left. I wanted to stay, but Summer told me to come back in the morning."

"Poor Logan," Ramey muttered with a shake of her head. "That man will do anything for you."

"Seems that way." Jenessa took another sip. "I'm worried about him. What if he has internal injuries and they have to rush him into surgery? Maybe I should go back to the hospital."

"He's in good hands. Besides, you look like you could use some sleep."

"It has been a horrible day." With what happened to Logan, finding out the private investigator wanted to give up searching, her issues with Michael, and then learning Summer was dying, the word *horrible* didn't even begin to describe it.

"What did Michael say?" Ramey asked.

"About what? Logan?"

"About the hit-and-run." Ramey's eyes narrowed and she cocked her head. "Never mind. You must be exhausted. Why don't we talk about it in the morning?"

"Good idea." Jenessa leaned her head back against the sofa and rested her eyes. "You said Sara was here? With Jake?"

"Yes, she brought him to swim."

"She seems to be babysitting Jake a lot these days."

Which surprised Jenessa. And maybe annoyed her a little too.

"I've never seen her like that before, like a mother hen with the boy. Nice she can fill in while Michael's folks are out of town."

"Yeah, nice," Jenessa murmured. Was she jealous of someone else spending so much time with the boy? Jenessa loved little Jake. He filled the empty spot left by the son she gave up. If she chose Logan over Michael, she would lose her relationship with Jake. The idea of it made her heart sink.

And Sara seemed to be spending a lot of time at Michael's house lately. Had he spoken to her about the bumps their relationship had hit? No, he wouldn't do that, would he?

Jenessa straightened and turned to look at Ramey. "Did Sara mention Michael?"

Ramey looked puzzled. "Mention Michael? I don't understand."

"Never mind." Jenessa waved her hand. "I'm going to bed."

"Wait. Why would Sara mention Michael?"

"It's just that she's been at his house quite a bit lately, and I simply wondered if maybe he was crying on her shoulder about our problems."

"Michael is a man, Jenessa."

"What do you mean by that?"

"He's not an emotional female that would be crying on someone's shoulder about personal problems with her boyfriend. Guys don't do that."

Jenessa rose. "I hope you're right, Ramey."

"You're jealous."

"I'm not jealous, just curious."

"I should never have told you she was going to ask him out last year."

"Doesn't matter." Jenessa yawned for emphasis. "I'm going to bed."

~*~

Michael drove home from the hospital, irritated by Jenessa's actions, how she was doting over Logan, her protector, her hero. The glowing porch light and the soft illumination of the lamp in the living room window was a comforting sight.

He lumbered inside and set his keys on the entry table. At almost ten o'clock, Jake was surely in bed asleep, but where was Sara? He crept down the hall to Jake's bedroom and found her tucking him into bed.

"I love you, Sara," Michael overheard Jake say in his small voice.

She kissed the boy on the forehead and said, "I love you too, Jake." Once she turned the lamp off, she moved toward the doorway, stopping short when she saw Michael standing there, watching them. She put a finger to her lips, motioning for him to be quiet.

Michael stepped back and Sara pulled the door almost shut. He followed her to the kitchen.

"Have you eaten?" she asked. "I made mac and cheese with some fish sticks for dinner for Jake. I could heat up the leftovers for you, if you're hungry."

"No, I'm not hungry," he sat down at the table, "but maybe I'll have a glass of red wine to help me relax."

"Okay, where are your wine glasses?" She opened a cupboard and stared in.

"Top shelf, but I can get it." He rose and moved toward her.

She stood on her tiptoes, stretching her petite five-foot-four frame. "I'm not tall enough."

"Here, let me." Michael stepped behind her and reached up, bringing down two wine glasses. "Join me?"

She took the glasses from him. "Sure. Why not."

Michael grabbed a bottle of wine and met her at the table. He uncorked it and poured the drinks.

"How's Logan doing?" She picked up her glass. "I've been so worried about him."

"You sound like your sister," he mumbled into his glass, then took a sip.

"What was that?"

He set his glass down. "I think he'll pull through just fine." There was a bitter taste in his mouth when he said it.

"How bad? A car accident, right?"

"Hit-and-run. Maybe on purpose."

She sucked in a quick breath in surprise, her eyes widening. "On purpose?"

"Possibly." Michael took a long drink of the wine. "Jenessa's fine too."

"Jenessa?" Her brows grew together in concern. "I didn't realize she was involved."

"Oh yeah, she's involved all right." He took another gulp.

"Why do you say it like that?"

"Like what?" He finished his glass and poured another.

"Like you're angry about something."

He lifted the goblet and swirled it around before taking another drink.

Angry. Hurt. Heartbroken. That about covered it. He was sure she was slipping away from him and he felt powerless to stop it.

"Michael, what's wrong?"

The concern in her voice told him he was doing a sorry job of covering his feelings. He downed the glass of wine and set it hard on the table. The stem shattered and sliced into the side of his hand.

"You're bleeding." Sara ran to the kitchen and stuck a dishtowel under the faucet. "Come in the kitchen." She turned on the water.

Michael spun out of his chair and met her at the sink where she wrapped the damp towel around his bleeding hand.

"Tell me what's wrong," she pleaded, applying pressure to wound.

"I'm losing her." His voice cracked as he said it. "It's that damn Logan Alexander. I know it."

"But you two are great together."

"That's what I thought, but lately…" He looked into Sara's kind eyes. He'd never noticed how much they looked like Jenessa's.

"Those two have always been drawn to each other," she said, looking up at him, her hands holding the towel around his wound, "like a couple of magnets."

"It seems Logan's pull is stronger than mine and I hate it," a tightness gripped his chest as he said it. "Our relationship seems to be changing and there's nothing I can do to stop it."

"Then it wasn't meant to be, Michael." Sara held his gaze.

"That's what Provenza said too." He dropped his head, too tired to argue the point.

"He's right." She gently cupped his cheek. Her hand was soft and warm against his skin. "You are a wonderful man, Michael. If my sister can't see that, then she doesn't deserve you."

He tried to look away, but she brought his face back to her.

"Someone else will come along," Sara said, "a woman who appreciates you, someone who is perfect for you. I promise."

His gaze dropped toward the floor. "But I thought Jenessa and I were perfect together."

"She's not the only woman out there that can make you happy."

He lifted his eyes and met hers, their faces mere inches apart. "You think so?"

Her intense green eyes peered deeply into his. "I know so."

He suddenly felt drawn to her. Instinctively, he lowered his lips to hers. They were as soft as rose petals and they tasted like cherries and red wine.

CHAPTER 26

THEIR KISS IGNITED SOMETHING surprising in Michael, a rush of heat in the core of his body, and he pulled back at the sensation. This was Jenessa's sister he was kissing. What was he thinking?

"I'm sorry," he muttered. "I shouldn't have done that."

"You have nothing to be sorry about." She gave him a little smile and stepped away from him. Walking toward the living room, she glanced back over her shoulder. "Remember what I said."

He followed her. "Which part?"

"If things don't work out with Jenessa," she picked up her sweater and purse from the sofa, "someone perfect for you will come along." With that, she walked out the door.

~*~

At five o'clock the next morning, Jenessa lay wide-awake in bed. The numbers on the clock glowed red and seemed to fill the room with light. At first she wasn't sure where she was, but as she came more awake, she recognized the wallpaper in her aunt's guest room.

As she laid there, her mind became fully alert with thoughts of the Nick Evans case and who might have wanted her dead because of it. Poor Logan, she thought, laying in pain in the hospital for taking the hit that was meant for her. He could have been killed. Hopefully the morphine was keeping his discomfort at bay.

With no chance of falling back asleep, she slipped on a robe and went downstairs to make a cup of coffee. It was too early to go back to the hospital to check on Logan, besides she had a sneaking feeling it was her day to stay with Aunt Renee. Maybe she could bring her along to see him.

After preparing herself a steaming cup of caffeine, she sat at the breakfast bar and opened the photo gallery on her phone, searching for the photos she had taken of the police file. She came upon the picture the old medical examiner had taken of Nick's upper right gum. With two fingers sliding across the screen in opposite directions, she tugged the photo larger. There it was, diagonal lines and a couple of curved shapes below them. Something definitely made the pattern embedded in his gum line and it wasn't from the water bouncing his body against the rocks. That piece of evidence had kept Detective Provenza from filing this case away and forgetting it for twenty years.

What did it mean?

The more she studied the pattern, the more familiar it seemed—but where had she seen a design like that?

Nothing came to her, so she moved on to the other photos for the time being—some pics of documents, some of the crime scene, and others of the victim. What was she missing? Where should she go from here?

Eventually, her aunt came downstairs and joined her. "Good morning, honey."

"Morning," Jenessa replied. "Sleep okay?"

"I did." Aunt Renee fixed a cup of coffee for herself. She paused and peered out the window that overlooked her rose garden. "Looks like it's going to be a beautiful Sunday. Got any plans today?"

"To spend it with you." Jenessa was anxious to get back to the hospital, but if her aunt needed her, she would be there for her.

"With me? Why?"

"It's my turn…on the schedule."

"Oh, Jenessa. I'm fine. You go about your day."

"No. You need someone to look after you and I'm it."

"I wish you girls would stop hovering over me and treating me like an invalid. I'm only fifty-eight, not eighty-eight."

"But your heart—"

"It's been days since the heart attack. Besides, I'm starting to feel like my old self again."

"But the doctor said—"

"I have my cell phone." Aunt Renee patted her pocket. "If I need help, I'll call nine-one-one."

"I would like to go back to the hospital to see Logan. You could come with me."

"Logan? I heard last night that he was in some sort of car accident. How is he?"

Apparently no one had told her he'd gotten *run over* by a car, one that was aiming at Jenessa. "Pretty banged up, but the doctors believe he'll be fine, eventually."

"So you were with him last night?"

Jenessa explained how she had been talking with him right before the accident happened, not wanting to give her aunt the full story with her delicate heart condition. "I went to the hospital after talking to the police."

"The police? You mean Michael and George."

Jenessa nodded.

"What did Michael say? He couldn't have been happy you were with Logan."

"He wasn't."

"I hope this doesn't cause a problem between the two of you."

"Too late." Not wanting to belabor the topic, Jenessa changed the subject. "You know they arrested Chet Monahan, don't you? Not for murder yet, only for assaulting an officer, but he is their prime suspect for the old murder I've been investigating."

"Yes, I'd heard about all of that on the news."

The TV news? No, she couldn't let them scoop her. That would be disastrous for her and the newspaper. She needed to get to the bottom of this story before they did. What information did she have that they didn't? They couldn't know that someone was trying to kill her.

But if Chet was in jail, he couldn't have been the one that attempted to run her down last night. And if Chet was, in fact, the murderer, then why had someone else tried to silence her?

Maybe she should ask Michael to help her find out. After what happened between them at the hospital, though, perhaps she would have better luck talking to George Provenza.

"Jenessa?" Aunt Renee questioned.

Jenessa's gaze flew to her aunt. "What?"

"You didn't hear a word I said. What's going on?"

"I'm sorry, what did you say?"

"It wasn't that important. You've obviously got something on your mind. Is it Logan?"

"I am worried about him, but no, I need to talk to Detective Provenza about the murder case. Are you sure you're going to be all right here by yourself?"

"I'll be fine. You go on and do what you have to do."

~*~

It was almost nine o'clock when Jenessa climbed into her Mercedes and dialed Provenza's cell number. After a few rings, it went to voicemail. Did she dare try Michael's? She had no choice. Three rings later it went to voicemail as well. She asked both of them to call her back, but she couldn't sit around and wait until they did.

Allison was the one who had pointed the finger at Chet, but with him in jail, he couldn't be the one who tried to stop her from pursuing the case. And if Chet wasn't the murderer, why had Allison said she saw him kill Nick? She needed to track the woman down and ask her. It was early Sunday morning, hopefully she could catch her at her apartment.

Jenessa began backing her sports car out of her aunt's driveway when her cell phone pinged. She stopped, grabbed the phone off the seat, and checked it. It was a text from Summer.

"Logan's out of surgery. Please come."

Surgery?

No one had told her he needed to have surgery. Something must have changed during the night. Summer made it sound urgent, like things did not go well.

Oh, Logan.

Her eyes became moist and her heart filled with an emotion she hadn't let herself feel for him in a long time. Was it love? Did it take the possibility of losing him forever to make her admit what she had worked so hard to bury? The passionate kiss they shared the previous night had stirred something in her that she had tried for years to suppress. Now it was pushing its way to the surface and she felt powerless to stop it.

Finding Allison would have to wait. Jenessa raced to the hospital.

~*~

"Good morning, big guy," Michael greeted as his little boy, dressed in his Spiderman pajamas, entered the kitchen. "I made some pancakes. Want a couple?"

Jake's eyes widened with delight. "Animal pancakes?"

"No, regular round pancakes."

"I like the way Sara makes me animal pancakes."

"You do?"

Jake nodded his head.

"What kind of animals?"

"Ducks, elephants, pigs. Mickey Mouse."

Michael was impressed. He had no idea. "I think I can do the Mickey ones, next time."

A huge grin lit up the little boy's face.

"You like Sara?"

"Uh-huh." Jake nodded as he said it. "She reads to me and plays games."

"Like Jenessa does?"

"Uh-huh, but Jenessa hasn't been here in a long time, Daddy."

"Well, not that long."

"Is she mad at me?"

Michael crouched down in front of his son and took him by the shoulders. "No, Jake, she's not mad at you. She's just been busy working, and then her aunt got real sick."

"I miss her."

Michael hugged the boy. "Me too."

"Can Sara come back?"

"Maybe." Michael stood up and went back to the stove, wondering if the kiss they shared would change things.

CHAPTER 27

"JAKE, DID YOU KNOW GRANDMA and Grandpa are getting back from their vacation tonight night?" Michael asked, trying to put Sara and the kiss out of his mind.

"They are?" Jake's face beamed with joy.

"Yeah, so you can spend some time with them tomorrow."

Jake bounced up and down with a big smile. "Can we go swimming, Daddy?"

"Sure, but that's tomorrow. Right now, let's eat this big ol' pile of pancakes before they get cold."

~*~

Jenessa shut her phone off as she entered the hospital. Down one hallway and then another, she made it to Logan's room. She knocked lightly and pushed the door open. The room was silent, he must be sleeping.

"Good morning, sleepy head," she sang as she stepped in.

She moved farther into the darkened room. The lights were not on, the room only illuminated by northern light peeking through the curtains. Her eyes adjusted and she saw the bed was empty, neatly made.

An acrid taste filled her mouth as her heart dropped to her stomach. Was she too late? Had he died and they'd already taken his body somewhere else?

"Can I help you, miss?" a woman said from behind her.

Jenessa spun around and found a sturdy, middle-aged nurse standing there. "Where have they taken him? Logan Alexander?"

"He's in the ICU."

A wave of relief rushed over her. "Can I see him?"

"Are you family?"

Family? Sort of.

"No, only a friend."

"I'm afraid not, then."

"What floor is the ICU on?"

"But you can't go in," the nurse insisted, her expression set.

"I need to see him," Jenessa gently grabbed the woman's forearm as she said it, "even if it's just through the window."

The woman's face softened, as did her voice. "You love him, don't you?"

Jenessa pulled her hand back. "What? Me? No, we're just friends."

The nurse dipped her head and peered over her glasses, giving Jenessa a look that said she didn't quite believe her. "Okay, honey, have it your way. Fourth floor, but you still can't go in."

"Thanks." Jenessa gave the woman a quick hug before tearing off down the corridor.

Once she arrived on the fourth floor, she headed for the nurse's station. Before she could ask for directions, she spotted Summer coming out of a room down the hall, her expression sullen. Jenessa raced toward her.

"Summer," Jenessa said as she bustled down the hallway. "I got your text. What's going on?"

"After you left last night, I sat with him for a while," she lifted her chin toward the door to Logan's room. "All of a sudden, alarms started going off and a couple of nurses came rushing in, then the doctor."

"Oh no." Jenessa's hand went to her heart. "What happened?"

"Apparently when he broke his ribs, one of them punctured his lung—not badly, but enough to do some damage without showing up on the X-rays they said—or the X-ray tech is a moron—I don't know which," Summer rattled on, "and the hospital certainly isn't taking responsibility for it. They got him into surgery and took care of it, but later a blood clot made its way near his heart and he almost died. They shot him full of blood thinners—Coumadin or something like that—and, thank God, they were able to stop it from killing him."

He almost died? Jenessa's heart was hammering when she stepped to the window and gazed at him lying in a bed, tubes and wires running from his body to the various machines. "Is he going to be all right?"

"The doctor said he's been through the worst of it."

Dark shadows below Summer's eyes showed she must have been up all night. Where was the rest of Logan's family? His mother? Summer's parents?

"Does Elizabeth know yet?" Jenessa asked.

"She's in Europe. I spoke to her last night on the phone. She's trying to get a flight out."

"What about Logan's dad?"

"I left word for him with the prison warden. I doubt they'll let him come, especially since Logan seems to be over the worst."

"And your mom and dad?"

"Mom said she would stay with the kids, but my dad should be here any moment." She glanced toward the elevator.

With Summer battling the disease ravaging her own body, the last thing she needed was this added stress. Jenessa slipped an arm around her shoulders. "Why don't you go home and get some sleep? I'll stay here until he arrives. I'm sure the doctor will fill him in."

Summer nodded. "Maybe you're right. I am pretty exhausted."

Jenessa watched as Summer plodded toward the elevator, her shoulders hunched under the weight of her tragic life. Once the doors glided shut, Jenessa's attention shifted back to Logan, who seemed to be sleeping peacefully. If only she could go inside.

She glanced up and down the corridor—no nurses or doctors in sight, except for the nurse at the desk with her back turned. Dare she slip into Logan's room? Perhaps she could have a moment or two with him before someone spotted her and ordered her to leave.

Slowly she pushed the door open and tiptoed to his bedside. The steady beep told her his heart was beating just fine. She wrapped her fingers around his hand, glad to feel the warmth of it.

"Logan," she whispered, not wanting to wake him but needing to know he was going to be okay.

His eyes fluttered half open then closed again as a small grin spread across his lips. He squeezed her fingers and her heart leapt.

"What are you doing in here?" a man spoke harshly from the doorway.

At the sound, Jenessa pulled her hand back and turned toward the door. There was a man looming there—Summer's father, no doubt—tall with broad shoulders, and he looked angry to see her.

"You're that reporter, aren't you?" he growled as he approached.

Just then a gray-haired doctor strode into the room, past the man. "Keep your voices down." Grabbing the chart at the foot of Logan's bed, he began to check the machines.

"I'm his uncle," said the angry-looking man. "The name's Walker. And this woman is a reporter for the newspaper, Doctor. This hospital needs to keep better security. We can't have the press in here, writing who knows what for the town to gossip about."

Obviously Logan's father had poisoned his sister and brother-in-law against Jenessa.

The doctor turned from the monitors, his attention riveted on her. "Is that true?"

"Yes, it's true, I am a reporter," she said with a nod, "but I'm also a close friend." Jenessa took a small step away from the bed and turned to face Mr. Walker, summoning up confidence she hoped would make a difference. "Your daughter just left. I told her I would wait with Logan until you arrived, so he wouldn't be alone."

James Walker's eyes narrowed. "And I'm supposed to believe you?" His tone was terse and unforgiving.

Not being family, Jenessa did not have the authority to be in the room, that was true, but why would he think she deserved to be treated so callously? *Only one reason—Grey Alexander.*

"Check with Summer," she said, not backing down from him. "She'll tell you—Logan would want me here."

He crossed his arms and expelled a harrumph in response, his fiery gaze trying to bore a hole right through her.

Time was up and she had to leave. She started for the door but turned back and gazed at Logan one last time before going, his eyes still closed, that silly grin still pasted on his lips. "Take good care of our guy, Doc."

~*~

It was a little too early on a Sunday morning for Jenessa to approach Allison Reagan—she was probably at mass—so she stopped by The Sweet Spot for a cup of coffee. Logan was not far from her thoughts. She hated to leave him in his condition, especially after the night he'd had, and she owed him for saving her life, didn't she? Surely there was something she could do to make him more comfortable, ease his pain in some way, even if it was simply holding his hand and sitting with him as he slept. But there was no way his uncle was going to let her stay.

When she strolled into the café, Sara was behind the counter waiting on a customer. Jenessa took her place in line until the counter was free.

"Why aren't you with Aunt Renee this morning?" Sara questioned, sticking the last customer's cash in the register. "It's your turn, isn't it?"

"She ran me off. Said we all need to stop hovering over her, so I did."

"Hmm." The expression Sara wore said she didn't think that was a good idea. "If something happens to her—"

"Not my call." Jenessa raised her hands in surrender, then glanced around the café. "Where's Ramey?"

"She slipped out a few minutes ago with Charles. Something about an errand to run."

Ramey and Charles. The thought of them together brought a smile to Jenessa's face. With all the turmoil in her own love life, she was glad to see her best friend finally find love with a good man.

"Could I get a medium mocha latté?" Jenessa asked.

"Sure." Sara moved to the machines to start the order. "Where are you off to so early this morning?"

"I just came from the hospital. I was checking on Logan."

Sara grabbed a cup and lid. "How is he?"

"Better. He had a rough night." It was probably best Jenessa didn't go into too much detail.

"Seems like you're seeing a lot of him lately," Sara said as she steamed the milk.

"He was badly hurt, Sara."

"I meant before the accident." Sara stopped what she was doing and locked on to Jenessa's gaze. "Why are you spending so much time with him?"

"Who told you I was?"

Sara looked down at the cup.

"Michael?"

Sara slipped the cup into a corrugated sleeve, but said nothing.

"When?"

Sara's gaze slid back to meet Jenessa's. "Last night, when he got home from work. I was watching Jake for him."

"And the two of you discussed me?" Heat began to spread up Jenessa's neck.

"Well, I don't know if I'd use the word *discussed*. More like mentioned."

Mentioned? So Michael had been crying on her sister's shoulder about the problems in their relationship. She could see it in the shiftiness of her sister's eyes, hear it in her unsteady voice. Jenessa's jaw tightened at the thought. What else had he told her?

"I wish he hadn't *mentioned* me," Jenessa snapped.

"I'm sure he didn't intend to, it just came out. You're hurting him terribly, Jenessa. He doesn't deserve to be treated like—"

"Like what?" Jenessa held her breath.

"Never mind," Sara muttered, turning back to clamp the lid on the cup. "I wish I hadn't brought it up."

Jenessa wished she hadn't either, but Sara was right about her. Michael did deserve better. "I think I'll take that coffee to go."

She laid a five on the counter, scooped up her drink, and went to the door, pausing as she reached for the handle. Turning back, she wanted to say something more to her sister, but what could she say in her defense? "See you later," was all she could manage.

~*~

Once Jenessa was back in her car, she got a call from Detective Provenza.

"Did you forget you owe me a statement from the hit-and-run accident last night, Miss Jones?"

"I didn't forget, Detective, and it wasn't an accident."

"Until we know for certain, we're calling it an accident. I will need your full statement before I can change that, assuming there's enough evidence."

"I'm happy to tell you all I know, but I don't think you're going to like it."

CHAPTER 28

DETECTIVE PROVENZA EXPELLED a low growl of irritation into the phone. "I won't like what, Miss Jones?"

"Well, I'm wondering if you're looking at the right person for Nick Evans' murder."

"Need I remind you that you're the one who brought an eye-witness to us in the first place?"

"I know, and I believe what she says she saw. Having Chet Monahan in the same room with her practically made her soil herself, but someone wanted to silence me last night, George, and it couldn't have been Chet."

"Then you'd better get yourself down here ASAP, before they try again. How soon can you come in?"

She looked at her watch—nine fifteen. She had hoped to track Allison down for any additional information she might have, but talking to Provenza might afford her some protection from whoever made an attempt on her life last night. "I could come now."

"We'll be waiting."

We? Michael must be there too. After the little skirmish she just had with her sister over him, facing Michael this morning wasn't what she had in mind.

~*~

Michael looked up from his computer when Jenessa entered the office he shared with Detective Provenza. "Good morning," he offered brightly, genuinely happy to see her.

"Morning." A little smile lifted her lips, but it failed to make it all the way up to her eyes. That wasn't the response he had hoped for. She was probably still miffed at him from the night before, at the hospital.

He got up from his chair and started to stretch his arms toward her but dropped them when Provenza came through the door behind her. "Sleep okay?" He sat back down. "You had quite a night last night."

"I've had better, that's for sure." She watched Provenza skirt past her and go to his desk. "It's Logan that had a terrible night."

"How is he doing?" It pained Michael to have to ask, recalling how she had fawned over the man the night before. He supposed he should be thankful though. It could have been Jenessa who got hit by that car.

Jenessa looked Michael in the eye, any trace of a smile had vanished from her lips. "He almost died."

"Almost died?" Provenza asked. "I didn't think he was hurt that badly."

"One of his broken ribs punctured his lung, not deeply, but enough to cause internal bleeding. During the night there was a blood clot that moved near to his heart and they had to act quickly before it lodged in his heart and killed him."

"You were at the hospital all night with him?" Michael asked.

"That's what you're focusing on?" she bit back.

"No, I just meant that——"

"I was not at the hospital when it happened, Michael." Her tone was cool and even. "Summer told me about it this morning."

Now he felt like a jerk.

Provenza picked up a file from his desk and shot his partner a disapproving frown. "Let's go into the conference room. It'll be more comfortable. The air in here is getting too thick."

"How about we go to visit Logan together, Jenessa, after we're done here?" Michael asked as they walked down the hall, trying to sound more sensitive. "Then we can both see how he's doing."

"Can't," she replied flatly. "He's in the Intensive Care Unit and only family can get in."

Michael hadn't realized how serious Logan's condition was. But was Jenessa being drawn to Logan because he was injured or because her feelings for him were growing? Michael felt powerless to do anything about it, for no matter what he said now about her relationship with the guy, it would be taken as uncaring and insensitive—and very likely jealous.

Was he jealous?

Absolutely.

Provenza opened the door to the conference room and stepped in first.

"We'll be right in," Jenessa said, stopping Michael in the hallway. "I spoke with Sara this morning. She told me about what happened last night, you and her."

The kiss!

"She did?" His chest felt heavy, and a thick layer of prickles ran down his neck and over his shoulders.

"How could you, Michael?" Jenessa's green eyes paled with moisture, her gaze steady on his. "I never thought—"

"I didn't mean to. It just happened. She was there, and I was upset." He couldn't believe Sara had told her about the kiss. "It didn't mean anything."

Jenessa's back stiffened and her brows knit together. "What didn't mean anything?"

"The kiss. That's what you're—"

"You kissed her?"

"I thought that's what you—"

"I meant your talking to her about what's going on between you and me." Tears filled Jenessa's eyes and Michael reached out for her. She pushed his hands away and ran down the hall toward the exit.

"Jenessa, wait!" Michael called out, but she kept on going.

Provenza came to the doorway. "What's going on?"

"I kissed Jenessa's sister."

"You did what now?" George gasped.

"I kissed—"

"No, I heard you the first time. I just couldn't believe you'd do such a numbskull thing."

"She wouldn't even let me explain."

"Can you blame her?" Provenza shook his head in disgust. "You really mucked it up this time, Baxter."

~*~

Jenessa stood at Allison's apartment door, still reeling from hearing Michael say he had kissed her sister. That was the last thing she had expected to come out of his mouth. Then her thoughts flew to Logan and her lips tingled at the remembrance of his mouth so passionately on hers. Did she have the right to be angry with Michael when she had done the very thing she was mad at him about? Maybe this was a sign that they shouldn't—

Head back in the game, Jones!

She gave herself a mental shake and knocked on the door, hoping to find Allison home. Instead, it was her sister, Kelly, who opened the door.

"You're that reporter, right?" Kelly asked, her expression friendly.

"Yes, Jenessa Jones."

"Why don't you come in?"

Jenessa stepped inside. Kelly motioned toward the sofa and Jenessa took a seat.

"What can I do for you?" Kelly asked.

"I was looking for Allison. Is she home?"

"No, she's at mass."

"You didn't go with her?"

"No, she's the good Catholic girl, not me."

Allison and her father and grandfather had all gone to Notre Dame, so it made sense the Reagans were a Catholic family. Apparently Kelly hadn't followed in the same footsteps.

"I heard the police arrested Chet Monahan for that old murder," Kelly went on.

"Something like that." Although he was under arrest, it wasn't yet for the murder, but she didn't care to share the confidential details with Kelly. "When will Allison be home?"

"I'm glad they finally figured it out. All this time I thought it might have been my dad that killed him." She let out a nervous giggle.

"Your dad? Why would you think that?"

"Well, it was the night Nick died that I told my dad that Nick was having sex with Allison in the boathouse. He was livid."

"I can understand that," Jenessa said. "Allison was only sixteen, right?"

"That's right."

"So how old were you?"

"I was eleven."

"How did you know?" Jenessa asked.

"I had overheard Allison talking to Summer on the phone about it. And when I heard the word *pregnant* I knew I had something I could use to get back at my sister."

Pregnant? "Allison was pregnant?"

"No," Kelly gave her head a slight shake. "Seems I misunderstood."

"What made you tell on her that night?"

"See, before Allison left that night to go meet Nick, she and I got in a terrible fight. I can't remember over what—probably I had worn something of hers and ruined it—that happened a lot. She told on me to our parents, and I got grounded. After she left to go and meet Summer," Kelly placed air quotes around the words *meet Summer*, "I told my dad where she was really going and why."

"I'll bet he was pretty angry about that," Jenessa said.

"More like ballistic, thinking his daughter was preggo."

Sure, he would be furious, but there had to be more reason for Kelly to suspect. "What made you think he might have killed Nick?"

"Well, I never knew that for sure, but I just wondered if he could have done it. After I told him about Allison and Nick, he ordered me to my room. I went to bed and didn't come out until early the next day. In the morning, when I went out the back door, I almost tripped over his muddy shoes on the back porch. They were still wet."

"Wet and muddy shoes," Jenessa muttered to herself.

"So you can see how, as a kid, I might have gotten the idea in my head that my father took Nick out."

"That's some story, Kelly." Could it be true?

Kelly shrugged at the comment. "But now that Allison admitted she saw Chet beat Nick to death, and the police have arrested him, I guess I've worried about it for nothing."

"Guess so," Jenessa agreed for the sake of conversation. Could Allison's father be the real killer? Was he the one who'd tried to run her down? "So when will Allison be back?"

"She didn't say."

Jenessa stood. "I'll give her a call later, maybe we can connect."

Kelly followed her to the door and opened it. "Any message you want me to give her?"

"Just that I'm anxious to talk to her again, as soon as possible."

Kelly promised to let her know.

As Jenessa passed through the doorway, she stopped and turned back. "Does your father happen to drive a small dark car?"

CHAPTER 29

ALLISON'S SISTER WASN'T SURE what her parents drove. "I'm not a car person," she had said. "I know it's a blue car of some sort…or maybe green."

Obviously, Kelly wasn't the sharpest knife in the drawer, but she had given Jenessa something to think about when it came to her father.

Once Jenessa was back in her car, she thought about calling Michael with the new information, but chose Provenza instead. She dialed his cell number but it went to voicemail. Should she call Michael? This was important to the case, but she couldn't bring herself to talk to him yet. No, she would wait for Provenza to call her back. Hopefully it would be soon.

As she sat there, she scrolled through the photos of the police file again. When she came to the picture of Nick Evans' damaged gums, she enlarged the photo and studied it. The pattern seemed vaguely familiar but she couldn't put her finger on it.

She put her phone back in her purse and started the car. Maybe she would have time to run by the hospital to check on Logan, knowing they wouldn't give her any information over the phone. She could try Summer, if she were up to talking.

As she tugged out her phone again to make the call, it began to ring. Caller ID showed it was Provenza. "Hello."

"What's up, Miss Jones? You ready to come back in and give me that statement?"

The statement? She groaned a little. "Uh, yeah, that's why I was calling. I'm on my way over...if the coast is clear."

"You mean if Michael isn't here?"

"Roger that, George."

"Oh, I sent him home, told him I'd call him if he was needed, so get yourself down here, young lady."

"On my way."

~*~

"Start at the beginning," Provenza said as he and Jenessa sat in the conference room.

"Like I said last night, Logan Alexander and I were standing outside of the newspaper building talking. I said I had to go, then turned and walked across the street toward my car. Before I knew it, Logan yelled my name and pushed me out of the way as a car raced by. I didn't get a look at the driver or the car, but I heard the bone-crushing thump of Logan's body being hit. As I turned I saw him thrown up on the car's windshield and then slide off the passenger side onto the pavement. I immediately called nine-one-one and waited for the ambulance and the police."

"And you have no idea of the make and model of the car, or the color?"

"I saw the tail lights speeding away. A small sedan. Dark color. Fairly late model, like within the last ten years, I'm guessing."

"Forensics said there were no skid marks showing the driver applying the brakes, so it appears the he meant to run you or Mr. Alexander down."

"It certainly seemed that way to me. The car didn't slow down at all. Maybe even accelerated. It's hard to recall, it all happened so fast. Logan might be more helpful."

"Something must have happened that made you dash across the street without looking for oncoming traffic. What was it?"

"I simply wasn't paying attention, like I should have been." She didn't want to tell him her private business.

"Seems like there's something you're not telling me. Something obviously upset you. Could it have anything to do with why this person would want to do you harm?"

"Nothing."

"I'm trying to help you here. You said you believe it wasn't an accident. What makes you say that? Why do you think someone wanted to run you down?"

"Maybe I'm getting too close to solving the Nick Evans case," she offered.

"Helping to solve it. I'm the detective here."

"Doesn't mean I can't figure out who killed Nick."

He eyed her for a moment, his lips pursed, as if wondering if he should argue the point.

"So, if we have Chet Monahan in jail, we know is wasn't him," Provenza said. "Maybe someone working for him? Someone he paid to do it?"

"What would be the point?" she asked. "If it was Chet, I'd think it would be Allison he'd want to stop from testifying against him."

"Maybe."

"What if Chet is innocent, George? What if someone else killed Nick?"

"But Allison Reagan said—"

"I know, but maybe she didn't stick around to see how things ended. Perhaps Chet and Nick did have a fight, but someone else finished Nick off."

Provenza's bushy gray eyebrows came together. "Someone like who?"

Jenessa pulled out her phone and showed Provenza the photo of the gum damage. "Whoever left this imprint."

"You took photos from the file?" Provenza looked none too pleased.

"To help with my investigation."

"What else do you have pictures of?" he barked.

"Only the necessary stuff to help you with this case." She wasn't about to tell him it was all necessary stuff. "So who, or what, could have made this imprint, George?"

"That's the million dollar question." He seemed to calm down. "That little fact is exactly why I haven't been able to file this case away. Got any ideas?"

"Allison's sister Kelly said something very interesting to me this morning."

"What was that?"

"That she had always suspected her father of killing Nick."

Provenza's eyes grew wide. "Patrick Reagan?"

Jenessa gave a nod.

"Why?"

"The night Nick died, Mr. Reagan found out that Nick had been sleeping with his sixteen-year-old daughter, maybe even gotten her pregnant, and he was livid, according to Kelly. In the morning, she saw her dad's shoes were wet and muddy on the back porch."

"There could be a hundred reasons for that," Provenza argued.

"Why are you defending him?"

"I have known that man for a long time. We went to Notre Dame together. I've been in the Rotary Club with him and played golf with him for over thirty years—so has Mayor Evans, for that matter. No, Jenessa," Provenza shook his head, "you must be barking up the wrong tree."

"You went to Notre Dame too?"

"You sound surprised."

"No, I was just wondering if you had a class ring."

"Why would you ask that?"

"I've been trying to remember where I saw the pattern in that photo of Nick Evans' gum and I think it's similar to a Notre Dame class ring I saw Allison Reagan wearing around her neck. So do you have one?"

"No, never got one." George paused and stared at her, like he was processing her line of thinking. "So if that imprint was made by the killer, he would have been wearing a Notre Dame ring at the time."

"Or she."

"What?"

"You said 'he' would have to been wearing the ring, assuming our killer is a man. Could be a woman, right?"

"I guess, but we may not have any way to match the size."

Jenessa sat back in her chair. "Does Chet have a ring from Notre Dame?" She paused for effect. "Probably not, since the fight happened while he was still in high school."

"But Allison said she saw him beat Nick to death."

"She saw Chet beat Nick, and she saw Nick fall and stop moving, but she didn't stick around. Maybe Nick got back up again and someone else finished him off. Seems he could have found more than one enemy that night. I'm thinking less and less that Chet's beating did it," she said.

"And you suspect Patrick Reagan might be the killer?"

"It's worth digging around a little more to find out, maybe get a warrant to check his vehicles for evidence of the hit-and-run."

"You'll need more than a hunch to get a warrant, Miss Jones."

That could be a problem. If Patrick Reagan was part of the mayor's circle of good ol' boys, there would have to be something concrete to show the judge.

"Now, back to your statement about the accident," Provenza said. "What were you talking to Logan about before it happened? Were you arguing or something?"

"No."

"Clearly something upset you so much that you dashed across the street without looking. I know you, Miss Jones, and you are nothing if not thorough."

Jenessa looked away. She didn't want to tell him. She forced herself to look him in the eye, make it appear as though she had nothing to hide.

Provenza's eyebrows rose. He wasn't buying it. Eye contact or no. He wagged a finger at her. "You were discussing Michael with him, weren't you?"

Now he was just prying. What did this have to do with the hit-and-run? He was a friend of sorts, stuck between her and Michael at times, but why did Provenza need to know?

"Jenessa?"

She held his inquisitive gaze, then finally caved. "I don't know what this has to do with the incident, but we were discussing the child we had together. The baby boy we gave up for adoption when we were teenagers."

"Oh, I'm sorry," he blustered. "I didn't know."

Maybe it was true that confession was good for the soul. She actually felt a little better getting that off her chest. At least Provenza was an unbiased confidante. He wouldn't judge her like Sara and Ramey would. "Well, you might as well know the whole story, George. The private eye Logan hired was close to finding the boy, but then he hit a dead-end and there were no more leads—zippo."

"No wonder you were upset."

"Then he kissed me," she blurted. Her heart jumped into her throat and she slapped a hand over her mouth, but it was too late. Why had she let that slip out? A little confession felt good, but this...this was too much redemption.

Provenza's eyes widened in surprise. "Come again?"

"You heard me," she mumbled.

"Seems to be a lot of that going arou—" Provenza's gaze shot above and behind Jenessa, his eyebrows quirked, then his face fell.

Jenessa spun around just in time to see Michael turn and disappear from the doorway. She sprang from her chair and ran to the hall, but his long, quick strides had carried him out of sight.

A warm hand descended onto her shoulder. "I'm sorry I didn't see him there sooner," Provenza said, standing behind her.

She stood still, her heart pounding, continuing to stare down the hall. "Don't blame yourself, George. It had to come to a head sooner or later."

"He loves you, you know."

"I know."

The question was, did she truly love him? Thoroughly and completely love him? She thought she did...until lately.

Both Aunt Renee and Ramey had brought up little Jake as playing a big part in her feelings for Michael. Maybe they were right.

First, Aunt Renee's words drifted through her mind. *The heart wants what the heart wants.*

Then Ramey's voice echoed through. *Cut one of them loose.*

That was easier said than done…

~*~

Jenessa rushed out to her car, climbed in, and paused before starting the engine. That wasn't how she wanted things to go with Michael. If she were going to break things off with him—and it was still an *if*—she would have had a quiet, private conversation with him, not like this.

Logan's image floated before her. He was often at the forefront of her mind these days. The kiss they had shared was spectacular, fireworks going off, even the memory of it brought back the feeling of every cell in her body coming alive.

Was that the way Michael had felt when he'd kissed her sister? And if it were, did that make her feel better or worse? Was all of this pointing to her starting an exciting new life with Logan, driving Michael to Sara? That thought made her shudder. Maybe she would be safer ignoring her rekindled feelings for Logan, staying with Michael—if he would even let her now…

But would that really be fair to Michael?

CHAPTER 30

WHEN JENESSA HAD FIRST RETURNED to Hidden Valley after a long time away, it was Michael who had swept her off her feet and she had loved every minute of it. Spending time with his little boy was a welcome bonus, she couldn't deny that, filling the hole that had been left by the baby she had given away.

They had worked well together, the detective and the reporter, solving crimes and writing about them. He had even saved her life on more than one occasion, for which she was immensely grateful.

But he wasn't Logan.

Her feelings for Logan had been buried deep in her soul for a very long time, so deeply she wasn't sure she could ever dig them out completely. Should she even try?

She thought of him lying in the hospital, his body broken and bruised, all because of his undying love for her. No matter how many times she had spurned his advances this past year, he never let it dull his determination to win her back. Michael was constantly annoyed at Logan's persistence, but Jenessa could not deny she felt a thrill whenever he was near.

Could it be that this was how Michael felt whenever his ex-wife came back to town? Did it stir in him a passion for her that he had tried to bury?

And what about what Jenessa had overheard him say to George the other day? That he had come very close to taking Josie back when she had visited a few months ago. Apparently he'd had doubts about his relationship with Jenessa as well. Then and now—if he'd kissed her sister...had he kissed Josie too? Or more?

She shook her head and stuck the key in the ignition, turning the engine over. Her first thought was to go after Michael, but he'd looked so upset before he'd stormed off. She should probably give him time to cool down before they spoke. Tracking down Allison Reagan seemed a better choice. She needed to get some answers from her.

Before Jenessa could back up, though, her phone started ringing in her purse. Dragging it out, she was delighted to see it was Allison. *Perfect timing.*

"Good morning, Allison."

"It is a good morning, knowing Chet is behind bars. My sister said you stopped by to see me. What can I help you with?"

"Can we meet? I'd rather talk in person."

"All right, at The Sweet Spot in ten minutes?"

Avoiding that place for the rest of the day was probably best. "How about we meet at Hal's Pancake World?"

"Okay. See you soon."

~*~

When Allison sat down at the table, the first thing Jenessa noticed was the ring hanging around her neck. From the side, as it dangled on the chain, Jenessa spotted the familiar design.

"Thanks for meeting me," Jenessa said, trying not to stare at the jewelry. "Would you like to order something?"

"Just coffee. I had brunch with my folks after church."

The cheery blond waitress stepped up to their table, pen and pad in hand. "What can I get for you ladies?"

"A blueberry muffin and coffee," Jenessa ordered, "and she'll have a cup of coffee."

"With cream," Allison smiled.

Once the waitress left, Jenessa jumped in. "I see you're wearing your college ring again."

Allison fingered it. "Yes, most days."

"You don't like wearing it on your finger?"

"Oh, no…it's too big. This was my father's ring. I had one, but I lost it a few months ago. I was heartbroken when I couldn't find it—my years at Notre Dame were the best years of my life—so he offered to give me his."

"He gave you his?" Jenessa muttered.

"Yeah, he wasn't wearing it. Kept it in my mother's jewelry box most of the time he's had it, so he offered it to me."

If this was Patrick Reagan's ring, and it had been stored away, it might still have Nick's DNA stuck in the crevices. Now, how to get it away from her?

"That was awfully kind of him. He must be a great dad."

"He is."

"I'll bet he was mad when he found out you and Nick were sleeping together."

Allison's eyes widened for a second, then her gaze momentarily dropped to her lap as she expelled a nervous giggle. "I didn't know you knew."

"Kelly told me. She said he was furious."

"Furious doesn't even begin to describe it. You know how dads can be with their little girls."

"What do you mean?"

"The screaming and lecturing. I thought I'd never hear the end of it."

"Yeah, my dad would have reacted the same way," Jenessa said, thinking back to when she turned up pregnant.

"You know he shipped me off to an all-girls boarding school for my senior year, don't you? To keep me away from temptation, he said."

"Yes, you mentioned that. Boy, that must have been hard, to miss your senior year of high school with all your friends."

"I was happy to be away from Chet Monahan, after what I saw."

"Here you go, ladies." The waitress set their orders on the table. "Let me know if there's anything else you gals need."

Jenessa waited for her to leave before resuming the conversation. "You're probably relieved he's in jail now." She wasn't about to tell her she had reason to believe Chet was not the killer.

Allison nodded as she stirred some cream into her coffee. "He'll finally get what he deserves."

Someone would, if Jenessa had anything to say about it. She just wasn't sure it would be Chet.

"What did you want to talk to me about?" Allison asked, then took a sip.

Jenessa couldn't tell her she had questions about the ring. She had to come up with something quick. "Um, well…yes, you must have heard about the hit-and-run last night…"

"I did. How awful for Logan Alexander. Do you know how he's doing?"

"I'm not family, so they won't tell me anything directly, but Summer told me he's in serious but stable condition."

"Poor man." Allison's brow dipped in confusion. "You wanted to ask me about the accident?"

"Not exactly. And I don't believe it was an accident. I think someone didn't want me snooping into this case and meant to run me down, but hit Logan instead." Jenessa stuck a piece of muffin in her mouth as nonchalantly as she could, trying not to show how much that thought rattled her.

"Oh no," Allison gasped. "Sorry, but I don't know anything about that."

"I just wondered if there was anyone you knew of that might want to keep me from poking around Nick Evans' death. You know who all was involved in his sex games and the people who were angry because of it—all the people the police questioned back then."

Allison sat back in her chair. "Maybe years ago."

"They all seem to still live here in Hidden Valley."

Allison crossed her arms over her chest. "Sorry, Jenessa, but I'm of no help to you there."

The woman's body language was telling her that she was closing off. Jenessa wasn't about to ask any more about her father and put Allison on alert. She and her dad seemed close and Jenessa couldn't afford to have Allison telling him she was asking about him, his car, or his ring.

Surely Detective Provenza would want to swoop in and question her if he knew the ring was her father's— that is, if he didn't let his decades-long friendship with the man get in the way. On the other hand, if George did interrogate her about her father, Mr. Reagan could get wind of it and that ring would disappear in a heartbeat.

No, Jenessa had to play coy in order for Provenza to take possession of this critical piece of evidence as soon as possible if they had any hope of getting it to the crime lab for DNA testing. It was time she wrapped this meeting up.

"No worries," she said, pulling another piece of muffin off. "Just thought I'd ask." She took another sip of coffee. "There's something else I wanted to talk to you about, but I need to use the restroom first." She glanced around for a sign pointing the way. "I'll be right back."

Allison checked her watch. "Okay."

Jenessa swiveled out of her chair and headed for the ladies room. Once out of Allison's view, she pulled her phone out and called Detective Provenza. She explained what she had just learned about the ring being Patrick Reagan's. "With any luck, there's still some DNA wedged in the ring's design. Will you please get a warrant and take the ring before it disappears?"

"If I can." George paused, likely mulling it over. "Judge McCormack is new, so maybe I can finesse my way into getting his signature on a warrant. No promises."

"You need to do it fast, George." Jenessa rubbed her temple, hoping to ease the pain growing behind her eyes. The stress of knowing someone wanted her dead was weighing on her. Not to mention everything else. "I don't know how much longer I can keep Allison here."

"Where are you?"

"Hal's Pancake World."

"It's Sunday, so I'll need to catch the judge at home. He won't like it, but I'll beg if I have to. Patrick is my friend, but if testing that ring for DNA will put to rest any doubts we have about his involvement, it's worth a shot."

"I've got the photo of the impression on Nick's gum on my phone, as well as a photo of the Notre Dame ring I picked off the internet earlier. I'll text them to you and you can show the judge. You do text now, don't you, George?"

"Yes, I'm not that much of a dinosaur."

"Did you find out what the Reagans drive? Check it for front-end damage?"

"I already know they own a dark blue Toyota Tercel and a silver Honda Accord. I drove by their house, but they must have them in the garage. I'll need a warrant to get a look at them."

"We're running out of time, George." She rubbed the back of her neck to relieve the tension.

"I know, but we don't have much to go on for these warrants."

"Tell the judge you've been trying to solve this cold case of the death of the mayor's son for the last twenty years and you've never been this close. Tell him this warrant could break the case wide open."

"I'll do my best."

Jenessa peeked around the corner to make sure Allison was still there. "Do it fast."

~*~

Jenessa returned to the table. "Sorry for the wait. Want some more coffee? I know I could use some." She waved at the waitress and caught her eye, then raised her cup to her.

The woman filled their cups and moved on.

"Are you sure you don't want something to eat?" Jenessa asked, trying to stall. "Best pancakes in town, I hear."

"You've never tried them?"

"Not yet. I try to stay away from too many carbs." She looked down at what was left of her blueberry muffin. "Unfortunately, I do love them." She popped the last morsel in her mouth. "You know, Allison, we don't really know each other very well. We say hello at the bank, but that's it. I'd love to get to know you better."

"You would?"

Too much? But she had to stall.

"I would. Why don't you tell me about yourself? Tell me all about those wonderful years you spent at Notre Dame."

Allison smiled, apparently touched that Jenessa wanted to know. She started in and told one story after another—the classes, the parties, the boys, the spring-break trips, and on and on.

"So, after graduation, what did you do?" Jenessa inquired.

Allison launched into another monologue about her career, boyfriends, a broken engagement, and other highs and lows of her life.

"Wow, that's quite a story," she said, trying to think what to ask next to keep her talking.

Allison checked her watch again. "I'd love to stay and chat longer, but I need to go to—"

"Sorry to interrupt," a male voice said, "Miss Reagan, Miss Jones."

Jenessa looked up, relieved. "Detective Provenza. It's good to see you."

Allison cocked her head, her expression puzzled. "Something wrong?"

CHAPTER 31

ALLISON GLANCED NERVOUSLY around the restaurant, shifting uncomfortably in her chair. "Detective?"

"Miss Reagan," Provenza began, "I have a warrant to take possession of the ring you're wearing around your neck." He laid the folded document on the table in front of her.

Her fingers closed around the ring. "I don't understand." She picked up the paper, unfolded it, and began reading.

"It's all there," he said. "It's potential evidence in the Evans murder case."

"What does Chet Monahan or Nick Evans have to do with my ring?" Allison asked. "I don't understand this at all."

"I'm not at liberty to explain right now, just here to get the ring. Don't worry, it should become clear in a few days."

With any luck, that's all it would take to get the DNA results and check Patrick Reagan's car for evidence he was the hit-and-run driver.

"A few days?" Allison unhooked the chain and slid the ring off into an evidence bag Provenza held open. "I will get it back, won't I?"

He sealed the bag and shot Jenessa a quick knowing glance before returning his attention to Allison. "Yes, eventually."

~*~

After Jenessa said her good-byes to Allison—who thankfully had not caught on to Jenessa's role in Provenza collecting her ring—she slipped behind the wheel of her car and blew out a long breath, anxious to get the detective on the phone.

"Good job, George," she said, rolling her shoulders to relieve some tightness. "I thought you'd never get there."

"That's Detective George to you." He chuckled. He apparently was done trying to get her to call him Detective Provenza. "I had to do some fancy footwork with the judge, but, in the end, I got him to see things my way."

"What about the warrant for Mr. Reagan's car?"

"Michael is there serving it as we speak. I'm headed over as soon as I drop off this evidence bag to be tested."

She took a deep calming breath. "I'd meet you at the house, but it's probably best I steer clear of Michael until he's calmed down and we have an opportunity to talk."

"Don't wait too long, Jenessa. These things have a way of festering."

"I know, I know," she agreed, "but I doubt he wants to talk to me this afternoon. I'm going to pop over to the hospital, see if there's any updates on Logan's condition."

"I promise not to mention that to Michael."

"Thanks, George. Let me know how things go with Mr. Reagan's vehicle, would you?" She pushed the door locks on her car. "I'd feel better knowing who it was that tried to kill me last night." Maybe then she could relax a little.

Now, to get busy on writing her story. Her editor was practically panting the last time she spoke to him, anxiously waiting for a big headline from her. At least she could temporarily appease him with an article about the hit-and-run from an eyewitness perspective, along with an update on the victim's condition if she could get the family's permission. The town would be voracious in reading about their number one son.

"Don't write anything that'll jeopardize this murder case." Provenza must have read her mind.

"I wouldn't dream of it." She smiled to herself. "Hey, Detective, do you know any good massage therapists?"

~*~

285

Jenessa looked through the glass and saw Logan alone in his private room, still in the Intensive Care Unit. Glancing down the corridor, one way and then the other, she found no one who might try to prevent her from going in. She pushed the door open and slipped inside, gently closing the door behind her. He appeared to be sleeping, with wires connecting him to various monitors that beeped a steady rhythm.

She tiptoed to his bedside, wanting to talk to him but not wanting to wake him. He looked so peaceful. Her fingers wove around his and his eyes fluttered open. A smile lifted the corners of his mouth.

"Hey," was all he said in a groggy voice.

"Sorry, I didn't want to wake you."

"Glad you did."

"How are you feeling?"

He ran a hand over his face, trying to wake up. "Like a bus hit me."

"I hear we almost lost you last night."

"We? Would it have made a difference to you?" he asked, his azure blue eyes becoming wide and alert.

"Of course it would," she replied, her heart pounding a little harder. "I—"

"You what?" He lifted a brow.

"I…I…" she stammered. How should she reply? "I care what happens to you, Logan."

"Maybe more than you want to admit." He flashed her a grin.

She thought of Michael, how hurt he was knowing they had kissed. "It's complicated."

His fingers closed tighter around hers. "I love you, Jenessa."

"Yeah, you keep saying."

"And I think you might feel the same if you would just let yourself. That kiss—"

"You kissed me," she said.

"You kissed me back. Don't deny it." He seemed pleased at the thought.

She couldn't deny it. She wanted to, but couldn't. Not any longer. She *had* kissed him back and she *had* thoroughly enjoyed it..

"You never knew this," Logan said, still holding her hand, "but, after the initial shock that you were pregnant wore off, I tried to convince my father to let me marry you and keep the baby."

"You did?"

"He threatened to cut me off financially, of course, and I knew I could never support a family working as a fry cook."

"If it came to that—"

"Let's face it, my dad owns this town and without his blessing I knew I'd never get a good job, even if I managed to find my own college money."

Why hadn't he told her this sooner?

"I guess, being young," he continued, "I thought I would come find you one day, and then our child. I was just a kid, Jenessa. I didn't know any better."

Tears filled her eyes at his revelation.

"But I know better now. That's why I hired the private eye."

His words touched her heart, she couldn't find the words to express how she felt. She blinked back the tears and heaved a sigh.

"I wish you had told me," she finally said, struggling to keep further tears at bay. "I have to go." She pulled her hand out of his and turned to leave.

"I'm sorry." Logan groaned in agony and she spun back to him. He had tried to sit up, tried to stop her from going. He dropped back against the pillows.

"Please don't go," he pleaded, clearly in pain. "Stay with me."

"I can't," she said. "I have to go and find out who did this to you."

"Let the police handle it, Jenessa. Stay with me."

"They are handling it, but I have a vested interest in finding out who tried to kill me last night. That person is still out there and I'm not safe until he or she is caught."

"Then kiss me good-bye, in case I'm gone when you come back."

Gone? Like dead?

He had almost died the night before. How would she have felt if she'd lost him? Especially knowing what she did now? But she never would have found out if he had died. Her throat tightened at the thought.

She bent down. "You're not going anywhere." She closed her eyes and kissed him softly on the lips. Still hovering inches from his face, she opened her eyes and met his gaze. She straightened slowly, their eyes remaining locked on each other's. "Be here when I get back."

"Sorry, are we interrupting something?" a woman's voice said.

Jenessa turned to leave as Summer walked in. "Hey, Summer."

Summer smiled. Her expression seemed happy, but the shadows below her eyes said her health was rapidly declining.

Grayson walked in behind his mom and stepped to her side.

"Hey, buddy," Logan greeted the boy with a smile. "It's good to see you."

The boy moved to Logan's bedside and laid a couple of magazines on his lap. "Mom thought these might keep you from getting too bored when there's nothing good on TV."

Watching them talk, the family resemblance was evident, as was Logan's affection for the kid. He might have made a good father after all.

"Where's your little sister?" Logan asked.

"At Nana and Pop's. Mom thought she was too young to come with us."

"Really, we weren't trying to interrupt," Summer said apologetically, standing beside her son, draping an arm around his shoulder. "Grayson just wanted to see how Uncle Logan was doing."

"*Uncle* Logan?" Jenessa asked.

"Well, he's really more of a second cousin," Summer replied, "but the difference in their ages makes it easier for Grayson to call him uncle."

"Anyway, I was on my way out—" Jenessa began to say.

"Didn't look like that." Summer glanced back at Jenessa, who had moved to the door.

"Really, I was," Jenessa insisted, feeling like she had to justify herself. "Logan, feel better and I'll come back to see you again."

"I'll be right here," he promised as she waved and walked out the door.

CHAPTER 32

THE INTERROGATION WAS ABOUT to begin. Jenessa stood in the observation room, unbeknownst to Michael. Detective Provenza had snuck her in with her promise not to say a word during the interrogation of Patrick Reagan or to write anything about it until he gave her the go-ahead.

She watched Michael march Patrick Reagan into the room and drag out a chair for him. "Have a seat." The man sat down, uncertainty in his expression. As Michael too a seat across the table from him, Provenza joined them, standing at the end of the table.

"Am I under arrest?" Mr. Reagan asked.

"No," Provenza jumped in, "we just want to talk to you, see what you know about our investigation."

"What investigation?" Reagan glanced up at Provenza, then shifted his attention to Michael. "You looked through my garage, inspected my cars, and then you hauled me down here without so much as a hint as to why." His gaze slid again to Detective Provenza. "What's going on, George?"

Michael opened the file on the table. "We want to find out what you know about the murder of Nicholas Evans."

The man's focus remained on his friend, Detective Provenza. "I'd heard you people were digging into that old case again, but, George, you can't think I had anything to do with it. Besides, aren't you looking at Chet Monahan for that murder?"

"He's our prime suspect at the moment," Michael said, "but there is some new evidence."

His gaze flicked to Michael. "What new evidence?"

Provenza walked around the table and stood next to Michael. "We have your college ring, the one you were wearing the night Nick Evans was killed."

"How would you know that?" Reagan asked.

Michael leaned forward and folded his hands on the file. "So you're confirming it?"

"I didn't say that."

"We're having the ring tested for DNA," Provenza said. "We fully expect the results to confirm that there is latent tissue evidence from Nick Evans in the crevices."

"You punched him out, didn't you?" Michael questioned. "Knocked him unconscious and dumped him in the lake?"

"No!"

Michael stood and leaned forward, hands on the table. "You walked his body out to the deep and gave him a shove."

"No! My God, George." His gaze once more went to his friend, his eyes pleading. "You have to believe me."

"Your wet and muddy shoes were seen on your back porch the next morning," Michael said.

"By whom?"

Michael sat back down. "You'll find out during trial...unless you want to make a full confession in exchange for a lighter sentence. I'm sure that could be arranged."

Reagan's expression went stoic. "Should I be calling a lawyer?"

Provenza came around to Mr. Reagan's side of the table and sat on the corner of it. "Listen, Patrick, right now is your best chance to make a deal. We know the story. You find out this college kid talks your prized sixteen-year-old daughter into having sex with him and you're out of your mind with rage."

"You would be too if you'd just been told she was pregnant with his child," Reagan blurted out.

Jenessa muttered the word *pregnant* to herself, alone in the observation room. Kelly had said she'd misheard the information, but her father thinking Allison was pregnant, whether or not it was later proven false, he would have gone postal at the time. Jenessa was all too familiar with that scenario.

"Pregnant?" Michael mouthed to Provenza, whose back was now to the two-way mirror.

"Now, Patrick," Provenza went on, "I'm sure you didn't mean to kill him, but after you slugged him a few times, he wasn't breathing, was he? No, he was dead."

"No, that's not right."

Provenza continued. "There was nothing you could do now but protect your daughter's reputation."

"You could smell the alcohol on the kid's breath," Michael said. "You figured people would assume that he had fallen into the water because he was drunk, or at least that's what you hoped the police would think. You must have been so relieved when the ME declared his death an accidental drowning."

Mr. Reagan hung his head and shook it several times. "I did not kill that boy."

"We know you didn't mean to do it," Provenza said. "I'm sure the prosecutor will take that into consideration."

"Do you really want a lengthy trial?" Michael asked. "Drain your family's finances? What will your wife live on?"

Provenza pushed off the edge of the table and walked around to Michael's side. "You want to drag your daughter's reputation through the mud? Have this story plastered all over the media? You know, don't you, that when the test comes back on that ring—your ring—that Nick Evans' DNA will be on it."

Reagan's stare was fixed on Provenza. "I'm not going to confess to something I didn't do."

"And then there's the matter of the hit-and-run last night." Michael sat back in his chair and crossed his arms. "Your car fits the description of the offending vehicle and you have some front-end damage on the passenger side."

Provenza placed his hands on the table and leaned forward. "You do realize it was Hidden Valley's fair-haired boy that you ran down, don't you? When our CSI unit is finished going over your car, will they find Logan Alexander's DNA on it?"

"Absolutely not! What possible motive would I have to do that? I have no beef with Logan Alexander," Reagan insisted. His voice softened. "How is he doing by the way?"

Was he trying to sound like he cared? Or was it simply a self-serving comment?

"We don't think you were aiming at him," Michael said. "More likely you were trying to keep a certain female reporter from digging into this story and exposing you."

"That's ridiculous."

"Is it, Patrick?" Provenza asked.

Jenessa was very interested to hear what Mr. Reagan had to say about that.

Reagan appeared uncomfortable as he squirmed in his seat. "That's nuts. Maybe someone was just trying to scare her."

"Is that an admission?" Jenessa mumbled to herself as she watched.

"Are you admitting to trying to scare her with your car?" Provenza asked.

"Of course not." Mr. Reagan shot Provenza a frosty stare. "Am I free to go?"

"Are you saying you don't want to help us?" Michael asked. "Are you trying to obstruct this investigation?"

"I think I'd better call my lawyer now, George. I'm not saying one more word until he gets here."

"Then make your call, Patrick," Provenza replied.

Michael closed the file and tucked it under his arm as he stood. "We'll be back."

~*~

"What are you doing here?" Michael asked when he saw Jenessa sitting in a side chair in their office. Seeing her was painful, finding out just hours ago that she had kissed another man. Hearing her admit to it was like a knife in his heart.

She perched on the edge of the chair. "I'm following the case, of course. I know you brought Patrick Reagan in for questioning, Michael, and I—"

"Who told you that?" Michael interrupted.

"I did." Provenza strode into the office. "I thought we could use her insight since she's been in close contact with both of his daughters." He sat down at his desk. "Well, Miss Jones, what did you think?"

"She was in the observation room?" Michael's irritation was hard to contain.

"I was." Jenessa eyed Michael before turning her attention to Provenza. "Kelly told me she had overheard Allison on the phone and thought she said she was pregnant by Nick, but found out later she misunderstood. But, and this is a big but, Kelly had told her father that Allison was pregnant and planning on meeting the guy that night. That was before it got straightened out."

"Well, that does put a little different spin on things," Provenza said. "But even if Allison hadn't been pregnant, finding out the guy was sleeping with his sixteen-year-old daughter could have been enough to make any father go ballistic."

"Pregnant, not pregnant. I don't know what difference it makes," Michael argued.

"A stronger motive, for one," Provenza replied.

Michael sat down at his desk and crossed his arms, leaning back into his chair. "Maybe."

"His comment about the hit-and-run sounded like he was trying to suggest he only meant to scare me, not run anyone over," Jenessa remarked, "but him seriously injuring Logan was a direct result of his actions, whether he meant to or not."

CHAPTER 33

PROVENZA'S DESK PHONE RANG. It was the medical examiner on the line.

"What did you find out, Doc?" Provenza asked, then paused and listened to the reply.

"We need to talk," Michael whispered to Jenessa.

"Later," she whispered back.

"You're sure?" Provenza questioned, again listening to the answer. "Okay. Thanks, Doc."

"Why was he calling?" Michael asked as soon as his partner hung up the phone.

Provenza went to the large crime board along one wall of the office and picked up a marker pen. He began sketching out what they knew, writing as he spoke. "From Allison Reagan's testimony, we know Chet fought with Nick outside of the boathouse, knocking him out."

"That's right," Jenessa said.

"Then, we believe Patrick Reagan found our victim. So, after Chet left, Nick must have gotten up off the ground in time for the confrontation with the irate father." Again Provenza made a note on the board.

"We know Mr. Reagan had to have fought with Nick because of his ring's impression on Nick's upper gum," Jenessa added.

"Somehow, after that altercation, Nick ended up in the water." Provenza made another notation.

"Okay," Jenessa concurred, "so what does this have to do with that call from the ME?"

"I had asked Dr. Yamamoto to review the old autopsy notes and photos." Provenza set the marker down and he scanned the timeline. "Maybe there was more to this than we're seeing."

"More?" Michael got up and went to the board, looking it over.

"I get it," Jenessa said, "something in his body that could prove who killed him—hence the medical examiner."

"So what did he say?" Michael asked.

"He said there was a tear in Nick's brain. He couldn't be certain, but his best guess is that the first fight made the tear, if it was as brutal as Allison had reported, and the second fight made it worse. Eventually, left untreated, the doc said, the first tear would have killed Nick anyway, even though he was able to get himself up off the ground. Then, after the fight we believe he had with Patrick, probably weak from his first go 'round, Nick may have been breathing, probably pretty shallow breathing, when Patrick Reagan left him, but he could have died very shortly after."

"But he didn't die, George," Jenessa said. "The original report says he had water in his lungs. That's why the old medical examiner eventually ruled it an accidental drowning."

"Which means Patrick Reagan didn't leave Nick laying on the ground," Michael said. "He put him in the water to cover up what he'd done."

"So you're saying Patrick is lying to us," Provenza said.

"I know he's your friend, George, but where's the big surprise?" Michael put a hand on his partner's shoulder. "Gee, a guilty person claiming he didn't do it."

"Is it possible there was a third person?" Jenessa suggested.

"Let's not go there," Michael said. "We could start guessing all kinds of things. Was there a fourth and a fifth one, too? No, let's concentrate on what we know."

"We know Chet fought with him," Jenessa remarked, "and we know Patrick Reagan had a good reason to."

Provenza shook his head slowly. "I hate to think my friend could have done this."

Jenessa rose and sat on the edge of the desk, facing the board. "At the very least, George, you should be able to arrest him for the hit-and-run—no?"

"Not until we have the CSI results on the car," Provenza replied, "assuming we can prove it was him behind the wheel."

"Who else would it be?" she asked.

"The wife, maybe."

"The wife?" Jenessa echoed. "Perhaps. She was pretty tight-lipped when I called for an interview."

Allison or Kelly? Not likely, because it was doubtful they knew what their dad had done the night Nick died.

"You fellas ought to check the phone calls coming in to the newspaper in the last twenty-four hours, see if any of them are from Patrick Reagan."

"Why should we do that?" Provenza asked.

"Well...," she hesitated, her gaze shifting away momentarily, "remember the threatening phone calls I mentioned? They came in on my desk phone, not my cell."

Michael turned to her, heat prickling his neck. "Remind me again, why didn't you tell me?"

"Because I knew you'd tell me to back off the story."

His jaw tightened. "And you would have been right."

"And Logan wouldn't be lying in the hospital if you had," Provenza added.

"I'm sorry, but—"

"It's too late for apologies, Jenessa," Michael interrupted, his throat feeling raw with anger. "The harm has already been done." Not that he cared that much about Logan's well-being, but it was the principal of it.

"You really should have alerted us when it happened," Provenza agreed.

"You wouldn't have the ring if I had told you guys," she said. "That could turn out to be the pivotal piece of evidence in this case."

"We'll have to wait for the DNA results from the ring to see if we can charge Patrick with Nick's murder," Provenza said. "I'm positive the DA will say the case won't fly without it."

Michael gazed at the board again. "His lawyer should be here before long, then we can take another run at him. Hopefully his lawyer will convince him to play ball and we'll get something more out of him this time." Michael went back to his desk, his eyes avoiding Jenessa's.

She huffed. "You know his lawyer's going to say that if his client is not under arrest, they're out of here."

"You're probably right," Michael shot back, his gaze sliding to her, "but we have to try."

"Technically," Jenessa came off the desk and stood before the board, studying what Provenza had written there, "if Chet caused the initial brain tear, which in time would have led to Nick dying, wouldn't he be legally responsible for his death?"

Michael and George looked at each other. "Good question," Provenza replied. "I'll talk to the DA and see what he has to say about it."

"So, unless Patrick Reagan confesses," Jenessa said, "you'll be keeping Chet in jail for the time being, won't you?"

~*~

It was almost four o'clock when Jenessa left the police station. She phoned her aunt to check up on her before heading to the hospital. Fortunately, Aunt Renee said she was doing just fine, Sara was there swimming with Jake.

Again? Jake's little face popped into her mind and it made her smile. She hadn't seen him in a week, but it felt so much longer.

"Jenessa," her aunt said, "you should go on with your day without worrying about me."

She said she would. Now, if only she could stop worrying about Logan.

Thoughts of him were filling her mind almost constantly it seemed, especially since his injury…but maybe that wasn't such a bad thing. Her relationship with Michael had hit a bumpy patch and things were becoming increasingly chilly between them. She did miss seeing Jake, though.

There was just too much going on in her life, too much to think about right now. How could she make sense of any of it? If she could just find the missing clue in the murder mystery, maybe the rest of the pieces of her life would start falling into place.

She headed to the hospital to check on Logan, hoping his condition was improving. As she drove, her mind replayed the passionate kiss they'd shared the night before, which suddenly morphed into a vision of Michael with his lips hungrily kissing her sister's. She shook her head to erase the image. It seemed they both had something to be mad and hurt about.

As much as Michael would like to ignore it, Jenessa and Logan had history, and a child together. Not that she was justifying her own actions, but still…why had Michael kissed her sister? Had he been secretly attracted to her as Ramey had said Sara was to Michael? Or had Jenessa simply driven him to it?

She needed to clear her mind. She had a murder case to follow and a story due to her boss. That had to take priority at this moment. Before she could see Logan, she had better stop by the jail to see if she could get Chet Monahan to give her an interview.

She peeked at her watch. Just enough time to swing by the jailhouse, make it to the hospital, and get her story to Charles by the deadline—if she hurried.

"Follow me, Miss Jones." The police sergeant entered the security code into the keypad and the lock made a loud click as the heavy metal door unlocked. He pushed the door open and she followed him through it. "Visitors' stations are that way," he said as he motioned to the right, through another door.

She took her seat behind a thick window and waited for Chet to appear on the other side. After pulling out her notepad and pen, she sat, trying to be patient. After a few minutes, Chet appeared, dressed in a jumpsuit with thick horizontal stripes of black and white. He dragged the chair out and took a seat.

She grabbed the phone on her side of the partition.

He picked up the receiver on his side. "Who are you again?"

"Jenessa Jones. I'm a reporter for the Hidden Valley Herald. We met briefly at the bank last week. Then I was at your house visiting Summer."

"That's right, but your hair was different." It seemed to come back to him. "Sorry, but a lot's happened since then. Why did you want to see me?"

"As you might have heard I'm covering the Nick Evans murder and I hoped I could interview you."

"Not without my lawyer present."

"I understand, but is there anything you'd like people to know about you?"

"That I didn't kill Nick Evans. He was alive when I left him. That's all I'm going to say."

Jenessa made a few notes. "Is there anything you'd like to tell me about yourself, unrelated to the case?"

His brows came together. "Why would you want to know that?"

"To let the readers get to know the real Chet Monahan, from a human-interest perspective. You must know the other newspapers and the media are demonizing you." He obviously wasn't going to talk about what happened the night Nick died, so why not try another tack? "It might help your case when it goes to trial if people got to know Chet Monahan, the family man."

"Hmm." He stroked his rough jaw as he considered it. Even in the jumpsuit with stubble growing on his chin, he was a handsome man with classic features—a banking executive with intelligence and charm. "You're not just trying to get me to talk?"

"Of course I want you to talk." Jenessa flashed him a friendly smile. "I want you to tell me about yourself."

He nodded and began telling her about growing up in Hidden Valley, in the less prosperous part of town, his difficult home life with his father, and how he had

306

fought hard to make something of himself. He had been faithful to the same woman for the almost twenty years and loved his children.

Jenessa wrote a few notes, but most of it she had already heard from Summer. She settled back in her chair and crossed her arms. "A man who loves his wife and children."

"That's right. Make sure you highlight that."

"Funny you should say that. I have reason to believe, Mr. Monahan, that you have been abusive to your wife and children over the years, that you have quite a temper on you." She studied him for a reaction.

"Who told you that?" he growled, a frown deepening a fold between his eyebrows.

"Doesn't matter. Is it true?"

"Someone is spreading lies, trying to set me up."

"Weren't you arrested in high school for assaulting another boy?"

"Yes, but that was a long time ago."

"Then let's talk about something more recent. Aren't you in here for taking a swing at one of the detectives?"

His face pinched into a scowl and he said nothing.

"I was wondering, was the spiral fracture of Grayson's wrist just someone making things up?"

His lips flattened into a tight, straight line as anger flared in his eyes. "That was an accident."

"There are other documented incidents."

His expression softened as his eyes moistened. He slid a hand over his mouth and looked away, giving no response.

"Do you truly love your children, Chet? Honestly?"

His gaze slid back to her. "I thought I could love them. I tried, but I never really felt like their dad."

That was an odd comment—not what she expected. "What did you feel like?"

"I don't know, just disconnected."

"Why is that?"

"They're not mine—but then you probably already knew that."

CHAPTER 34

NO, SHE DID NOT ALREADY KNOW THAT.
Jenessa sat across from Chet, the jail's Plexiglas window
standing between them, completely stunned by his
surprising admission. Had Summer cheated on him?
That wouldn't be completely unreasonable. After all, she
had cheated on him with Nick. Or maybe Chet was
infertile and they'd used a donor.

"No, I didn't know anything about it," she said.
"Why would I?"

"I just thought...well, I assumed, Summer
had...maybe you should ask her about it yourself."

Jenessa's mind was spinning. Why would he think
his wife had told her about this? She considered Summer
a friend, but not a close one. "Is there something you're
trying to hide?"

He did not respond.

"I know Summer is sick and she's going to..." Jenessa paused to consider her words, "that Summer has terminal cancer. Is that why?"

With eyebrows lifting, Chet raised both hands briefly, the phone in one, as if in surrender. "I've said all I'm going to. You figure it out." He glanced over his shoulder and called out, "Guard!" Then he hung up the phone.

~*~

Jenessa stepped off the elevator and hurried down the hall to Logan's room in the Intensive Care Unit. She surveyed the area, looking for anyone who might try to stop her. No one. Through the window, she noticed the curtain drawn around his bed. She slipped in and tiptoed toward his bedside. Pulling the curtain back a little, she gasped, finding a frail old man curled up on his side, right where Logan had lain.

The man's eyes grew wide in surprise.

"Oh, sorry to disturb you." She dashed out the door and strode to the nurses' station.

A young nurse in blue scrubs stepped behind the counter. "Can I help you?"

"Logan Alexander. He isn't in his room anymore. Do you know where they've taken him?"

The woman typed something into the computer and ran her finger down the screen. "Looks like they've moved him to the third floor. Room three fourteen."

"Thank you," Jenessa smiled and headed for the elevator. The sound of the nurse urging her to check in at the nurses' station when she got there echoed down the hallway.

When she reached room three fourteen, Logan was sitting up, carrying on an animated conversation with young Grayson, who sat in the chair beside him. He turned toward Jenessa as she entered, a bright smile on his face, his eyes a clear, sparkling blue.

She couldn't help but smile back as she approached Logan. "You look a lot better than the last time I saw you."

"He's been playing video games with me," Grayson said, holding out his device to show her. "But I'm winning."

Logan ruffled the top of the boy's hair. "Only because I let you win."

"I thought Summer would be here," Jenessa said, hoping to ask her what Chet had been referring to.

"She wasn't feeling good," Grayson said. "She went to get a cold drink in the cafeteria."

Summer had seemed especially tired the last couple of times Jenessa had seen her. The cancer was likely taking its toll on her. How much longer would she last?

"And what about you, mister?" Jenessa gave Logan a light, playful punch in the arm. "When are you going to get out of this place?"

"The doctor said I might be able to go home tomorrow, assuming I keep improving." He took her hand and turned serious. "Have the police figured out who ran me down?"

His touch sent a warm sensation dancing up her arm. Her first instinct was to pull her hand back, but she didn't.

"They're working on it," she said. "They've got a good suspect, but can't arrest him yet."

"Who is it?" Grayson asked, eyes wide.

"I can't say. The cops'll know who leaked it." She offered the boy an apologetic smile. "Hey, I visited your dad today," she said, changing the subject.

The boy's expression fell. "Do you think he really killed that guy, like everybody says?"

She glanced over to Logan briefly, before replying. "I don't know. He swears he didn't do it, but we may not know what really happened until the trial."

Conflict ricocheted in the boy's eyes—love for his dad, no matter the abuse, fighting against the shame that his father could be a killer.

"Listen, boys, I've got a story to finish up before deadline, so I honestly can't stick around." She gave Logan's hand a squeeze before letting it go. "I hope to be back later to check on you."

"Uncle James." Logan's attention moving to the door as Summer and her father walked in.

She seemed more frail that she had the day before, the color of her skin a bit grayer.

"How are you doing, Logan?" James Walker asked, his voice deep and resonant.

"A lot better." Logan's gaze slid back to Jenessa. "You know Jenessa, don't you?"

Before Mr. Walker answered, she stuck out her hand to him. "Good to see you again, sir," she said, not wanting to wait for his response.

He took her hand and gave it a weak shake. "You too," he said flatly, clearly not meaning it.

Jenessa looked past him to his daughter. "How are you, Summer?"

"Tired."

"Here, Mom." Grayson got up from his chair. "Sit here."

"Good man," his grandfather praised.

"Thank you, sweetheart." Summer slumped down in the chair and blew out a breath.

Jenessa had hoped to get her alone to talk, but now was not that time. She'd have to look for a better opportunity—and soon.

"Well," Jenessa's attention traveled back to Logan, "like I was saying, I've got to get going, so I'll leave you to your family."

Logan grabbed her hand again. "But you will be back, right?"

"Probably. After I put the story to bed, I'm going to drive up to the lake and check out the boathouse again, see if I'm missing something." She untangled her fingers from his, feeling the chill of his uncle's glare.

She glanced over her shoulder and confirmed he was definitely shooting icicles at her with his eyes.

Grayson must have sensed the rising tension. "Mom, Jenessa said she went to see Dad today," changing the topic of conversation.

Summer straightened in the chair. "How is he?"

"How do you think he is?" James barked. "He's sitting in jail for murder."

Well, he hadn't been officially charged with murder.

"I warned you not to marry that trash," the man went on.

"Dad!" Summer snapped back with a frown. Her hand went out to her son, but her eyes remained fixed on her father. "Don't listen to him, Grayson. Grandpa's just in a bad mood."

James glowered at his daughter. "I'm going to get some coffee." He turned and marched out the door.

It seemed there was a lot more to the story of Summer and Chet than Jenessa knew. Was it that her family thought she married beneath her station? Or was it something more?

She'd have to leave those thoughts for another day, she had a deadline looming. "Well, I'm off," Jenessa said, once more trying to leave.

Logan shifted in the bed, trying to sit up. "You have to promise me you'll be back."

"I don't know. It might be past visiting hours."

"Promise me." He was like a little boy who would not be denied. He leaned closer to her and lowered his voice. "We have things to discuss."

What things?

Now she was intrigued. "Okay, okay, I give you my word."

Logan crossed his arms with a satisfied grin and leaned back against the pillows. "I'll be waiting."

~*~

Jenessa stopped by The Sweet Spot on her way out of town.

"Hey, Jenessa." Ramey's face lit up with a big smile when she walked in. "What are you up to today?"

"Working, as usual."

314

"On a Sunday?" a booming male voice asked.

She turned to find her boss, Charles McAllister, standing beside her. "I didn't expect to find you here," she said.

"We're closing soon and Charles stopped by to make plans for later this evening." Adoration twinkled in Ramey's eyes as she looked at him. Her gaze moved back to Jenessa. "What can I get for you?"

"An iced mocha."

"Coming right up." Ramey stepped to the coffee machine. "Got plans for tonight?"

"I'm going home to finish my story and get it in—" Jenessa started to say.

Charles clicked his tongue at her. "Your boss is such a task master."

Jenessa nodded and smiled. "Yeah, but I can handle it. After I email you the story, I'm going to take a drive up to Jonas Lake and walk around the boathouse where Nick Evans was killed. Maybe there's something I can figure out just by being there."

"After twenty years?" Ramey asked, setting Jenessa's drink on the counter. "What do you think you'll find after all that time?"

Jenessa collected her cup of coffee. "I won't know until I go up there. Maybe nothing, but then again…"

~*~

"It's James Walker you should be talking to," Patrick Reagan insisted, his attorney seated next to him. "Nick Evans was having his way with his daughter too."

315

"We know that," Michael replied, "but you're the one with the Notre Dame ring. It matches the impression left on—"

Patrick huffed a laugh, cutting Michael off, then pressed back in his chair. "You really think I'm the only one who has one?"

"What do you mean?" Michael asked.

"James Walker went to Notre Dame as well," Patrick replied, "graduated a different year, but he has one." He turned his attention to Provenza. "You've got one too, don't you, George?"

"No, I couldn't afford it."

"Listen to my client," the attorney said. "It's James Walker you should be questioning."

Patrick crossed his arms over his chest and seemed to relax. "I've always wondered if he killed that boy."

"Really. You wondered?" There was a hint of sarcasm in Michael's voice.

Provenza glanced to his partner before returning his attention to the suspect. "Why is that?"

"Because it was his daughter that Nick Evans got pregnant." Patrick paused and tipped his head. "Didn't you know?"

Provenza leaned forward over the table. "You said he got your daughter pregnant."

"No, I said I thought he did. My younger daughter overheard Allison on the phone with Summer and misunderstood. She told me her sister was pregnant, but it was all a mistake. It was really Summer Walker."

"A mistake?" Michael echoed, his voice raising a bit.

"Kelly was only a kid at the time," Patrick said.

Provenza leaned over to Michael and whispered, "That might change things."

"I think my client has told you enough," the attorney said. "Either you charge him or we're leaving."

"Wait," Patrick said.

"Don't say any more," his lawyer warned.

Patrick leaned over and whispered something into the man's ear and the attorney nodded. "James drives a car pretty similar to mine," Patrick went on. "You should be checking his vehicle for front-end damage, not mine."

"But you were seen leaving your cabin about the time Nick was killed, boiling mad about your daughter and Nick," Provenza said.

"And your wet, muddy shoes were seen on your back porch the next morning. How do you explain that?"

Patrick looked to his attorney, who nodded his approval to proceed. "You're right, I was angry, furious, in fact, but I knew if I found that boy in my state of mind I might do something I'd regret. So I did not go down to the boathouse. Instead, I headed for the road and went to Jack's Place, at the marina, and had a few beers to calm down."

"Can you prove you were there that night? Did you talk to anyone?"

"Sure. Jack, the owner. Business was slow at that time of night, so we cracked open a couple bottles of beer and sat in some chairs on the deck, overlooking the water, and talked for a while. He's got to remember that."

"After twenty years, you really think he'll remember, if he's even still alive?" Provenza asked. "He was no spring chicken even back then."

"I'm telling the truth," Patrick moaned. "I did not lay a hand on that kid."

"We'll have to check out your story," Provenza said.

Michael closed the file with a snap. "What about the wet, muddy shoes?"

"That's enough, Patrick." The attorney stood. "Let's go."

"No, I want to explain, then I'm done. I was a bit tipsy by the time I walked home along the beach. I can only assume I stumbled into the water a few times."

"How convenient," Michael remarked.

Patrick pulled up out of his chair, his lips tightening as he spoke. "I'm telling you, I did not murder Nick Evans. You need to be checking out James Walker."

~*~

After Jenessa finished polishing her story and emailed it off to Charles, she hopped in her Mercedes and was off to the lake. She rolled the windows down and let the mild evening breeze float through her hair. It was exhilarating how the MLK Sportster her father had left her in his Will hugged the turns like a racecar.

Her phone rang in her purse. She plucked it out and saw it was Michael. She'd call him back later.

All the way to the lake, she kept checking her mirrors for any sign of red-and-blue lights flashing behind her as she pushed the speed over the limit. The grass on the rolling hills was still a lush green. The crystal blue lake began coming into view off to the right.

She turned the corner for Jonas Lake and came to a fork in the road. If she turned right, it would take her to the sandy beach and the nearby marina, where visitors could fill up their boats with fuel and get food and drinks. To the left was the road that led to the summer homes and cabins that dotted the pristine shore.

She chose the one to the left and began searching for the boathouse Michael had pointed out to her when they had been out on the lake recently. She passed Logan's family's lake house, a two-story white clapboard with lots of tall windows. The sight of it instantly took her back to her seventeenth summer when she was so in love with him she would have done whatever he asked. They were there alone one evening, not long before he was to leave for college. One long and sensual kiss ignited a passion in her that she had never known. Before she could regain her senses, she had given her whole self to him.

Though that night changed the course of her life, she couldn't help but wonder if she would ever feel that white-hot passion again. Would it be with Michael? Perhaps. Or would it be with Logan? Something about that possibility made her smile.

She continued down the road until she spotted the old boathouse. The sun was setting behind the rolling hills, but it was still light enough for her to take a walk around the property. She parked off the road and descended the gentle slope, through the trees, down to the water's edge.

Standing on the shore near the boathouse, she looked out over the expansive lake. The ground closest to the water was soft and muddy, the moisture beginning to seep into her sandals.

She took a step back, to firmer ground. "So this is where he died," she muttered to herself, imagining Nick and Chet exchanging angry punches. Or was it Patrick Reagan's blows that finally did him in?

With not much daylight left, Jenessa climbed the few steps to the wooden decking that ran from the shore to the end of the boathouse. She tried to peek in the windows, not sure what she might find there after all this time, but she had to look. The curtains were open, but it was dark inside.

Snap!

The sound of something like a twig cracking came from somewhere on the bank. She turned, but saw nothing. After a moment, she turned back and tried the door, but it was locked.

Snap!

There it was again. She spun around and scanned the bank, and up the little hill to the road, her heart beating faster, but still saw nothing.

CHAPTER 35

WITHOUT SUFFICIENT PROOF, Michael and Provenza could not arrest Patrick Reagan—at least not yet.

After he and his lawyer were gone, Provenza asked Michael what he thought of Patrick's story and his assertion that James Walker might be the better suspect.

"Until the DNA testing comes back on Reagan's ring and the CSI guys give us the results from going over his car, there's no harm in checking out Mr. Walker," Michael said. "If it was his daughter that Nick had gotten pregnant, that's a pretty strong motive."

"I know I'd tear the head off any man that knocked up my little princess," Provenza said.

"You have a daughter you've been hiding away?"

"No. I'm just sayin', *if* I had a sixteen-year-old daughter."

Michael gave a nod. "Oh, gotcha."

"And then there's the fact that Walker had access," Provenza continued. "It was his boathouse and he told the police he and his wife were at their lake house that night."

"How would he have known Summer was pregnant?" Michael questioned. "Was there no mention of it in the old interviews?"

"None. What we do know is that Allison was talking on the phone with Summer about it. Maybe Daddy overheard. Or maybe she took one of those home pregnancy tests and he or his wife found it in the trash."

"Yeah, it could have been any one of those, which would mean it is possible it could have been James Walker that tried to run Jenessa down." Michael closed the file and picked it up off the table. "If that's the case, then I'd better let Jenessa know to be on the watch for him."

"That's assuming it was him behind the wheel," Provenza added, heading for the door. "It's all conjecture at this point."

"Still…"

"I won't lie, Baxter, I'd rather it was James than Patrick."

"Why is that?"

"Because Patrick is a friend and a good man. On the other hand, that James Walker," Provenza gave his head a shake as if disgusted, "there's just something about that man that I've never trusted. For years it has galled me to no end how he always uses the fact that he's the brother-in-law of the great and mighty Grey Alexander. Yeah, we'd better check him out, just in case."

"You go on ahead and get started." Michael pulled his cell phone out of his jacket. "I'm going to try to reach Jenessa to warn her."

Provenza nodded and left the room.

Michael dialed her number. After a few rings, it went to voicemail. "Hey, this is Michael. I wanted to warn you that there's a possibility it was James Walker that tried to run you down. Please be careful. Call me and let me know you got this message."

What if she wasn't picking up because she saw it was him calling, thinking he wanted to talk about the kiss? He hoped not.

But what if she wasn't answering because something had already happened to her? Surely Walker wouldn't be stupid enough to try it again, especially since he ended up running down his own nephew—that is, if he was the driver.

Michael poked his head into the office he shared with Provenza. His partner was typing something into his computer and looked up when Michael appeared.

"I'm going to pop over to The Sweet Spot before they close and get some coffee." Maybe Ramey knew where Jenessa was. "You want anything?"

"A luscious blonde and a million dollars," Provenza replied with a smirk.

"Ha-ha. I meant some coffee or a doughnut."

~*~

On the way to The Sweet Spot, Michael phoned Jenessa once more. Again, it went to voicemail. He pulled his car over in front of the coffee shop and hopped out, finding Ramey at the door, locking up.

He rapped on the glass and she looked up, surprised by him.

She unlocked the door and opened it. "I'm closing, Michael."

"No problem," he replied. "You haven't seen Jenessa by chance, have you? I've tried her cell, but she's not answering. I wondered if—"

"She went to Jonas Lake. She said she wanted to check something out up there."

"The boathouse?"

"Yeah, I think that's what she said." Ramey cocked her head. "Is something wrong?"

"Not if I can help it." Michael rushed back to his car and jumped inside.

He stomped on the gas pedal and turned the siren on. He radioed Provenza what he suspected and asked him to meet him at the Walkers' boathouse. "Bring a couple of officers with you."

"I'll have the tech guy ping James' cell phone, see if he's there first," Provenza said.

"Tell him to call you with what he finds." Michael flew through town. "You can always turn back if his phone shows him somewhere else. We've got to hurry."

"Calm down, Michael. We're only talking about a few minutes."

He was approaching the city limits. "I've got a bad feeling, George. If we wait, we could be too late."

"You don't know that."

Michael pushed the gas pedal harder. "Are you willing to gamble with her life?"

~*~

The sound of something snapping in the otherwise quiet woods sent a chill down Jenessa's spine. She turned, but saw nothing—again. She tried to dismiss it as no big deal.

Probably a squirrel.

She turned back and went to the end of the wooden deck, looking out over the expanse of the lake. There was still enough light to make out the cropping of rocks that Michael had shown her from the boat. It was where Nick Evans' body had been found the next day, he had said.

What a waste of a young and promising life.

She stood there for a few minutes, her gaze traveling to the edge of the water, imagining what might have happened to him, how things could possibly have played out. First Nick's encounter with Chet, the angry boyfriend, there on the muddy shore. Then, shortly after that, an altercation with a furious father, likely in the same place, or at least nearby.

Jenessa imagined Nick lying motionless on the ground, bloody from the blows to his face. But Nick wasn't dead when someone dumped his body in the water. The medical examiner had found water in his lungs, which had to mean he was still alive.

Though it wasn't up to her to decide who was guilty, she had to come up with a way to write her story that the readers could follow and understand, or at the very least would seem plausible to them. She leaned her arms on the railing and continued to stare out over the water, considering the details of what happened.

What she needed was that final piece to the puzzle. Who threw Nick in the lake?

It couldn't have been Chet who put him in the water, because Nick was still alive when Patrick Reagan fought with him. It had to have been Mr. Reagan who drowned him.

Although, the ME had said it was the tear in his brain, likely from the first fight, the one with Chet, which would have eventually killed him if he hadn't drowned. So how would they determine fault?

Chet Monahan was right now sitting in jail—but was he the one who would eventually go to prison for it? Someone else in town had something to hide. Why else would they have tried to run her down?

The sound of wood creaking came from behind her and she twisted around. Standing before her was James Walker, looming over her actually, his angry eyes blazing with the reflection of the sunset. His piercing stare bore through her, and her heart began to pound in her chest.

"Mr. Walker," she said, willing herself to stay calm. She tried to work up a friendly smile, glancing past him to nearby cabins, hoping to find any with their lights on, anyone who might hear her scream—but no.

It was Sunday night in late spring. The places naturally would be vacant. Weekenders gone back to town, no one to hear her holler for help. "I didn't—"

"You couldn't leave well enough alone, could you?" he growled, taking a step closer, a gun peeking out from inside his open jacket.

She gulped, being already at the end of the deck she had nowhere to run. He was twice her size, how was she going to fight him off? "Now, Mr. Walker, I just wanted to—" Her hands flew out, grabbing hold of his jacket. She jerked him toward her as she jammed her knee up into his groin with everything she had in her.

He buckled over in pain, cursing her for what she'd done, and dropped to one knee.

If she were going to get away, now was her chance. She tried to squeeze past him on the narrow deck, but his arm flew out low to block her. She tripped over it and hit the deck hard.

He grabbed at her ankles as she tried to scurry away, catching one of them and dragging her back. She rolled on her side and kicked at him, which just seemed to make him angrier.

Hovering over her, his sizeable fist came crashing into the side of her mouth, like he wanted to take her head off.

Her head began to spin from the blow and she could feel herself start to lose consciousness, slumping back onto the deck. Everything was going black and her eyelids slid closed. She fought unconsciousness with all her strength, but she was losing the battle.

A thick lump grew in her throat at the sound of heavy feet shuffling around on the wooden decking near her. Then the man's large hands grabbed her under the arms. Was he going to hit her again? Was this the end?

Instead, he picked her up and heaved her over the railing, splashing into the cold water below. Did he think she was dead? Or that she was unconscious and would surely drown?

Only half-aware of what was happening, with her mind fuzzy from the wallop, she only knew she couldn't breathe. The frigid waters began to revive her and she swam up to the top, flailing a bit as she broke the surface of the lake. A loud gunshot rang out and something whizzed past her in the water. Was he shooting at her? Was she going to die?

An ominous feeling consumed her. Did anyone know she was there? Would her body ever be found?

Was this how it went down for Nick Evans?

She dove below the water and swam for the deck, coming up for air between the pilings below it as another bullet zipped by her. Trembling, she got her head above water, hugged a wooden column, and tried not to make a sound.

CHAPTER 36

ANOTHER SHOT RANG OUT as Jenessa clung to the piling under the deck, shivering and terrified, as the cold water lapped against her head, trying to keep as much of herself as possible buried in the dark water. Would he see her through the boards? Hear her teeth chattering? Shoot her through the decking? Every muscle in her body tensed and trembled.

She heard someone yell something, a deep voice in the distance, but she couldn't make it out with the water rising and falling over her ears. There was another shot, she was sure of it, then the sound of something heavy dropping onto the deck above her, followed by quick-moving footfalls drawing closer. She didn't dare look up between the slats and expose the whites of her eyes in the darkness. She wasn't going to help him find his target.

Someone mumbled something she couldn't make out. Who was it? Pulling herself higher on the piling, she strained to hear.

"Jenessa?" a man's voice called out.

Michael?

"I…I'm here," she stammered excitedly, shivering in the chilly waters.

"Where are you? Are you all right?"

"Here." She swam out from below the deck. "I think I'm okay." Although her head was throbbing and she tasted blood.

He shone a flashlight on her as she swam to the shallow water and trudged to the shore. He scrambled down the walkway and met her there, then draped his jacket about her trembling wet shoulders.

She looked over to the deck and saw her attacker, lying face down, in handcuffs. "Is he dead?" she asked before thinking it through. The handcuffs wouldn't make sense if he were. The pain in her head muddled her thoughts.

"No," Michael replied. "I only shot him in the shoulder. I ordered him to lay there and not move a muscle or I would shoot him again."

He tugged out his radio and called for an ambulance. It would be at least twenty minutes before it arrived from town, the dispatcher replied. Fortunately the wound wasn't serious, Michael told the woman. "Through and through," he added.

"You know," Jenessa said, once Michael was off the radio, "he must have been the one who tried to run me down," still shaking from the experience.

"Yeah, I figured that out, but I couldn't find you until Ramey told me you came up here." He put an arm around her and walked her toward the deck. "Are you sure you're okay? Your mouth is bleeding."

Jenessa nodded, comforted by the warmth and safety he provided. "I will be." Now she could finish her story, for she had finally found the last piece of the puzzle.

Provenza came running down from the road above, followed by a couple of patrolmen. "You okay, Jenessa?"

"Why, George, I didn't know you cared," she said with a little smirk.

He grinned. "Yeah, you're okay."

"There's James Walker, over there." Michael lifted his chin toward the man. "I had to shoot him, but he'll be fine. I just called for an ambo. I'll explain it all on the drive back to town."

Provenza glanced over at the man lying on the deck. "I've never seen James Walker so quiet." He chuckled. "Never did like that blowhard."

Michael instructed the two patrolmen to get him on his feet and escort him to the road to wait for the paramedics. "There should be some bandages in the first aid kit in my car. Apply some pressure on that wound so he doesn't bleed out. We need him healthy for the trial."

"Yes sir," one of the men responded.

"Then one of you can drive Miss Jones' car back to Hidden Valley," Michael added.

"I can drive," she protested, although she still felt a bit woozy.

"I'm not so sure," Michael said, lifting her chin with a couple of fingers and studying her swollen and bloody mouth. "I'm taking you to the hospital to have you checked out, see what the doctor has to say."

"I'll be fine."

"Do you have to argue about everything?"

She touched her lips and winced from the pain. Perhaps he was right.

~*~

Once the ambulance arrived, James Walker was put on a gurney and loaded into the vehicle. Provenza said he'd ride with the suspect, maybe he could get him to confess. Michael figured it was more so that he and Jenessa would be alone to talk.

They drove for ten minutes or so with neither saying a word. The atmosphere in the cruiser was filled with an air of hesitancy, neither him nor her wanting to start a conversation. When Michael could stand it no more, he broke the silence.

"I don't know what's happening with us, Jenessa."

She squirmed in the seat and stared out the side window. Was she thinking about their flagging relationship too?

"I love you, Jenessa, but I'm not sure how you feel about me these days."

She turned toward him and he glanced at her, their eyes meeting briefly before he had to return his attention to the road. He expected her to say something, but nothing came.

"What are you thinking?" he asked.

She didn't answer right away. "What I'm thinking is this—if you love me, why did you kiss my sister?"

"I told you. I was upset about what's been going on between us, and she was all emotional over her breakup with Luke. It was late, we were commiserating over a few glasses of wine and the alcohol was taking effect. We were standing there talking about things and when I looked at her, her eyes looked so much like yours...I don't know, it just happened."

"I don't believe things just happen for no reason, Michael. Maybe you don't love me as much as you'd like to think you do."

He looked at her briefly. "What's that supposed to mean?"

"I overheard you talking to George last week. You forgot to hang up the phone after leaving me a voicemail. You said you almost took your ex-wife back when she was here a few months ago."

"You heard that?"

He saw her nod out of the corner of his eye. "I think you misunderstood."

"Did I?"

She didn't believe him. He could tell. Should he explain? How could he, when he wasn't even sure himself? Josie had managed to get his thoughts and passions all twisted up. But he had to come up with something to say—and quick.

"I won't lie to you, Jenessa. I was madly in love with Josie—that's why I married her—and then totally devastated when she left me and little Jake for her career in Hollywood. Probably some part of me will always love her, but I was only considering taking her back for Jake's sake, not mine."

He glanced at her again as he drove. She appeared to be mulling over what he said, but she did not reply, so he asked the burning question that had been consuming his mind all afternoon. "I've told you what happened on my side, at least the best I could. Now, I'd like to know why you kissed Logan." His throat tightened at the thought.

Out of his peripheral vision, he saw her head snap toward him. He expected her to say something in response, but she held her tongue. He snuck a quick peek at her, catching her gaze, then slid his focus back to the road ahead. She was staring at him, her pale jade eyes holding an intense expression that said she had something she wanted to say but seemed to be having a hard time putting it into words.

He slowed the car, pulled it over to the shoulder, and threw it into park. With trepidation, he twisted in his seat to face her. "So, can you tell me why?"

~*~

Jenessa swallowed hard and pushed her damp tresses back over her shoulder. How could she explain what happened? Without hurting him, that is. She had to find a way, because she had put it off too long. It wasn't fair to him to treat him like this, to string him along anymore.

"Michael, I think you're a wonderful man," she noticed his jaw twitch at her words, "one of the most wonderful men I have ever met."

"But…" His chocolate-brown eyes looked sad as they shone in the glow of the dashboard lights.

She held his gaze. "But I don't think this is leading where you want it to go."

"You said you loved me." His eyes began to glisten.

"I do have love for you, but not the burning, passionate kind of love that you deserve, the kind that will last a lifetime."

"It's Logan, isn't it?" He looked straight ahead when he said it, as if he couldn't bear to look at her when she answered.

"I'm sorry it took me so long to realize—"

"Realize what?" he broke in, turning sharply back to her.

"That I gave my heart to Logan years ago, just like you did to Josie, and, although I've done my best to deny it, I have never really gotten it back. It's not fair to you, Michael, not fair for me to continue our relationship when it's Logan who holds my heart."

"Jake adores you, Jenessa." His lips became tight with emotion. "I warned you when we started dating that you would break his heart if things didn't work out between the two of us."

"And I adore him," she countered, "but I can't continue to be with you because of him. Would you want that?"

He paused and stared at her, then his gaze fell to his lap. "No, I wouldn't, but I thought…"

"Michael, you're a great guy in so many ways. The right woman is out there for you. A woman that will give you her whole heart…as long as you both shall live."

His eyes raised to her, almost in surprise. "That's what Sara said." He wiped a hand over his mouth and turned away. "Exactly what she said."

CHAPTER 37

THE REST OF THE DRIVE BACK to Hidden Valley was done in relative silence. Michael pulled up to the emergency entrance to the hospital and stopped.

"Go on in," he said. "I'll park and meet you inside."

"No, Michael." Jenessa put a hand lightly on his arm to stop him. "You've done enough for me. I can handle it from here."

He put his hand over hers. "We would have been good together, you, me, and Jake."

What could she say to that? She worked up a bit of a smile as she pulled her hand back. "You go on home. I'm sure Jake and Sara are waiting for you."

"I will, but I wanted to make sure you're okay."

"I'll be just fine. Go home, Michael."

"I've got to go back to the station to finish up."

"Have it your way." She opened the door and slid out, turning back before she closed it. "Sara cares for you, you know."

~*~

Once Jenessa was seen by one of the ER doctors, she kept her promise to Logan and went upstairs to check on him. When she walked in, an older nurse was helping him out of his bed.

"Are visiting hours over?" Jenessa asked.

Logan looked up and his face lit up at seeing her, but just as quickly his expression changed as she stepped closer.

"You've almost missed it," the nurse said, not looking at her. "I was just taking Mr. Alexander for a walk."

Logan's brows knit together. "What happened to you?"

The nurse's head bobbed up. "Oh my."

"I'll tell you later. So, you're going for a walk, huh?"

"It seems I have to be able to do certain things by myself before they'll release me."

"I can take him," she said to the nurse.

The woman took a step back from her patient. "Just once around this floor will be sufficient."

Jenessa took his arm and the nurse left them alone in the room. "Where would you like to go?"

"The fourth floor," Logan replied.

"What's up there?"

"Summer. She was admitted a few hours ago."

"I thought she looked awful this afternoon."

"She's refusing treatment." Logan curled his arm around Jenessa's waist and she slipped her arm around his to help steady him. "She always said she wanted to spend what time she had left enjoying her family, not in and out of the hospital feeling lousy."

She looked up into Logan's face, awash with concern for his cousin. "Let's go visit her."

"Won't Michael be upset you're spending so much time here with me?"

Jenessa's heart both sank with sadness and filled with hope at the thought of how she would answer him. "That's no longer a problem."

"What do you mean?"

"Michael and I are no longer together. I broke things off with him tonight."

He pulled her around so she was facing him. "Did he do this?" His eyes were roving over her injured mouth where the doctor had applied Steri-Strips to cinch together her split lip.

"Of course not. Why would you think that? Michael's not capable of—"

"All right, all right. It's just that you said you broke up with him and then you show up here like someone punched you in the face."

"Not Michael."

"Then who?"

"I don't want to talk about it now." His face was only inches from hers. "I want to go to see Summer."

He gently kissed beside her wound. "We're not leaving here until you tell me. Who did this to you?"

She hung her head. How could she tell him it was his beloved uncle? The father of his dying cousin, who was like a sister to him?

He tipped her head up, searching her eyes for the answer. "Is it that awful?"

She nodded, feeling tears coming to the surface. She blinked them back. "Let's go see Summer. Then we'll talk."

~*~

When Jenessa and Logan reached Summer's room, her mother and children were saying goodnight. She looked frail and weak. Her long blond wig replaced by a knit cap.

"I don't know where your father has gone off to, honey," Summer's mother said. "I'll send him over as soon as he surfaces." She kissed her daughter's cheek and took little Lily by the hand. "We'll be back in the morning."

Grayson hugged Logan hard, tears in the boy's eyes. "I don't want her to die," he whispered.

Logan wrapped the boy up in his arms. "I know."

Jenessa stood by, feeling like an observer, knowing so much that would hurt this family, yet not wanting to speak a word of it.

As soon as Summer's mother and children were gone, Logan and Jenessa came closer to her bedside.

"Goodness, girl, what happened to you?" Summer gasped.

"Just a little accident." Jenessa wasn't about to tell her the truth. "How are you?"

"Not good." Summer grasped Logan's hand. "Those kids are going to need you when I'm gone." Her gaze shifted to Jenessa briefly, then back to Logan. "Remember what we talked about. Are you up for it?"

He gave her a nod. "I'd do anything for those kids."

"They're going to need a mother, Logan." Summer's eyes closed as her head rested against the pillows. "Especially Lily."

Jenessa looked at Logan, then Summer. "Won't your mother be taking the children?"

"My parents are too old. They'll still be their grandparents, of course, but the kids need someone younger to keep up with them. I asked Logan, and he said yes."

"What about Chet?" Jenessa asked. "I heard the police have another person they're looking at for Nick Evans' murder."

"Who?" Logan asked.

"I'm sworn to secrecy...sorry." There was no way she could tell him now, in front of Summer. "It may not turn into anything, so Chet may still be the one on trial."

Summer's eyes came open. "Either way, I don't think he'll have any trouble signing over his parental rights."

Thinking back to her conversation with Chet, Jenessa knew he felt no fatherly obligation to these children—they weren't his—but she still had no idea why. Maybe now Summer would explain.

"Why do you say that?" Jenessa questioned.

"Because they're both adopted. He never really bonded with them like a real father would."

Adopted? She did not see that coming. Fertility treatments, sure. Even the thought that Summer had cheated on Chet during their marriage. But this?

"Adopted?" Jenessa repeated. "Why did you adopt, Summer?" she asked. "If I'm not being too personal."

"Well," Summer tried to sit up and Logan tucked another pillow behind her, "no one knows this, so please keep it under your hats, but I was pregnant when Nick died."

Summer was the one that was pregnant. That explained her father's actions. Did James Walker also have a Notre Dame ring that may have left an imprint on Nick's gums?

"Please don't tell anyone about it."

"Oh, no, of course not," Jenessa said.

"My folks went to a lot of trouble to keep it hidden. They'd be mortified if anyone found out."

So, clearly, her parents had known about Summer and Nick. But the pregnancy explained her not wanting to admit it to Jenessa. She, of all people, could understand keeping *that* secret. Still, she had to know more—the child would be nineteen by now. "What happened to the baby?" Jenessa asked.

Summer's expression turned sad. "My dad forced me to have an abortion. I was sixteen and he said he wasn't going to let me ruin my life because I made some stupid choices."

"I'm sorry," Logan said, squeezing her hand. "I didn't know."

"It was the worst thing I could have done. Things went badly, blood everywhere, and pain—so much pain.

In the end," her voice cracked with emotion, "I was no longer able to have children."

"So Grayson and Lily are adopted..." Logan said, as if he were learning about it for the first time.

"I never would have guessed," Jenessa remarked. "I mean, Grayson looks so much like you—"

Suddenly the family resemblance Jenessa had seen between Grayson and Logan took on a whole new meaning. The boy was around the right age...

Jenessa's heart leapt into her throat. *Could it be?*

"If you don't mind my asking, how did you come to adopt Grayson?" She glanced at Logan, whose quizzical frown said he was wondering where she was going with this. "Did you use an agency? Were you on a list for a long time?"

"So many questions," Summer replied, closing her eyes again. "I'm so tired. Can we talk about this tomorrow?"

But how many more tomorrows would Summer have? What if she slipped away in the night and Jenessa never found out?

She pitched a passionate, pleading gaze at Logan, hoping he would get on the same page as her. Finally a light seemed to come on in his eyes, as though he understood her line of questioning.

"I know you're tired, Summer," he said, his eyes on Jenessa, "but if you could tell us when and where Grayson was born and who put you together, then we'll say goodnight and let you rest. After all, I am going to be his dad."

"All right," she huffed. Her eyes fluttered open again. "I wanted a baby so badly and I was getting depressed because I couldn't have one. My dad told Uncle Grey about our situation and he called me one day, said he knew of a baby that was going to be born in a few months, one that would be perfect for us. He said that if Chet and I wanted to adopt the child, he was sure he could arrange it. That's why we named him Grayson, after Uncle Grey."

"Please, where was Grayson born?" Jenessa pressed.

"Santa Rosa, California."

The anticipation was eating at her. This moment felt so surreal. It looked as though the answers she had been searching for all these years might be right in front of her, and Jenessa could barely breathe. She was desperate to know but afraid to know, all at the same time. She took a deep breath and looked at Logan. His eyes communicated the very thing she was feeling inside, so she pushed forward. "His birthday, Summer? When is his birthday?"

"April sixth."

"Oh my God." Tears flooded Jenessa's eyes. Logan put his arms around her and held her tight. She pressed her face into his shoulder and began to sob.

"I don't understand," Summer muttered. "What's wrong?" It seemed she wasn't aware of who Grayson's parents actually were.

"Nothing." He kissed the top of Jenessa's head. "Absolutely nothing."

"If you don't want to tell me—"

"Tomorrow," Logan said. "We'll tell you tomorrow, when you're feeling better."

"I am tired, but there's one more thing I need to tell you, in case there isn't a tomorrow."

Jenessa straightened and ran her fingers under her eyes to clear away the tears. Was Summer truly that close to death?

"I have to get something off my chest before I die."

CHAPTER 38

"DON'T TALK LIKE THAT, Summer," Logan said, letting go of Jenessa to take his cousin's hand. "I'll stop by and see you in the morning before I check out."

"Listen to me. There's not much time." There was an urgency in her voice that seemed to make Logan stop and pay attention.

Jenessa sucked in a breath and held it.

"The night Nick died," she paused, as if she were having difficulty getting the words out, "I saw who killed him."

"What?" Logan gasped.

"It wasn't Chet."

"Are you sure?" Logan looked at Jenessa, his eyes widening.

"I heard voices and peeked out the window, through the curtains."

Had Summer been unaware of Chet and Nick's altercation? Possibly, but she was aware of Allison's allegation that she had seen Chet do it, yet she never said anything.

"Who was it, Summer?" Jenessa was sure she knew, but she wanted her to say his name.

"I don't want to get this person into trouble, so I won't tell you, but after he left, I ran out of the boathouse and down to the shore. Nick was dead and I was frantic."

"What did you do?" Logan asked.

"I dragged Nick's body to the lake and shoved it out into deeper water. He was already dead, so what was the point of destroying another life?"

There was no way Jenessa was going to tell her Nick was still alive at that point, not in her frail condition, but he had drowned because of her actions. Believing all these years that her father had killed him, because of her, was torture enough, in Jenessa's mind. Could it be that this insidious secret that had been eating away at Summer for so many years may have precipitated the cancer? How sad, if that were true.

"And you've carried this secret for the past twenty years?" Logan questioned.

Tears rolled from her eyes as she nodded.

"What I don't understand is why you let the police accuse your husband of the murder," Jenessa said, "knowing he didn't do it."

Summer closed her eyes, drew in a deep breath, and expelled it slowly. "I couldn't tell anyone, I just couldn't. If I had, it would have brought a good man's whole life crashing down, destroying his family."

There was so much Jenessa knew that she could not say—it was hard to keep quiet, but she had to. She glanced up at Logan. "But Chet…"

Summer opened her eyes again and her weak gaze met Jenessa's. "The honest truth is that I saw it as my opportunity to get the kids away from him. I did it for my children." Another tear trickled down her cheek. "Can't you understand that?"

Yes, a mother protecting her children, Jenessa could understand that, but Summer was also protecting her father. Clearly, she loved him and could never turn him in to the police, but to let her husband be accused of a murder she believed he did not commit was just plain wrong.

"What if the police were to determine Chet is innocent?" Jenessa asked, the only one in the room knowing James Walker was now under arrest. "He could be released and then he'll expect to get the children."

"Not to worry." She pulled a tissue from the box on the night table and wiped her eyes.

"But I am worried," Logan replied.

Summer clasped her hands over her abdomen and closed her eyes again. "My father already made arrangements with our attorney."

Logan and Jenessa looked at each other in question.

"What arrangements?" Logan asked.

Summer sighed softly, as if it were exhausting for her to talk. "Whether Chet goes to prison or not, papers have been drawn up for him to sign upon my death, relinquishing his parental rights in exchange for a hefty sum of money. If it comes to that, I have no doubt Chet will take it."

How sad that a man did not love his children, adopted or not. Fortunately for them, their mother's dying wish was that they would be raised by someone who would love them. Tears welled in Jenessa's eyes, feeling torn between the sorrow of inevitably losing her new friend and the overwhelming joy of having finally found her son. She looked away so no one could see.

"I'm spent, guys. Can we talk about this in the morning?"

"Sure," Logan replied, "about this and the children."

Jenessa snaked her arm through Logan's and nodded her agreement to him, assuming—hoping—Summer would still be with the living when the sun came up again.

~*~

Jenessa walked Logan back to his room.

The surly nurse stood outside the door, her arms crossed, wearing a perturbed expression. "I said once around the floor. I expected you back long ago."

"Don't worry so much, Betty." Logan flashed her a smile and her angry façade melted away. "We were visiting my cousin on the fourth floor."

"The cancer floor? I'm so sorry." She even managed to work up a small smile. "Let's get you into bed." She took Logan by the arm.

He winked at Jenessa over his shoulder as she followed them into the room. "I know visiting hours are over, Betty, but Jenessa and I have things to discuss," he climbed into the bed. "You don't mind do you?"

The nurse gave Jenessa a once over as she adjusted his blankets. "I guess it'd be all right. Fifteen minutes." She moved toward the door. "I'll be back to check on you."

Once she was out of earshot, Jenessa squealed with excitement. "We've finally found our son, Logan." After all they had done to try to find him, now, to discover he'd been in Logan's family the whole time was astonishing.

"I'm as thrilled as you are," he said. "But, there's something I need to clear up first."

"What could possibly be more important than finding out Grayson is our child?"

"I need to know who hurt you."

Standing beside his bed, she looked him in the eyes as she considered what to say. The expression on his face told her that even with the injuries marring her lips, she was still beautiful to him. She could tell now, without any doubt or hesitation, that Logan truly did love her. And she was finally ready to admit she felt the same about him.

"Well?"

He was going to find out eventually, but why did she have to be the one to deliver the terrible news.

"Jenessa?" he pressed. "Who are you protecting?"

She leaned down and kissed his forehead. "You."

"Me?" His eyes widened in surprise. He took her hand. "Hey, I'm a big boy. I can take it."

"But, Logan—"

"Just tell me."

"Well…" she paused to measure her words, "if you

must know…it was your uncle." There, she had said it. She steadied for his response.

"Uncle James?" He shot up in bed and clung to her hand, surprise choking his speech. "What? Why? What happened?"

She poured out the whole story to him, probably saying more than she should have. George and Michael would just have to deal with it. Logan had the right to know, didn't he?

When she was done, he slumped back against the pillows, a stunned look on his face. "I am so sorry, babe."

Babe? He hadn't called her that since she was seventeen. It felt kind of nice.

"No wonder you didn't want to tell me."

Jenessa rested her head on his chest and his hand rubbed over her back. "I couldn't tell Summer either." She paused as she thought about how much the woman was already dealing with. "She will find out, though." She pulled up straight. "She'll need us when she does."

"Us?" Logan said with a smile. "I like the sound of that."

"It's been a long time coming."

Logan slipped out of the bed and held her face in his hands. He kissed her long but gently, sending a thrill rippling through her body. Then he slid down on one knee and took her hand.

"What the heck is going on in here?" Nurse Betty bellowed.

"I'm about to ask this woman to be my wife," he said, his gaze not leaving Jenessa's.

"Oh my," Betty said sweetly. "I'll leave you to it. Go on ahead." She waddled out.

Jenessa expelled a nervous giggle. "It's a bit soon, don't you think? I mean, we haven't even been dating."

"I've been waiting for you for thirteen years, Jenessa. I think this is long overdue."

"Well then, go ahead and ask."

He looked up at her, hopefulness shining in his eyes. "I don't have a ring today, but, Jenessa Jones, will you do me the honor of becoming my wife and the mother of our children?"

"As long as we have a long engagement, so we can really get to know each other again."

Logan winced as he got to his feet, continuing to hold her hand. "I think we already know each other better than anyone else does, and it'll be hard enough to wait while you plan a wedding. Besides, Grayson and Lily will need a mother very soon."

"But, Logan—"

"Marry me. I love you."

"Oh, Jenessa, go ahead and say yes already," a familiar woman's voice came from the doorway.

Jenessa and Logan both spun their heads in her direction.

"Aunt Renee?" Jenessa gasped, seeing her sister, Sara, standing beside her aunt, beaming. "What are you doing here?"

They entered the room. "We heard you were almost killed and we hadn't heard from you—"

Jenessa cut her aunt off mid-sentence, looking at her sister. "You spoke to Michael?"

"Yes, he told us everything."

"Everything?" Jenessa questioned.

Sara nodded, unable to hide a small grin sweeping across her lips. "They're expecting you at the station for your statement."

Aunt Renee stepped closer. "We were worried, so we came looking for you."

"I'm fine."

"Yes, I can see that." Aunt Renee smiled brightly, eyeing Logan. "I told you that the heart wants what the heart wants. I always knew that deep down it was Logan you wanted."

"You did?" Jenessa smiled at Logan, seeing love written all over his face.

"Now you've finally gotten what your heart wanted," her aunt said. "What are you waiting for, Jenessa? Put the dear boy out of his misery and say yes."

She looked at her aunt, then her sister, before turning her attention back to Logan. "Ask me again."

He stood close to her, holding both of her hands in his. "I promise to love you till the day I die, to protect you, and to make you smile every single day. Jenessa, will you marry me?" His words came with such a warm tenderness that it cut through any objections she might have.

"Yes, Logan. Absolutely yes."

THE END

Thank you so much for reading my book,
The Boat House Secret.
I hope you enjoyed it very much.

Debra Burroughs

The highest compliment an author can get is to
receive a great review, especially
if the review is posted on Amazon.com.

Debra@DebraBurroughs.com
www.DebraBurroughsBooks.com

Other Books

By Debra Burroughs

The Lake House Secret, a Jenessa Jones Mystery, Book 1

The Stone House Secret, a Jenessa Jones Mystery, Book 2

Three Days in Seattle, a Romantic Suspense Novel

The Scent of Lies, Paradise Valley Mystery Book 1

The Heart of Lies, Paradise Valley Mystery Book 2

The Edge of Lies, Paradise Valley Mystery Short Story

The Chain of Lies, Paradise Valley Mystery Book 3

The Pursuit of Lies, Paradise Valley Mystery Book 4

The Betrayal of Lies, Paradise Valley Mystery Book 5

The Color of Lies, Paradise Valley Mystery Short Story

The Harbor of Lies, Paradise Valley Mystery Book 6

The House of Lies, Paradise Valley Mystery, Book 7

ABOUT THE AUTHOR

Debra Burroughs writes with intensity and power. Her characters are rich and her stories of romance, suspense and mystery are highly entertaining. She can often be found sitting in front of her computer in her home in the Pacific Northwest, dreaming up new stories and developing interesting characters for her next book.

If you are looking for stories that will touch your heart and leave you wanting more, dive into one of her captivating books.

Sign up for Debra's New Release & Giveaway eNewsletter at:

www.DebraBurroughsBooks.com

You will never be spammed or your email address sold.